THE URBANA FREE LIBRARY
3 1230 00855 6009

D1112796

THE CHAPEL WARS

Also by Lindsey Leavitt

Sean Griswold's Head
Going Vintage

THE CHAPEL WARS

Lindsey Leavitt

BLOOMSBURY

NEW YORK LONDON NEW DELHI SYDNEY

First published in the United States of America in May 2014
by Bloomsbury Children's Books
www.bloomsbury.com

Library of Congress Cataloging-in-Publication Data
Leavitt, Lindsey.
The chapel wars / Lindsey Leavitt.
pages cm
Summary: Sixteen-year-old Holly's grandfather leaves her his financially strapped Las Vegas wedding chapel in his will, along with a letter asking her to reach out to Dax, the grandson of her family's mortal enemy and owner of the chapel next door, who is both cute and distracting.
ISBN 978-1-59990-788-8 (hardcover) • ISBN 978-1-61963-232-5 (e-book)
[1. Wedding—Fiction. 2. Family-owned business enterprises—Fiction.
3. Family life—Nevada—Las Vegas—Fiction. 4. Inheritance and succession—Fiction.
5. Las Vegas (Nev.)—Fiction.] I. Title.
PZ7.L46553Ch 2014 [Fic]—dc23 2013045821

Book design by Amanda Bartlett
Typeset by Westchester Book Composition
Printed and bound in the U.S.A. by Thomson-Shore Inc., Dexter, Michigan
2 4 6 8 10 9 7 5 3 1

Caroline Abbey

Have you heard this one? An editor and an author walk into a wedding chapel and . . .

THE CHAPEL WARS

CHAPTER 1

Inheritance. I hate that word. Translation: Sorry someone you loved kicked the bucket; now here's your present. It's like getting hit by a car, only to make a fortune in the lawsuit. People constantly remind you what a financial *blessing* that accident was, such a sweet silver lining, when the truth is, you still got hit by a car.

I couldn't possibly find good in a reality so wrong. Grandpa Jim was gone—passed away, no longer with us . . . dead. Grandpa Jim, the person I shared my good news with before anyone else, who used to send greeting cards or even singing telegrams for the most ridiculous holidays, like an oversized paper card on Arbor Day. Made me wonder what he would send now—maybe a condolence card that played music when opened. I would guess "Celebration," with the inscription, "Just because I'm dead doesn't mean we can't celebrate good times!"

Anything would have been better than the *Instructions*. Capitalized. Grandpa planned his will reading two years before his passing, after he'd watched a *60 Minutes* special on celebrity funerals. *Why should celebrities get all the pomp and circumstance?* he'd asked. The next day he'd bought a faux gold casket. We thought he'd live until a hundred, but he didn't even clear seventy.

I was told to wear something "chipper," which ended up being a yellow Little Bo Peep–gone–streetwalker tragedy that Mom found at Goodwill. Here are more of Grandpa's strange Instructions:

1. No tears or tissues.
2. Brass band in the front. Make sure the trumpet wails.
3. The lawyer should wear a three-piece suit. Navy, with pinstripe.
4. Be ready for a surprise.

Our family wasn't told to meet in the lawyer's office, where normal families read normal grandfathers' wills. No, the Nolan family met at four p.m. on a crisp November Friday inside the Rose of Sharon Wedding Chapel. My grandpa Jim's wedding chapel.

I tugged down on my dress as I followed my mom over the bridal bridge, counting the thirty-two steps it took me to get to the chapel. My little brother, James, glanced back to flash another Look of Death. At thirteen, James's angst had the pubescent power to crack the bridge in half. Not that we would drown—the only thing under the bridge was concrete.

I picked up my pace, reaching the chapel door the same time as James.

"That dress looks like you stole it from a child beauty pageant loser," he said.

That face looks like you stole it from a serial killer. I elbowed him in the ribs and made it to the front pew first. Today I would not let him win. I hoped Grandpa Jim left him that bridge and maybe a gold-spray-painted urinal for good measure.

"Did you just elbow your brother?" My mom leaned over her seat, her high black ponytail swishing from one shoulder to the other. Our older sister, Lenore, sat by Mom, sketching another possible tattoo design onto her wrist. "LOVER" inside a goldfish.

"I'm sorry. It was an accident."

"Holly broke my rib," James said. "When did she turn abusive?"

"Your sister wouldn't hurt a flea."

"I don't care about fleas, I'm talking about my ribs," James said.

Mom glanced down at her cell phone. "I'm just going to call your father and see where he is. Be nice to each other."

"I *am* nice," I said, more to myself, as Mom scooted to the end of the pew and covered her ear with her finger.

James scowled. "You're a retar—"

"Don't say it," I said.

Lenore didn't look up from her pen tattoo, just sighed louder than a feminist during the last song of *Grease*. "Do you know how *offensive* that word is?"

"Do you know how offensive that word is?" James mimicked.

"What you say is a reflection of who you are. Are you even aware of the full historical context of that word?"

Oh, and Lenore was in a linguistics class at her Liberal Arts College You've Never Heard Of. In case you couldn't tell.

"Shut up, Lenore," James said. "I'm sick of your face."

Lenore aimed her pen at James's chest. There was a nine-year age difference between them, but they both defaulted to five-year-olds during conflict.

I stuck my arms out between them, annoyed that I'd already lost ownership of one of the few fights I'd started. "You guys, come on. This is serious."

The brass band started up right then, which didn't do much to prove my point.

Mom slid back down the bench and bumped her knee against mine. "Are we getting along better now?"

"No," James said. "Lenore is trying to act like everything is all Skittles and ballerinas."

"Have I ever acted like anything is Skittles and ballerinas?" Lenore asked. "What TV show did you get that from?"

"I do other things besides watch TV."

"Your school suspension record could attest to that." Lenore sniffed.

"Listen." Mom wrapped her arm around James's shoulder. "It's going to be okay."

James actually leaned into her, which had to be a first in years. It might have been a sweet moment if the band hadn't burst into another loud number. I needed to have a serious discussion with Grandpa about his musical choices.

But . . . no. There would be no discussion about music anymore. There would be . . . nothing. Just last week we got in an argument over brands of hot dogs—seriously, *hot dogs*—and then came the heart attack and the quadruple-bypass surgery, which obviously didn't go as we'd hoped. There's hearing that someone's dead, and then there's that gut-shredding moment when their death becomes real.

"I still expect him to jump out any minute," Lenore finally said.

James bowed his head, covering his face with stringy hair. "He shouldn't have left like this."

James was right. You expect ordinary people to die in ordinary ways. People who have regular nine-to-five jobs leave wills that don't have Instructions or mysterious surprises. Grandpa deserved a great tragedy to end his life, like an attempt to stop a burglary or a skydiving incident, not a sterile hospital room with a few get-well cards and half a dozen sagging balloons.

As if on cue, the band switched to a somber minor key, not the kind of music usually filling this room. Since 1987, the Rose of Sharon Wedding Chapel was, hands down, the most delightful and tasteful chapel on Las Vegas Boulevard. No pink Styrofoam angels or Elvis impersonators entered this building. In fact, Grandpa Jim issued a strict ban on anything Elvis nine years ago when a groom showed up drunk in a glittery seventies jumpsuit and threw up on the marble floor.

The interior was designed after an Irish Cathedral—columns, arched doorways, a gilded ceiling, frescoes, and a small but brilliant stained-glass window. Unlike some of the more stereotypical chapels, in ours Grandpa Jim insisted on using fresh flower sprays, and he redesigned the marble entry himself. TV shows were filmed here. *Bride* magazine named us "a charming oasis amongst the sea of Strip tackiness." We'd had people from around the world say "I do" in front of the antique candelabra.

The band stopped and the lawyer cleared his throat. His face was plump and pocked like an orange, the roundness expanding even more when he drew in a breath to start. "I've practiced law for twenty-six years in this town. I thought I'd seen everything. And then Jim gave me these Instructions." He held up the stapled sheets of paper. "A lot of hoopla. He was planning on having a funeral too, right?"

The chapel doors burst open, and Dad sailed in, his cologne reaching us first. "The funeral has a script. Seventeen pages. I think he has me break dancing at some point."

Lenore gave Dad a nod. "Andrew, so nice of you to join us."

"It's Dad, Lenore."

"Well, biologically, no."

"Legally, yes," Dad said.

Lenore's biological father was Nigerian and came to see her every few years. My dad—our dad—adopted her when she was four.

Lenore flipped her braids. "I just think now that I'm an adult, I should use your Christian name."

Dad ignored Lenore. "Hey, kids. Lana, good to see you."

Mom flicked on a smile, the kind you flash to people on an

elevator. Or ex-husbands. "You too. I'm so sorry about your father."

"I appreciate that." Dad patted her shoulder. "How are you doing?"

"Oh, don't worry about me. I'm more concerned about your family."

"Did you cut your hair?" he asked. "It's nice."

"I did. Thanks for noticing."

"You're late," Lenore said.

"Something my dad taught me. Make an entrance." Dad stuck his hands on his hips, his legs far apart in his signature pose. He wore his usual uniform: faded jeans, untucked dress shirt, and scuffed shoes that matched his disheveled hair. Yet those clothes hung on him, his smile hung on him, like he was just an impersonator from a Vegas show headlining as my father.

The lawyer rattled his pages. "So . . . everyone's here now?"

"Donna, Dad's . . . secretary, just couldn't come. She raises alpacas, one was sick—"

"Which one?" James asked. "Not Daryl, right?"

Dad gave James an odd look. "She named an alpaca Daryl?" Dad shook his head. "Never mind. And my mom said Dad wasn't worth the drive from Mesquite." Dad flopped into his seat. "Trust me. Her absence is a courtesy to us all."

"Well, your mom was the first on the list," the lawyer said. "And it is probably best she isn't here. Your father asked . . . please excuse me, I'm just reading his wishes, but he wanted me to offer a rude gesture to his ex-wife and say . . . some unkind words." The lawyer unbuttoned his suit coat and fanned himself with the will. "Is everyone fine if we skip that part?"

Dad barked a laugh. "Jim Nolan. Son of a gun."

The lawyer barreled through the rest.

The highlights:

Lenore: A $500 savings bond

James: A leather bomber jacket

Mom: An antique writing desk

Secretary Donna: An heirloom watch

Minister Dan: Grandpa's saxophone

Dad: Grandpa's decked-out golf cart

"Whatever isn't in here, Donna can sell. Money goes to my trust. And trust all goes back to the chapel." The lawyer looked up at us. "That's it. The band is supposed to play now."

No mention of my name. Was that the big surprise? It made no sense; I'd always been the favorite. Maybe he gave me nothing because he knew I wouldn't want anything. *Something* would just be a reminder he was gone, and besides, I had my greeting cards.

"Oh, wait!" The lawyer set down the Instructions and retrieved a padded mailer from his briefcase. "There is one more page. But before I read, he left Holly this envelope. There's nothing about it in the will, but he gave it to a hospital nurse. Open it alone."

"Why?"

"You think I know any whys, kid? That's just what he said."

My family stared at me, all questions, but I didn't have one answer. Unless . . . was this filled with greeting cards? That had to be it. I'd probably open only one each holiday, and based on how thick the thing was, I had loads of warm wishes ahead. I hugged the envelope tight, relieved that I'd gotten exactly what I wanted.

The lawyer went back to the will. "I didn't forget you, Holly. I just wanted you to sweat it out. Are you sweating? Did you buy a ridiculous dress for this pomp and circumstance? I hope it's periwinkle."

"It's yellow," I said out loud, like the lawyer was some medium and my grandpa could actually hear me. "And there are frills."

"Periwinkle with frills. You need more frills," the lawyer read.

My family laughed. He knows me—knew me—so well.

"Finally, I leave my granddaughter, Holly Evelyn Nolan, pause for dramatic effect." The lawyer furrowed his brow and read the line again to himself. "Oh, sorry. I think he was telling me to pause. Okay, I leave my granddaughter, Holly Evelyn Nolan"—this time he did pause, and it was clear he'd been in a courthouse once or twice and knew his pauses—"the Rose of Sharon Wedding Chapel. This place is all yours, Holly Bean. Now. Keep me in business."

CHAPTER 2

Later that night, I jogged up to the man-made lake in our master-planned community creatively titled the Lakes. We lived in crappy apartments on the northern outskirts of the community. James and I had nicknamed our "home" The Space, all stark walls and empty dreams. Sometimes I would sneak into the wealthy lakeside neighborhoods, just to see how long it took for security to stop me for a serious offense like walking on the sidewalk or looking poor.

The sun was setting, the dry air crisp. I burrowed into a patch of threadbare grass behind the Sail 'N shopping plaza, my own private spot. The building was a revolving door for businesses, the most recent being a wedding and banquet center. A garland of plastic flowers drooped over a gazebo on the gated deck. I'd only witnessed one wedding there from my patch, and it was pretty. Fake pretty. A lakeside wedding by a non-lake summarized Vegas's authenticity painfully well.

I counted sixty-three blades of grass, then switched to the pattern the lights made in the water—bright, bright, dim, bright, bright, dim. Next I thought of viable guesses concerning the contents of the still-unopened envelope resting on my stomach. Zero.

"Holly!" James was offshore, kicking the wheels of a paddleboat he must have "borrowed" from someone living on the lake. James was good at "borrowing" without getting caught. "Come on, pull me in."

It was darker now, the sun almost gone. I uncurled from my grass bed and helped maneuver him in with a large stick. He tied the boat rope onto the minidock. No one actually used the lake for anything other than prime real estate. The water was shallow, murky, and filled with bugs. I liked to catch and count the guppies that never seemed to grow into actual fish.

"How'd you know I was here?" I asked. "Were you following me?"

"Oh, is that what's in Grandpa's envelope? The deed to the dock? This is public property."

I jutted my thumb toward the No Trespassing sign.

"Whatever. I can be here if you can." James squeezed a hand into the pocket of his tight jeans and yanked out a bag of sunflower seeds.

I glanced at the road, wondering if I should do this at The Space. Home, where he could barge into my room anyway. When

I actually wanted to talk to my brother, he disappeared for hours, but when something interested him, there was no shaking the kid.

"Are you mad I got the chapel?" I asked.

"You know, for a genius, you ask stupid questions."

"I'm not a genius."

"Whatever, academically advanced. You know I don't care. The chapel smells like old ladies." He flicked a shell into the water. "I still want to know *why* you got it."

So did I.

"I'm supposed to open this alone."

"Grandpa wasn't talking about me." James spit out three shells in practiced syncopation. "He meant Dad and Donna, and that's because Grandpa knew all the adults would be mad you got the chapel. I bet he thought you'd be thirty or something when he died. Thirty and still working at that chapel. What's it like, being predictable?"

Miserable. Of course I would still work at the chapel. Rose of Sharon was my life. I would marry the chapel if marrying buildings was a thing, and I'd have Minister Dan do the ceremony. "I'm not predictable; I'm loyal. You should try it sometime."

"That's what Therapist Whitney said. She also said I should bond with you more." A sliver of shell hung from his lip. "So let's bond. Open it."

We huddled on the grass, the envelope between us. There was an old-fashioned light on the dock, but it was more for looks than function. James took out his cracked cell phone to illuminate the package.

"What if . . . what if I can't . . ." My voice caught. Whatever was inside here was going to change my life, and with that change, good or bad, there might be tears. I rarely if ever cried, and I didn't want James to pounce on the emotion if I finally did. Besides, I'd had enough sorrow this week, enough grief, and I still had a funeral to attend.

"I'm growing a beard waiting."

I was too nervous to make a puberty joke. Three more seconds, then I tore it open. We stared at each other before James tentatively beamed his cell phone inside. I pulled out an envelope with the name Dax on it.

"Who is Dax?" James asked.

I tapped the envelope against my hand. An old war buddy? U2 tribute band member? Grandpa Jim's life was freckled with interesting people. Dax could be anyone.

"Wait . . . there's a Cranston named Dax," I said. "We get their junk mail by mistake sometimes. But why would Grandpa leave something for someone related to Victor?"

"Bet there's anthrax in there," James said.

Our chapel shared a parking lot with Victor Cranston's chapel, but not by choice. If you got Grandpa raging on about Cranston, the conversation never ended. "It can't be the same Dax then."

"How many Daxes are there? Maybe you should open the envelope and see if there's a clue." James fumbled in his pocket again, this time unveiling a Swiss Army knife.

"Put that away," I said. "You'll hurt your hand."

"Everyone always says that and I never do."

James played the piano. He borderlined on prodigy. "Borderline" is a good overall descriptor for my brother.

"Where'd you get a knife?" I asked.

"Boy Scouts say you should always be prepared."

"Last time you went to Boy Scouts, you were eleven and your scoutmaster caught you smoking behind the rec center."

"Doesn't mean I didn't listen when they talked about things that mattered." James stuck the knife into his back pocket.

"Grandpa wouldn't have sealed the envelope if he wanted me to read it. Besides, look at this." There was an identical envelope inside addressed to me. This. This was what I'd been waiting for. Dreading. This letter would explain Dax, the inheritance, maybe even why Grandpa had to go and die when no one was ready for it. I eased my pinkie nail slowly along the fold, trying to keep the envelope as intact as possible. Grandpa Jim's small, neat handwriting cut into the thick ivory paper.

I counted the twenty-six "thes" appearing in the text, but it didn't do much to stop the harsh burst of emotion. So strange, the way handwriting outlives a person.

"If you want, I can leave you alone to read." James's face softened, like the handwriting had hit him too. "Get us some chili dogs."

My stomach was already twisted. Chili would not help. "No, no. I'll read it out loud. I'll stop if he says anything too, you know, personal." I paused, rather dramatically I must say, and read.

Holly Bean,

If you are not already freaking out about the chapel, then your dad or Donna will for you. I'm sure it was a shock, but hey. At least you didn't just take a defibrillator to the chest. There wasn't a white light, by the way. I'm a little worried about that. Good thing I like warm weather, right?

I'm doing this all wrong. No, I *did* this all wrong. The truth is, you're not just inheriting the chapel. You're inheriting a mess. It's a problem that I've been trying to fix for years, and in that attempt, I made it worse.

Let me explain: In the mid-2000s, the wedding business was booming. Literally, everyone and their mom was getting married (sometimes in back-to-back ceremonies). The money was ridiculous. Las Vegas started refinancing their loans, loans on their houses, on their businesses. Rose of Sharon was valued at double what I'd bought it for, so I refinanced the commercial mortgage with a balloon payment. Basically, I got a lot of money up front with the understanding that I would make small payments before paying a lump sum in seven years. I used that cash on the chapel. Okay, I also used the cash to take care of gambling debts and lost some more sports betting (stupid Lakers!), but most went to the chapel. Marble isn't cheap, and with how things were rolling, there was no end in sight.

Then the end became desperately visible. Apocalyptic. The economy crashed. People weren't coming to Vegas to get married; they weren't coming here period. Businesses failed, homes were lost. And the value the bank had put on my business didn't exist anymore.

I've been struggling to come up with money for the past couple of years and it's just not there. My savings are wiped, my assets laughable. I paid myself scraps to get by so I could still get money to your parents and other employees. No one has seen the books. No one else knows what situation we are in.

When it comes time to refinance this spring, I have to pay off the balloon payment or risk defaulting on the loan. They might refinance me again, but they will value the business at much less, and I will have to pay the difference back or lose the chapel.

Here, the handwriting switched to a bubbly cursive.

I'm feeling too weak to write, so I had this lovely nurse finish for me. Her name is Kiki. She's a keeper. And beautiful. Hey, if I make it out of this surgery, can I take you out for a steak dinner?

(From Kiki: Your grandpa has flirted with every nurse on this floor. He has a lot of steak dinners in his future.)

I don't know HOW you're going to keep the chapel in business. You'll have to talk to financial people, clue Donna in (I'm glad I'm dead so she can't kill me). Come up with a game plan to make some money. Believe me, if I could have fixed it alone, I wouldn't have to write this pathetic letter or the letter I need you to hand deliver to Dax Cranston.

Anyway, I'm sorry. I'm sorry I'm leaving this to you. I'm sorry I didn't tell you earlier. I'm sorry that your chances of success aren't great. I'm sorry because if you're reading this (and I really hope you never read this), it means I'm gone and our time together is gone too.

I'm sorry.

I love you, Holly Bean. You care about this chapel as much as I do. You know what this place means to our family. As for me, U2 said it best: "Home,

I can't say where it is but I know I'm going home."

Grandpa Jim

My brother's eyes were wide and alien-like in the dim cell phone lighting. "I can't believe he was dealing with all of that and he never told anyone."

My throat felt like I'd swallowed James's Swiss Army knife. "Me too. He was . . . he was drowning. Since we were kids. The whole time we've known him, like, really *known* him, he's been dealing with this."

"Poor Grandpa." For all my brother's toughness, he was a sweet kid. Reminded me of Pony Boy from that old book/movie *The Outsiders*. He talked big but had these chubby little cheeks. No matter what he did, I figured his cheeks would save him from too much destruction. Unless he joined a gang and they started to call him Baby Face. "That was probably the last thing he ever wrote."

"If the chapel closes . . ." I swallowed that painful "if."

"It's just a building."

"No, it's home."

James tossed a rock into the lake. "Home isn't a place, Holls."

I folded up the envelope, then smoothed out the four creases. Folded, unfolded. How desperate did he have to be to leave a failing business to his seventeen-year-old granddaughter?

James dumped half a bag of the seeds into his mouth and chomped, shells and all. His cheeks bulged. "Well, at least we know one thing."

One thing. One thing was a start. One thing could turn this crushing burden into a ray of hope. "What?"

"You're so going to screw this up."

CHAPTER 3

I woke up Saturday and enjoyed a good three seconds before I remembered that my grandpa was dead, just like he had been the morning before, and today . . . today I was going to attend his funeral. I stared at my alarm clock for five minutes, watching each minute march along, marveling at the power of time to just keep happening no matter what was going on in the world, no matter who was dying or living.

We had to take a hearse *to* the funeral. Grandpa Jim said he had to pay for one anyway, might as well get the full use. The vintage car had removable seats, so we all fit, but no seat belts. Irony there, riding a death trap to a funeral. Of course, the seats would need to be removed to fit a casket en route to the gravesite, and our family would have to bum rides.

The sun shone manically, oblivious. I leaned against the

window of the hearse and tried to block out my mom's voice. She was dreading this as much as her children were, but instead of the normal reaction of sullen silence, my mother prattled. At least she was trying *something*, which was more than I could say for my dad. He sat in the front with the driver, talking football like this was some leisurely Sunday drive.

"Your grandfather asked that all flowers be ordered through your subcontractor, what's her name?" Mom asked.

"Flowers by Michelle. Or Bunny's Boutique when Michelle's schedule is packed." I kept my eyes glued out the window, no matter how much I wanted to squint.

"Right. Michelle. Well, she was so touched that she's offering us a discount now for a year. The wedding community is great that way. Jim knew how to reach out."

Prattle. Prattle. Prattle. The responsibility of the chapel was almost as crushing as the funeral, so why did we have to talk about either?

"Mom," Lenore interrupted. "It's clear to all parties that you're trying to diffuse the situation by filling the void with mundane details."

"Lenore," Dad called from the front. That's all he ever said, "Lenore," like stating her name would magically change who she inherently was.

"I just think we're entitled to our grief," Lenore mumbled. James nibbled on a hangnail, his cuticles a short, bloody mess.

I picked off the sixteen pieces of lint on my skirt, wondering if it really was grief that Lenore was feeling and if that grief was anything like my own sharp hollowness. Whatever emotion was puncturing my insides, it was something I should be allowed to feel *inside*, not something to display at a funeral. We shouldn't have to be in this hearse right now, we shouldn't have to be around anyone; we should have quiet or solitude or music or patches of grass. Whatever we needed. Individually.

Instead, we had a whole day of dreary events, beginning with the family reception. "It'll be an intimate gathering area," Mom said, quoting verbatim the package pitch for the large meeting room behind the chapel. Over the past week, she'd carried around the mortuary's brochure in her purse until the creases ripped.

The wallpapered room was divided into work people, poker pals, U2 cover band members, and family, which was further divided by the invisible line between my parents that they swore did not exist.

Then there was a boy by the entrance who didn't seem to fit into any group. He was ungroupable. Unclassified. Aloof, alone . . . unworldly.

He shoved his hands into his pockets, shirtsleeves rolled. His hair was cut so short it was almost buzzed, and although he was average height at best, he was possibly an inch or two taller than me. Built, though. I could see that even in his dress shirt.

He didn't look like he knew anyone in the room or anyone knew him. Also, and I'm probably shallow for noticing this at a funeral, but he was not the ugliest guy I had ever seen. If looks were America and ugly was Los Angeles, this boy was comfortably Kentucky. West Virginia when he smiled.

He glanced up and caught me staring, and although I should have looked back at a picture of Grandpa's high school graduation, instead my instinct was to do this really lame . . . wave. And it was totally one of those moments where he looked behind him, because *I did not know him*, so why would I wave at him, right? But grief makes you do odd things at awkward times because you've forgotten how to act like a functioning human being. This boy happened to be within my age range and, again, not ugly, and I don't know, maybe I just wanted to talk to someone about something besides that time when I was five and Grandpa Jim made me sing at his wedding to his second wife, a story I'd already heard three times today.

I took a quick swallow of my cranberry cocktail and was working out this whole explanation, that my grandpa had this secret handshake that started with a wave and ended with air pumps, and I'd be happy to teach it to him. We'd laugh, but softly, because we were still aware of our surroundings. Then the funeral director would come to escort the family and I would say, "That's me." He'd give me a go-get-'em-tiger look, and I would never see him again, but that would be okay, because at least I was more in his memory than just a wave.

The boy (who wasn't really a boy, maybe a man . . . an in-between boy/man) looked back at me and instead of waving did a salute. It was the only possible thing worse than my wave, which made it the perfect gesture. I was about to head over and teach him my new secret handshake when he slipped into the hallway. I actually started to follow him before Sam and Camille blocked my exit.

"Holly!" Camille waved. Full force.

I blinked at my friends. It took a second for me to process that they were there, that people were really communicating with me, that I was standing where I was. "Hey, guys."

Sam crossed the room in three monstrous steps and gave me a bear hug. I stood there stiffly as he gathered me up. I breathed in that mix of piney soap and fruit Mentos that was Sam. "There's a country song, Garth Brooks, 'The Dance,' that says—"

"That song's depressing," Camille said. "Don't be depressing."

"I'm just saying, if Holly wants to cry or talk, do it now, before the big sob fest starts."

They both stared at me expectantly, like I really was going to break down. And I wavered for a second, almost told them about the money problems that I didn't even understand. But for what? What would it do? Make me think about it more? That wasn't even possible. It's like a neon sign was lit in my brain flashing CHAPEL! CHAPEL! CHAPEL! every six or seven seconds. "I'm . . . I'm whatever. It's a funeral."

"And it sucks." Sam reached down and tugged my hair like he used to during middle school math competitions. "Don't forget that part, Holls."

Camille sat on the edge of a wingback chair because that's all the space she took up. She was the girl who ate a half piece of gum and couldn't finish a whole soda to save her life. It wasn't a diet thing, she was just a Victorian lady like that. "I was going to get you something," she said out of nowhere. "Like, for support? But I didn't know what to get. I've never had someone in my life die. So how has it been so far? On a scale of one to ten, ten being the worst."

"Seventy-four. Seventy-five if you count the fact that Victor Cranston still needs to show up."

"I don't know who that is," Camille said. "Do we hate him?"

I loved how she did that. Declared someone her enemy if I told her to, as some strange display of loyalty. She did that with Sam too, asked which bands *they* liked, what *they* thought on different political issues.

Sam shifted. "Cranston's the guy who owns the Cupid's Dream Chapel."

"Oh, we *do* hate him then, right?" She twisted a strand of strawberry blond hair.

"Yes," Sam said. "Well, sort of, since I've never actually talked to him. If hate were a person, we'd be second cousins."

"First cousins for me. Maybe even an uncle," I said.

"Did your grandpa mention Cranston in the Instructions?" Sam asked.

"What instructions?" Camille asked.

"Of course," I said. "Cranston is supposed to show up drunk and make some shameful public display. I'm surprised Grandpa didn't print it in the program."

Sam guffawed. A man cleared his throat behind us. Sam wasn't trying to be irreverent, he just didn't know how to laugh softly. "Remember that time Jim sent him cheap wine for Christmas with that note? 'Cheap wine for a whiney cheap.'"

I cracked a smile. "Cranston came over waving that bottle. Thought he would smash it on Grandpa's head."

"When was this?" Camille asked.

"I don't know, Clarice was still working here."

"Remember Clarice?" I asked.

"I think Donna fired her because she didn't know what an alpaca is."

"She called it a llama." I laughed. "That's when Donna started hanging up all those alpaca calendars around the office, like she was going to educate Clarice."

Camille stuck out her bottom lip in a mock pout. "You guys have so many memories together."

"Camille, we have memories too." Sam rubbed her shoulder. "Different memories."

Hooking-up memories. Our friends called Sam and Camille "Peter and Cottontail" because those two were always going at it. Camille was homeschooled, with crazy-strict parents, so she wasn't actually even supposed to date Sam. They'd had this secret, forbidden relationship since the beginning of last year. It was all very romantic/dramatic/stupid, but I loved Sam, so as a favor, I begged Grandpa to give Camille a job working clerical. The number-one problem was Camille sucked at the job. She was great with people, but she misfiled things all the time and was terrible with the computer program. Grandpa kept threatening to fire her, but he didn't have it in him.

Now I guess Camille had more job security since I was the boss.

Ugh. *I was the boss.*

The funeral director cleared his throat. "Friends and family, as per Jim Nolan's Instructions, we'll now make our way into the chapel for the memorial service. His body will be available for viewing afterward. Graveside service is for immediate family only. Oh, and the bar will remain open until four this afternoon."

An open bar at a funeral.

I hoped this was the end of his crazy Instructions. The end after I delivered that letter to Dax Cranston, of course.

CHAPTER 4

I wish I could say the program was meaningful and special, but an hour of watery remembrances paled in comparison to the man my grandpa was. Plus, the open bar made everyone sloppy, and it was hard to tell if some of the memories were real or fictionalized.

Afterward, my bleary-eyed dad ushered the guests to the reflection room to ruminate over Grandpa Jim's legacy/get more drunk. Still no sign of the mortal enemy, which meant someone else was needed to do something dramatically stupid to appease my grandpa's ghost. With this crowd, I wasn't too worried.

Mom pulled me away and nodded to the door. "The viewing room is empty. Why don't you say your good-byes?"

"I did. Before he passed." I looked away. "He's gone, Mom."

"He's not gone for good. Just gone from here. Go on in. It'll help."

I sat in a foldout chair across from the casket, trying to muster the courage for a chat. The room was chilly, filled with dying flowers to cover up the scent of a dead person. The program may have been upbeat, but that didn't change the fact that everyone else got to walk out of that room and Grandpa would be in his faux gold box forever.

I chipped the black polish on three fingernails before I finally approached the casket. Grandpa Jim looked like a shriveled Bono from U2—red hair dyed black and cut short, with the signature tinted sunglasses, skin waxy and cold. I'd fought Mom and Dad on the open-casket thing and obviously lost. They said it brought emotional closure. Whatever—if they wanted healing, then the casket should be the thing closing, forget emotions.

Still, this would be the last time I would see him, or a version of him, and it was kind of nice to have this final moment. I reached down and readjusted his sunglasses.

"He's getting buried with his glasses?" Victor Cranston drooped against the doorway. "Wanna know why? His eyelids. Baggiest I ever saw. And he knew it. Bono, who likes Bono? Thought those shades gave him an air of mystery." He hiccuped. "Mystery, my foot, Jim Nolan."

"Grandpa Jim will be so glad you came," I said. "Drunk, just like he'd hoped."

Victor bought the chapel next door in the late nineties, a

decade after Grandpa Jim started his business. Cupid's Dream's previous owners were elderly lesbians who still sent us Christmas cards. But then came Victor, adding five themed chapels and a drive-up window and a stretch Hummer with cheesy cupids painted all over it and drunk patrons and everything that gave Vegas weddings a bad name.

He swayed into the room, lips curled around a full-dentured smile. "Did I interrupt something? You saying good-bye to this piece of garbage?"

I didn't realize how much I hated him until we finally met. Formally. There were all the times in the parking lot he'd flipped me off.

I blocked the casket. The man was still six feet away, but I could smell the alcohol. Alcohol and burned beef. "Grandpa Jim wanted more people around when you had your drunken fit."

"I'm hurt, darling. I'm here to pay my respects, just like anyone else." He charged over to the casket, literally pushing me away.

I counted to twelve. Twelve is usually my calming number. "You never showed him respect when he was alive. Why start now?"

"Poppy?" I was just snorting to myself about how stupid calling anyone "Poppy" was when the man/boy from the wake hurried into the room. His voice was higher than I'd imagined it would be, but it's hard to sound deep and throaty when uttering a word like that. When he saw me, he did the same kind of wave I'd done earlier. It made my heart soften. Skip. There was an unexpected skip. "Oh. Hi."

"I, uh . . . I wasn't trying to wave at you. Earlier." Quite possibly the only thing worse than waving was mentioning the wave and cementing myself as Wave Girl forever. "I thought you were someone else."

"Yeah, that salute wasn't for you either." He spoke with a southern accent, warm and mushy like a bowl of sugary oatmeal. "There was a veteran standing behind you."

"There was?"

He cracked a smile. It took me one unfortunate syllable before I got the joke. "A veteran. Salute. Cute." I tried to think of a funny line to follow it up, but it—him, here, this—was all too much.

Cranston cleared his throat. "Dax, you done flirting? Can I finish up my business here?"

Dax. This was Dax. Grandson Dax. Here was this short moment, a small breath that didn't burn, and I shared it with Dax Cranston. Great, Grandpa Jim. Who doesn't leave a sealed envelope for their enemy's lovely grandson?

Victor stuck his sausagey hand into the casket and snatched Grandpa Jim's sunglasses. "That's better. Now you can meet your maker in all your saggy glory."

The adrenaline kicked in. If Grandpa Jim wanted a scene, I would deliver. I would gouge Victor's ferrety eyes, yank his oily hair, rip his cheap suit. I would do it, and I would enjoy it. "Put those back."

"Come on, this is stupid," Dax said. "Shake everyone's hands and let's go. You're better than this."

Clearly arguable.

Victor twirled the glasses around his fingers, sizing me up. I did not squirm, although one look from this man made me want to jump into a tub of hand sanitizer. "So . . . what I really want to know is, what happens to the chapel?"

"What do you mean? People come in, they get married, we make money. Does it work differently for you guys?" I couldn't believe how calm my voice sounded.

"It's the make-money part that you aren't too good at. It's going to be fun to see that place nosedive under new ownership. Who's in charge now, that secretary of his or your dad?"

"None of your business."

"That's where you're wrong. This is all business. And I'm watching. Remember that."

"Whatever." I wanted to follow that up with "suck it," but I kept it classy.

"We'll see you in the parking lot, darling." He snapped the glasses in half and tossed them into the casket. "Rest in peace, Jimmy."

I was panting, but I didn't hear it until Victor and his scent left the room. I was going to . . . I was going to run after Cranston and tackle him to the floor. Go blind fury, taking full advantage of the don't-hit-a-girl rule.

Before I had a chance to attack, Dax stepped in front of me. "Hey. Hey. Don't go after him. It's not going to help."

"It'll help his face when I punch it."

"Seriously, just stay here with me for a second. He's a mean drunk. Let him cool off. Breathe."

I seethed at the now-empty doorway. "Those were his favorite sunglasses."

"Poppy gets a mind to destroy property sometimes. Can I pay for them?"

I blinked at Dax. "It doesn't matter, I guess. My grandpa is dead either way."

"Right." He scratched his close-cropped hair like a dog with a behind-the-ear itch. "Look, I'm sorry for your loss."

"Yeah. Me too." I was sorry that he was witnessing my loss too. My loss and my anger and my awkwardness. So I went back to the anger. "Your grandpa is a prick."

"He can be." He shrugged. His left shoulder rose higher than his right. "I've heard some stories about your grandpa too."

"Don't lump my grandpa into the same category as that man."

"Your grandpa filed four different lawsuits against mine for nothing."

"I never heard that," I said.

"Just because you didn't hear about it doesn't mean it didn't happen."

I stuttered. "W-well . . . Victor probably deserved it."

"Probably not, but that's how it was with our grandfathers. They weren't at their best around each other. Everyone has some prick in him."

"My grandpa is right in front of you!" I pointed toward the casket, like Grandpa would have my back. "Don't speak ill of the dead."

"Right. Forget I said anything. . . ." His voice skidded away. Maybe I could tape the glasses back together. It's not like Grandpa needed them to block the sun underground.

"Well, anyway," I said.

"Yeah. Anyway."

He didn't leave. He just stood there, all moody expression and toned arms. Not that the arms had anything to do with his expression.

"Listen." Dax hesitated before launching into a ramble. "Do you *really* think the dead can hear us? Are they sitting there now, hanging on our every word, worried what the living think about them? Then the longer you live, the more people around you die, and you have all these ghosts judging your every move. Pee in the shower, your great-aunt Mildred knows about it. It's creepy thinkin', right?"

"I don't think the . . . the deceased listen to everything that we say," I said. Who was this kid? "Maybe they just tune in for special events. Like at graduation or when someone says, 'Your great-aunt Mildred is smiling down on you.'"

"Sure." He rubbed at his jaw, which had enough stubble that I couldn't tell how old he was. Eighteen? Nineteen? Older. Older than me. "But if we're going to enlist in the life-after-death camp, then we should go my-own-private-paradise with it. Great-Aunt Mildred doesn't have time to see the messy birth of her great-great-niece. She doesn't care if you thought she was sweet or mean. The lady is busy. She's up there munching on Kit Kats with a lesser-known president and knitting sweaters out of clouds."

"A cloud sweater," I repeated.

"Cable-knit."

"But if the person who passed away can't hear us," I reasoned, "then why are we here? God must have invented funerals so the dead people could watch them. Otherwise, it's just a room full of people trying to convince themselves that they cared enough about the dead person, or that the dead person had cared about them. It's a joke."

He looked at me then, for the first time, right in the eye. It's not like I usually made a lot of eye contact with strangers—not salesclerks or people passing on the street, certainly not men/boys with eyes the color of cloudless sky. "I'm sorry I was joking. It doesn't make this a joke. Whatever you're feeling . . . that's not a joke. I just know sometimes . . . it helps. Maybe not right now." He puffed out a breath. "Did I go too far with the cloud sweater? You should be alone now, right?"

"Alone with a dead relative? No. The only thing worse than the funeral is a viewing. It doesn't make anyone feel better."

"My advice?" His voice went quiet. "The only thing that is going to make you feel better is time. And even that doesn't help much."

I lowered my voice too, the words almost too hopeful to utter. "But it does get better?"

"Better is a strong word." He swallowed. "But you're fixing to be okay. Soon."

I had never seen this boy in my life. I had no idea how he knew so much about death. The only thing I knew about him was that his poppy was Satan. Yet he'd invented a great-aunt Mildred to prove a philosophical point. His reassurance was better than anything my friends or family had said to me so far.

It was like he'd sliced this tiny slit through the curtain of death that had been hanging over my heart.

It would have been the perfect time to tell Dax about the strange letter, but there was a loud crash in the hallway. We hurried outside. Victor was waving his cane around at my dad, who weaved under it and pummeled into Victor's chest. My mom screamed and James jumped in and starting clawing Victor's arm. Lenore even got a kick or two in there.

"Not again." Dax lunged forward and pulled Victor back. I stood in the doorway, too stunned to move.

"Poppy! Stop it! Go get in the car."

"I'm taking your chapel down!" Saliva dripped from the corners of Victor's mouth. "Just wait, you won't last a year." His comb-over was no longer combed over but flopped in front of his sweating forehead.

"Scum!" Dad jammed his finger at Victor's chest. "You can't touch us. Our chapel is fine."

"Jim Nolan hasn't been *fine* in years. You think I don't know? Do you have any idea who I know, what I can do?"

Now the funeral director tried to get in on it. "Gentlemen, if you would please—"

"We were just going." Dax veered his grandpa to the door. He stopped in front of my mom and offered a weak smile. "Ma'am . . . our condolences."

"Nolans are garbage!" Victor hollered, and Dax pushed him outside. Dax glanced back at me and mouthed "*Sorry*" before the door closed. His mouth was . . . it was beautiful.

The guests tutted behind us. Mom grabbed me in a squeeze. "Who was that you were talking to?"

"Dax. His grandson."

"What a terrible family."

"No, he was trying to be nice."

Dad wiped blood off his mouth. "I can't believe he smashed Dad's picture like that. What a lunatic. I'm taking legal measures this time—it's a funeral. Who does that?"

I wandered away from the chaos, back to my grandpa's casket. With all the cleanup, I probably had time now to get new glasses or tape his old ones. He deserved glasses, and I deserved to know what was going on. "Okay, if you really are sitting on a cloud, listening, please tell me, why am I delivering a letter to that really cute Cranston? Why give me all of this? Seriously, what were you thinking?"

Grandpa Jim didn't answer. But even dead, he was telling me something. I just didn't know what.

CHAPTER 5

We still had to work that night, so Donna, Dad, Minister Dan, and I headed back to the office. This particular ceremony had been booked out for six months, and the couple was flying in from England, so we couldn't cancel, funeral or not.

Our golden-hued reception area was still warm and welcoming despite Grandpa's absence. Chairs were arranged in a conversational circle around the stiff-backed brocade couch, with a screen on the coffee table so that Mom could break down package options.

The couple before us tonight was, blessedly, of a forever nature. Scientifically, forever. Oh, and romantically, I guess. After each ceremony, I wrote down details into different categories, details like dress style, body language, duration of dating, age, groom's shoe size . . . you know, just the typical stuff you notice at a wedding. Then I plugged that into a formula I created that estimated within 2 percent the marriage success rate of each couple. Of course, I'd only been tracking for five years, so I'd have to wait decades to see who would survive, but I kept up with our couples, and most of those with percentages under 20 were already divorced.

Not that I *wanted* them to get divorced, mind you, but it's a great feeling knowing I was right.

Charlie and Emma Dean, though, these two had it. They held hands without groping, they laughed at each other without laughing *at* each other. They'd only walked into the building ten minutes ago and already I'd given them a 79 percent. If they nailed the vows, they were well on their way to their golden anniversary.

Donna wore her work bun and work smile. "Do you have any more questions?"

"Can you take a picture of our rings?" Emma asked. "Something with the bouquet, or on top of lace would be nice."

"It was my mum's," Charlie explained. "And she'll massacre us all if we don't do a picture."

Dad laughed. "You have me and this chapel to yourselves tonight. We can do any picture you want."

"Brilliant." Charlie stuck his wallet into his back pocket. "Mind if we clean up first?"

"Of course," Donna said. "I'll show Emma to the bridal room. The bathroom is on the right."

Charlie left but poked his head right out. "The loo has gold urinals."

Emma beamed at her fiancé. "Only the finest for you, love."

I wanted to bundle the Dean family into my pocket and pluck them out from time to time just to listen to their accented banter. I loved accents, like Dax's southern drawl. He'd obviously lived somewhere else long enough to develop that accent, so maybe that geographical distance meant he wasn't close to his poppy. Maybe he didn't even like his grandpa. We could sit around and hate the man together.

"Do you have a moment?" Donna led me into the photo studio. Dad was switching out backgrounds.

"Dad? Can you leave?" I asked.

Dad harrumphed. "I still can't believe Cranston pulled that at the funeral. I have half a mind to march over there now."

It was the fifth time he'd made a similar threat. As kind as both of my parents were, they had a blind spot when it came to Victor Cranston. "Don't leave the chapel, just the room. Please."

"Fine." Dad dropped the curtain. "Make it quick, boss."

"So how are you doing?" I asked once Dad left.

"Two of my alpacas, Milton and Clarabelle, were depressed today. I shouldn't have broken the news about Jim. He always brought them treats."

I filed away the alpaca comment to share with James later. He was obsessed with Donna's alpaca obsession. "But how are you?"

"I'm a mess." Donna didn't look like a mess. She looked exactly the same every time I saw her: a different colored suit for each day of the week (Saturday: lavender—seasons and funerals be damned), nude tights, cloggish shoes, and hair too aggressively blond to be natural.

"I'm sorry. I know you and Grandpa were . . . whatever you were."

"We dated on and off for nine years. Let's call a spade a spade."

Gross. We all knew there was something more between Donna and Grandpa, but no one ever came out and said it. Probably because the idea was disgusting—he had to be twenty years older than she was. And he was her boss. And he was my *grandfather.* "Sorry. Right."

"And while we are speaking frankly, let's discuss the chapel."

"Are you . . . are you okay? That it went to me?"

"You're seventeen. No one is okay with it."

I sucked in a breath. "Oh."

"It's nothing personal to you. Look at the facts. You're still in school, you have other obligations, you lack life experience, independent contractors aren't going to take us seriously, you are now essentially your parents' boss, and—"

"I get it."

Donna puckered her lips. "But it doesn't matter how I *feel* about it, because you legally and lawfully are in charge. What matters now is that I would like to keep my job."

I laughed softly. "Donna. You still have a job. I'm not changing anything."

"Well. You need to change *something.*" Donna leaned in closer. "I looked at the books for the chapel. It's bad."

My stomach dropped. Part of me would rather talk about

her relationship with Grandpa. "I know. Grandpa explained things in his letter."

Donna frowned. "I've been talking to the bank. There's debt. Lots of it. Jim owes about seventy thousand dollars; we have eleven thousand in cash, but he was behind on the last two months' payments. We're not going to come up with that kind of money before the balloon payment is due in March, but the financial guy I talked to said we could probably pay some of the debt and refinance if we can show the bank we're profitable under new ownership."

"What are you two talking about?" Dad popped his head back into the room. "I thought you were talking women stuff, but this sounds like business."

"Were you spying?" I asked.

"Yes." Dad ran his hand through his hair. I'd seen many happy-with-their-husband brides blush when my dad did that hair thing. "Did Cranston do something else?"

Donna gave my elbow a squeeze. Sixth Cranston comment. One-track mind.

Donna told Dad about the loan. His bloodshot eyes reddened to demonic. We shouldn't be having this conversation now, not the day of the funeral, not with Charlie and Emma outside, waiting for the happiest moment of their lives.

"Sixty thousand? How is my dad in the hole sixty thousand on this place?" Dad asked.

"Fresh flowers aren't cheap," Donna pointed out.

"So what do we do?" I asked.

"By my calculations, we need to double our ceremonies. That should get us in the right ballpark."

Double? The thing is, if we knew how to make money, we would already be doing it. I didn't know how much we brought in a month, but I knew doubling the ceremonies would mean doubling time and resources we just didn't have.

"And what if we don't get another loan?" I asked.

"Then we . . . then we default."

And we lose the chapel. That was the real ghost in the room, the haunting truth that none of us said out loud. If we didn't come up with a plan, and fast, my grandpa's legacy, and my entire family's source of income, would be gone.

"It's the slow season," I said. "We have New Year's and Valentine's, a few Christmas breakers. If it were June, I wouldn't be worried, but now . . ."

"We have Angel Gardens," Dad said. "They give us so much business, maybe we can talk to more reception halls?"

"Yeah, that's good. We'll have to think what else we can do differently, even if it means fake flowers and cutting corners. I'm scheduling a brainstorming meeting with the rest of the staff Monday."

"Holly, no." Dad grabbed a camera lens from his bag. "I had no idea this was going on. This is too big for you. Let Donna and me figure this out."

Donna nodded. "I'm so glad you said something."

"He can say all the 'somethings' he wants, but this is still my responsibility."

"And I'm still your father," Dad said. "There's your schoolwork to think about, your time with your family."

I almost laughed. What time with my family? All those daddy-daughter dates we never went on? "Grandpa explained this in his letter."

My upper hand. Neither of them got a letter or special instructions to see that Cranston grandson I was supposed to automatically hate. Grandpa had groomed me for this job, even if the job came sooner than we all thought. I had never let him down when he was alive, and I wasn't about to do it in his death. I opened the door. "The Deans are waiting. You know what Grandpa would say. Let's go make some memories."

Dad and Donna exchanged a contemplative glance. Finally, Dad shook his head and walked out.

It was a small moment, but a victorious one.

Now I just had a war to fight.

The Deans had no wedding guests. They'd spent all their money to get to Vegas, the city Emma had wanted to get married in since she was eleven and saw the Nicholas Cage movie *Honeymoon in Vegas.* Charlie laughed at the absurdity of the dream but saved for seven months to make it happen anyway. Emma wore a simple sheath dress, Charlie a gray suit. They shimmered.

"Hey, you," Charlie whispered when Emma walked down the aisle.

"Hey, yourself."

"We're actually getting married, Em."

Emma acted confused. "Is that where this dress came from? I wondered why that blimey minister was standing there."

And so it went.

They wrote their own vows, filled with inside jokes and tearful moments. Minister Dan went off script, sharing earnest advice based on his own thirty-five years of marriage. The light from the candelabra danced on their faces.

"As long as you both shall live?"

"Absolutely." Charlie glowed. "Since we're here anyway."

"You're supposed to say 'I do,' you twit." Emma squeezed his hand.

"I do."

"And do you, Emma, take Charlie to be your lawfully wedded husband, to have and to hold, for richer and poorer, in sickness and in health, as long as you both shall live?"

"I do." Emma giggled. "I do!"

They kissed before Minister Dan told them to.

Donna dabbed at her eyes. "What are their chances?"

"Ninety-two percent." The ceremony was a drop of rain on a day dry of hope. Charlie and Emma were the reason we were in this business, and the reason we had to *stay* in business. "Don't worry about the chapel. It's going to work out."

"Honey, I know you take business classes at school, but—"

"No. It will. Remember what Bono said."

"Great." Donna groaned. "Tell me what Bono said."

"The job of life is to turn your negatives into positives."

"I was hoping the Bono quotes would die with your grandpa."

"The quotes stay." I smiled as Emma and Charlie skipped down the aisle. "And so will the chapel."

I believed my words right then, I really did. I believed them about 63 percent.

CHAPTER 6

I didn't go to a normal high school. Normal in the way that high school movies portray schools, at least. As a magnet school, West Career and Technical Academy didn't have a homecoming game or even organized sports. If we wanted to participate in any of these things, we did it at the school we were zoned for. There were kids who shuttled back and forth between their academic and social zones, but not me. West was a hard school. There wasn't extra time for extracurriculars. I tried cross-country at another school my first year to get a PE credit, but I didn't like making something like running competitive. There's enough competition in life as it is.

I enrolled at West for a few reasons. Sam was a year older than me, so I'd already heard all about the school. I inherited all his older friends, making my freshman year relatively seamless.

Most of the guys were in the Sports Medicine elective, which was filled with sports enthusiasts and premeds. Sam was in the Biotechnology program, which was just as sexy as it sounds, and promised to breed the next generation of biologists and geneticists and other careers ending in "-ist." The main reason I went to West was because of the Business Management program. It was geeky how much I loved my classes. I guess if a seventeen-year-old had to run a business, I was more prepared than most.

We shared some core classes with other programs, one of which was advanced calculus. I couldn't be more excited for our test Monday, an entire period devoted to equations, beautiful and simple, all without any symbol or number representing a chapel or deceased grandparent or divorced parents or *D A X*.

Except for, you know, when you're actually solving for *X*.

"You look way too chipper for a Monday morning," Sam said as we pushed through the front doors.

"Calculus," I said.

"Of course. Who doesn't love a good test? I'm surprised the whole school isn't dancing around, what with all the amazing things like tests and pop quizzes raining down on us."

"It really is a great school," I agreed.

"Sarcasm, Holls. Sarcasm."

I headed straight for my locker, the seventh one on the right of the fourth hallway. It was the same thing I had done every weekday morning previously, all those mornings before I'd inherited my grandpa's drama.

Sam followed me, even though his locker was two hallways over. "You didn't text me back yesterday," he said.

"I know. I cocooned all day."

"What marathon did you do?" he asked.

"Little House on the Prairie."

He cringed. "I'm buying you new DVD boxed sets for Christmas. I promise you'd love *Game of Thrones* if you'd just get into it."

"Don't bother. Everything you watch is a downer. When I'm cocooning, I want happy and safe."

"Isn't that show about pilgrims? What's happy about pilgrims? They killed all the Indians."

"I would correct you right now, but there are too many things to correct."

The need to cocoon was something I could better explain to a girl friend or even a sister who was not Lenore. Surely most females understood the importance of wrapping oneself in a large duvet for a solid five hours with nachos and a high-quality series about homesteaders. Not *pilgrims.*

But it'd been a while since I'd had a close friend who was a girl, which wasn't even a conscious choice. There hadn't been some epic junior high fallout with an evil bestie, and I didn't grow boobs so early that the girls were jealous. No boyfriend had been stolen from me, and I'd never stolen someone else's.

I just didn't fully understand my gender. Socially, I could tell there were things I was supposed to say or feel and I was always a beat off. One-on-one, I was fine, but in groups I struggled to follow the conversation. With my guy friends, emotions weren't discussed. We stuck to topics. I was a huge fan of conversational topics.

Sam's face lit up, and I could already sense the boys lumbering down the hall.

"Kiss her!" Grant yelled for only the fifty-seventh time this month. Yes. That was an exact count.

"He's never going to give up on that," Sam said.

"Maybe he'll give us a break if you marry Camille."

Sam actually blushed. "Yeah, and you'll be the best man. Then Grant will go back to asking me if you're a lesbian."

"I have short hair, understand sports, and hang out with dudes. Grant's never going to be convinced otherwise."

"Maybe you should kiss *me* and prove me wrong," Grant said.

I turned around. I could make a joke about Grant's hair today—pigtail braids—but he wanted it too much. I wasn't one of those girls who ran my fingers through his luscious locks, asking to brush and style them, the whole time Grant purring like a cat in heat.

He was with Porter and Mike, as always, like that dog in Harry Potter with the three different heads. After Sam, they were my best friends, and when it came to everyday things, like wakeboarding at Lake Mead or game night at Buffalo Wild Wings, they were amazing company. Part of the reason I loved my school so much was because of them. But sometimes, like the Monday after my grandpa's funeral, the combination of them was just too much.

"Dude, you look like crap," Porter said in disgust, taking in my faded black yoga pants and UNLV hoodie. "What happened to your face?"

I glanced at the mirror in my locker, at the dark circles under my green eyes, my freckles stark against my hollow cheeks. I'd put lip gloss on that morning to combat the sorrow, but it looked cartoonish on my pale face. I slammed my locker. "Shut up."

Grant tried to shove him. Porter, who was nicknamed Portly until his chub turned to muscle in tenth grade, didn't even budge. "Her grandpa just died, dickwad. Of course she's going to look like crap."

"Thanks, Grant."

Mike slid his arms under my backpack straps and gave me a hug. "You hanging in there?"

Stupidest thing to ask. "Yeah."

"You want to talk about it?"

Porter snorted. "Holly doesn't talk about things like that. That's what makes her cool."

Things like what? Death? Does anyone talk openly about that? "You guys are really making this a big deal."

"Because it is." Mike hugged me closer. I barely came up to his shoulders. "Whatever you need. I'm here."

Mike and I dated for four days my freshman year, a lukewarm relationship at best, and yet he'd spent the two years since believing we had this sacred bond, that he understood me in ways no one else could. Nine times out of ten, his efforts came off as forced, but sometimes there was a flash of authenticity, and I wondered if maybe he did know me better than the others, if I should have hung around.

This was not one of those times. The hug lingered much longer than a sympathy hug should and ended with an awkward back tickle. I pulled away and cut Sam a look. He swallowed back a smile. He knew all about what I called the "Mike Ickies."

"Thanks, Mike. I . . . appreciate it."

Mike gave a modest shrug. Even his shrugs perved me out.

"Okay, hate to break up this team huddle, but I have a calculus test, so I'll see you guys after fifth period," I said. "Are we doing late lunch after school? Where?"

"Costco for hot dogs," Grant said.

"Hawaiian barbecue?" Mike asked.

"My turn to pick," Porter said. "I'm broke. So Sam's house for sandwiches."

"You guys ate all the leftover enchiladas last week," Sam whined.

We grinned. His mom would make more. She always did. Sam's 293,023-square-foot house (estimate) had been hangout Mecca since Sam hosted middle school math club there.

And listen. Number Crunchers was a *cool* math club. We ate fraction pie, like, every day.

"Uh, since we have you here, together"—Sam fiddled with the zipper on his backpack—"we wanted to give you something."

The boys shuffled into a solid line. The five-minute bell rang, and I shifted my weight, counting the nine seconds it took Sam to open his bag. Christmas was still a month away, but that didn't mean they weren't giving me a prank present. Valentine's last year they bought me a blow-up doll; my birthday was an old tube sock Grant found under his dad's bed.

"I have to get to class, guys."

Sam pulled out a piece of black paper. On it, in white chalk, he'd written "RIP JIM NOLAN." When I looked closer, I realized it was a tombstone. If it was a joke, it was sick, but if this was an act of kindness, well . . . that would be a big if. Sam flipped it around. On the back were a few hacked-up pictures of my grandpa and me, obviously printed off the computer.

"We got these online," Grant said. "For you to hang in your locker."

"Sort of a memorial," Mike said. "I know how close you were with Jim."

"Don't call him 'Jim' like you knew him," Sam said.

"My mom got mad that I used her scrapbook paper for the tombstone," Porter said. "But it's that stiff kind."

"Stiff." Grant snickered.

"It's called card stock," I said. One of the taped pictures fluttered to the ground. I knelt down to pick it up and stopped, staring at the grainy photo. Sam took it on 12/12/12, one of our biggest moneymaking wedding days to date. Grandpa and I painted 12s on our cheeks and made the numbers 1 and 2 with our fingers, although Grandpa got his mixed up so it's twenty-one.

I swallowed and looked up at my friends. "Thanks."

"Come on, Holls, zip up your hoodie a little." Porter scrunched up his face. "I can see your bra."

"Ah, she's wearing the green one," Mike said, like he ever saw my bra, and like I had the same bra I did freshman year.

I stood up and used a piece of gum to stick the tombstone in my locker. They'd never done something like this for me. It made the hurt bigger and smaller, if that makes any sense.

✦ ✦ ✦

I did well on the test, not because I had laser focus going in, but because I couldn't fail a calculus test if I tried. I actually *did* try, last year, in trig, when my parents first told me about the divorce. Midway through I got so bothered that I erased all the wrong answers I'd meticulously biffed and zipped through it again. I screwed up the class curve with that test.

My cry for help wasn't even a meow.

The day went downhill after that. It was that stupid envelope I'd been carrying around ever since the funeral, like I was going to run into Dax at the grocery store.

After school, I spent seventeen minutes pacing across no man's land, a.k.a. the parking lot separating Rose of Sharon and Cupid's Dream. The half-finished condos a block east cast a shadow across the asphalt. Grandpa and I used to wager bets when they'd start construction again, but after three years the skeletal structure still remained undressed, a looming reminder of the still-anemic economy.

I'd never looked between the two chapels and imagined

why a bride or groom would pick their garish monstrosity over our quaint slice of heaven. I honestly tried to look at both chapels objectively, but even from that in-between vantage point, the only positive thing about Cupid's Dream I could think of was that Dax worked there. And I was the only one, in my family at least, who would view that as remotely positive.

Eighteen minutes in, and I finally crossed the invisible line between the buildings. Too bad Grandpa's brass band wasn't there to signify that moment. There should be something heralding my visit to the dark side besides the traffic noises from the Strip.

I would walk in, hand Dax the envelope, walk out.

Walk in. Hand over. Walk out.

I'd only been in Cupid's Dream once. There'd been a power outage, and Grandpa Jim had sent me over to see if Victor had the same problem, or "if that SOB cut my power line." The power was out block-wide, so I'd only seen the dark lobby before running back to Grandpa.

Lighting didn't help the space much. Every one of Grandpa's rules was broken. Fake flowers, mauve and hunter-green decor. The front desk had a phone ringing off the hook, there were papers everywhere, and pictures of Victor with various celebrity patrons peeled off the wall.

I sat down on the bench and noticed the faux finish was chipping off. The counter had a display case, like a jewelry store, selling garters and mugs and mini top hats that said, "I got hitched at Cupid's Dream!" Behind the desk was this refrigerator with wilted bouquets on sale for $9.98. Hey, the marriage might not last, but at least the couple wouldn't go into the double-digit price point on floral design.

"Whattya need, sweetie?" a voice asked from behind a pile of paperwork. A woman's purple-gray coif sprouted above the mound like a feathery petunia.

I stood up so I could see the woman behind the counter, but all I got was more hair and the top of her glasses. "Lot of work, huh?" I asked

She shuffled a stack to the side so she was finally visible. Her smile was coffee-stained but kind. "Big sci-fi convention in town this weekend. Drive-through chapel had more traffic than the I-15."

This was another way our chapels differed. Grandpa was about quality; Victor was about quantity. Yes, Cupid's Dream ran the marital equivalent of a McDonald's value meal, but they still killed us when it came to revenue. Grandpa, purist that he was, swore that didn't matter, but when we faced losing the chapel, well, money . . . it didn't hurt.

"Busy's good though," I said.

"Life will get even busier if the boss gets his way."

Did his way have anything to do with my chapel? I wanted to ask her more, but she cut me off.

"You here for a ceremony or tour? I know you ain't getting married, unless your daddy is nearby to sign permission."

"I need to see Dax," I said.

She smirked. "One of Dax's girls, are you?"

"I'm not anyone's girl," I said, a blush rising in my cheeks. "One of Dax's girls" meant there were multiple, right?

"He's setting up in the Gable-view chapel. Down the hall, right one on the very end. Gunslingers at sundown."

I ignored her final cryptic comment. Gunslingers was likely slang for clients with an illegal source of income. Here, I wouldn't be surprised.

Sweat trickled down my back as I crept through the hallway. Victor could barrel through one of these doors at any moment and kick me right to our shared curb. The first door opened to their "traditional chapel." I poked my head in for a quick assessment.

Their biggest chapel was still much smaller than ours. I'd guess most of their clientele didn't come with a large wedding party. And ugh . . . the faux marble columns. Why, why, why? I won't even discuss the dust on the plastic carnations. Couldn't they at least spring for roses? Carnations are the weeds of the wedding world. And white folding chairs. What was this, the Elks Lodge?

"Looking for someone?"

I spun around. Dax startled when he recognized me. I did more than startle; I might have screamed. But he was dressed up like a frickin' cowboy, with a plaid shirt, leather chaps, and revolvers. Guns. Gunslinger.

He patted his chaps. "I'm in charge of the Old West wedding. Starts at sundown. When the preacher asks if anyone objects, I stand up and fire blanks. It's a big seller for us."

"Classy," I muttered.

Dax smiled down at me. I avoided eye contact by staring at his chaps. Which didn't help. Apparently, I had a thing for chaps.

"I'm surprised to see you. Especially here," he said. "Did you come for a tour?"

"No. I need to talk to you."

"Sounds promising."

"It's business." I kept an edge in my voice.

Dax glanced back down the hallway and opened the door to the right. He flipped the switch, lighting a room with black chairs, lace curtains, red candles, and dead, really dead, flowers.

"Grandpa sells it as Paranormal Paradise. Thank God for *Twilight*."

"What? He thinks a couple should be joined in holy matrimony in *this*?" I wrinkled my nose at the room.

"So y'all think a wedding has to be all stiff and buttoned-up?" Dax scratched his cheek. I stared in wonder at his throat, covered with stubble. The last boy I dated, Thomas, worked on his mustache for months, and it was still nothing but blond fuzz. Got to the point that I didn't want to kiss him, just thinking of that muff ball on his lips. And here Dax was, with dark specks of wonder all along his jawline.

"Of course it should be. A wedding is an occasion." My voice grew stronger as I echoed Grandpa's favorite sales pitch. "Not a pit stop."

"But a wedding should match the couple's personality," Dax said. "Some people want to say 'I do' dressed like Princess Leia and Han Solo. So what? Shouldn't the happiest day of your life be fun?"

"Can't it be fun *and* classy?" I asked.

"If that's what you want it to be," Dax said. "I'm just saying we cater to a different clientele."

"Clearly."

He sat down and nodded at the seat next to him. "So tell me why you are here, Jim Nolan's mysterious granddaughter."

"Holly. I'm Holly." Why was I there? Because my grandpa told me to be. I was honoring a dying request. This was the truth I could share with anyone, like my family if they'd seen me in the parking lot and asked what I was doing.

The secret truth had something to do with all the things I couldn't help noticing about Dax, like the way he breathed—deep and with purpose. Like air was a gift, not a reflex.

I was just noticing these things, like you do with an actor or a boy band member, someone you would never think to be with but still don't mind staring at in glossy pages. I knew who Dax was, and who I was, and was very aware of the differences and divisions between us.

I had hormones, but I also had *standards*.

"I have a delivery." I pinched the thick envelope in my purse.

Walk in.

Hand the envelope over.

And . . . what was the last thing? Stay and watch him open it, right?

Dax set the envelope in his lap. "Thanks. And I'm glad you came by. I wanted to talk about that, uh, spectacle with Poppy the other day. I know y'all won't believe it, but he's going to miss your grandpa too. He's grieving in his own way."

I snorted. "I guess it's hard to be the villain without a hero."

"Ouch."

Okay, I was on Victor's home turf. Sitting in that morbid and themey room just made me bitter. Seriously, was that formaldehyde I smelled? *Why would anyone ever want to get married here?* "Sorry. I think I'm mechanically engineered to say stuff like that without thinking. I won't condemn you for your relations anymore."

He breathed out. "Neither of us will. It's just a last name. A rose by any other name would smell as sweet."

"What?"

"Shakespeare. It's the only line I know. I probably shouldn't tell you that so you think I'm smarter than I am."

I had no Shakespeare to shoot back, so I stayed quiet as he tore off the right end of the envelope, making sure not to rip the paper inside. He shook out the letter, glancing at the signature at the bottom. "It's from your grandpa."

"Yeah. When he died . . ." I paused. That might have been the first time I'd said that word out loud. "He left me some things. One was that letter, with instructions to hand deliver it to you."

Dax set the paper down on his lap. The envelope was open, but he hadn't read it.

"I mean, why?" he asked.

"Why what?"

"Why me?"

"I wish I could tell you." I rubbed my hands against my shirt. Why was I so hot? Victor Cranston should spend less money on heating the building and more on his floral arrangements. "Things haven't made much sense since he died."

"I'm sorry again." He meant it.

"That's your tenth apology," I said.

"I use them all up at the beginning. Don't expect more."

I rolled my eyes but couldn't keep from smiling.

He smooshed his lips together. "I don't understand this. I've never even met your grandpa. Why would he leave something for me?"

"Read it and find out."

Dax looked down at the paper. "It says I'm supposed to read this alone."

"Mine said that too."

He glanced up at me. "It specifically says without you here."

This crazy mystery was never going to be solved. I shook my fist at the ceiling. "Grandpa Jim! I'm going to come knock you off your cloud!"

"It's fine. I just won't read it out loud." Dax did that brow-furrow thing as he scanned the letter. He looked older, like all the wisdom and sorrow in the world were embedded in the wrinkle between his eyes. He folded the paper into thirds, sticking it in his back pocket like I'd just given him directions to IHOP.

"Well, then." He brushed off his chaps. "That makes sense now."

"Sense? There is nothing about me sitting in a gothic wedding chapel with a ridiculously handsome cowboy reading a secret letter from my dead grandfather that makes *sense.*"

"Ridiculously handsome?"

"I meant to say ridiculous." Handsome like a celebrity I would have no real-life interest in. Not that he was *celebrity* handsome. Not that it mattered what breed of handsome he was anyway.

There was a cough in the hallway.

"Get down." Dax jumped across the chairs and flipped off the light switch, somehow dragging me with him. We crouched in the corner as the cough got louder and closer. Someone opened the door for a second but didn't look all the way in to see us. I had only met Victor that once, but I couldn't imagine the receptionist's cough being that deep and phlegmy.

What if he had seen me? What then? I wasn't doing anything wrong. I didn't want my family to know, but that didn't make being here wrong.

Right?

We slid down the wall in that blackened room. Dax rested his hand on my knee. I pretended I did not feel the weight of that hand, didn't notice the calluses on his palms. I'd changed into my black work skirt and boots with no tights so it was just his skin on mine. I'd come in contact with plenty of boys, but I couldn't remember responding, physically responding, to touch like this before. It's like he'd flipped on some switch inside my brain's sensory center, and suddenly my kneecap had a million nerve endings.

"I think that was Poppy."

"He should get something for that cold." It was the nicest thing I could think of to say.

"He doesn't have a cold. He has emphysema, and who knows what else. He's been smoking and drinking for over forty years."

It didn't seem right that a man abusing his body like that still got to live while my seemingly healthy grandpa was gone. Miraculously, I stayed quiet.

"Before you go, I need to ask you something," Dax said.

"Yeah?"

"It's relevant. Trust me. It's just . . . what's your opinion on marriage?"

"My opinion on marriage? Who asks that? You're so weird."

"And you're so . . . up-front." He grinned. His hand was still on me. My kneecap almost exploded. "Come on. It has to do with something your grandpa said."

This was clearly not the question I'd been anticipating. The heater picked up and ruffled his bandanna. How many guys can rock an accessory like that? I watched the bandanna flutter in the manufactured breeze and considered his question. Maybe it was his unexpected friendliness, or the leftover adrenaline and darkness, but I decided to be the raw kind of honest with a stranger.

Also, that *Twilight* chapel . . . it does things to you.

"All right. Marriage. I love my job. Love the chapel more than any place in the world. Being a part of someone's wedding day . . . it's like the joy of delivering a baby without all the blood. I like the promise and the hope and waking up knowing *that* day will be a forever kind of memory, whatever happens."

"That's your opinion of weddings. What about marriage?"

I fiddled with the small silver loop in my left eyebrow. I'd never really considered the difference. Get too deep, *think* too much, and the possibility of what could happen to those couples made the job less enjoyable. "Marriage . . . marriage is different. My grandpa was married four times. My parents got divorced this year. So I honestly don't know how I feel about the 'after' in 'happily ever.'"

"So you're iffy on marriage, but you love the chapel. Why?"

Because it's the only constant left in my life. Vegas morphed into something new every day, erasing anything familiar in the process, and I needed to know that one place, *my* place, could stand the test of time, divorce, and death.

Not that I could ever say that. Out loud. To anyone, except maybe Grandpa.

"No. Your turn. Tell me what you think of marriage and chapels. Tell me what's in that letter so I can go back to work. This room . . . it's giving me a headache."

Dax smiled, a genuine smile, a smile I wanted to bask in, to lie out in for hours until the light of that smile freckled me whole. "You're such a romantic."

Curse him, I blushed. "You haven't answered me."

"What do I think about marriage? I happen to have a very different opinion than you do. I know we disagree on the execution of the wedding ceremony, but marriage . . . I think it has the power to be the most right thing a person can experience."

It wasn't the answer I was expecting. Forget prowedding, how can he be promarriage after working here day in and day out? I would have to devise an entirely new marriage success formula for their drunken three a.m. ceremonies, most of which wouldn't even hit 2 percent.

"Well, glad to know where you stand on marriage and death," I said. "What's next? Global warming or politics?"

"Religion. And then maybe a breezy conversation about gun control issues." Dax checked his watch. "Your grandpa was right about you."

"Why, what did he say?"

"Oh . . . things."

"Vagueness is not a good look for you," I said.

"I'm just honoring a dead man's wishes." He stood. "I've got to go set up for that ceremony. Maybe we could talk more about this another time."

"Oh." I fumbled. Another time. He wanted to see me another time? No. This was our only time.

Dax squinted at me. "Thanks for coming by."

"Sure thing."

"Y'all have a beautiful chapel over there. I hope it succeeds. Really."

"And your chapel . . ." I glanced around the room. There was a weathered cardboard cutout of Edward Cullen standing by the altar. "I'm sorry. I think your chaps are nice, but that's the best I can do."

"These chaps make us money. So does this room. You really have to get over yourself if you want that place to stay in business. I know you're not making that much."

"Excuse me, Mr. Paranormal Paradise? Did your poppy say that? What does he know?"

"I'm not talking about him. This is just what I've seen. We share a parking lot, remember? I know how many couples go in there, and unless you're charging a thousand a pop, you're not doing great. And now, as hard as it is with your grandpa's passing, it might be a good time to change things up."

"But . . . but that's not us." How could I explain how "not us" that was? How the reason we were in debt was because Grandpa loved his chapel so much that he took out money just to improve it? "That's not what Grandpa Jim wanted."

"Sometimes you have to focus on what you *need* and forget about what you *want*."

"Says the boy in chaps."

"You can always trust a man in chaps." He took my hand, glancing both ways down the hallway before leading me to the back entrance. Maybe he was one of those touchy guys who always held hands with girls, boys, strangers, who knows. Even if he did, at that moment, it was my hand he was holding. And as treacherous and dangerous as it was, I liked it.

"I'll . . . see you around, I guess?" I said.

He leaned on the doorway and flashed a quick smile. "I'll wave from the other side of the parking lot."

"Okay. So. Good-bye," I said with formal finality.

He tipped his cowboy hat. And that was it.

Standing in that parking lot, I felt like I was losing my grip on something I'd never even held. I counted the seventeen cars parked next to his building. That's a lot of blushing brides.

There were only three on our side.

CHAPTER 7

For the next three weeks, I read every book on small business I could find. We had to cut some corners on our overhead and increase marketing. Sam took on the website, and I got everyone to agree to three hours of extra work with no pay. James started coming in to do clerical things, clean a little. We had our reputation and our contract with the Angel Gardens reception hall to produce some business, but there still wasn't a change in the bank account. No uptick of ceremonies.

The first weekend in December was the Bridal Spectacular, a perfect chance to advertise and network. Early Saturday morning, Mom and Dad settled into the booth while Sam and I fiddled with the sign.

"Your divorced parents look like the poster children for marriage," Sam observed.

We watched them laugh. "Doesn't it make you wonder why they ever got divorced in the first place?"

"They're probably acting happy to overcompensate for deeper feelings. It's the same brave face I'd wear if Camille and I ever broke up."

I analyzed them a beat longer. "I don't know. They have really happy-looking brave faces."

The biannual Vegas Bridal Spectacular is a decent show, but using a word like "spectacular" only leads to a letdown. Cashman Center is nothing like the planet-sized buildings on the south side of the Strip. It's old, you have to hike a hill to park, and the homeless trail up and down the street. Cashman is located even farther north than the wedding chapels, past downtown Las Vegas and the I-15, in a little nest of city buildings and museums. It took some bridal imagination, walking through wedding-dress and florist booths in this old convention center that smelled like old convention center, but tons of Vegas brides came, and we were one of the few chapels on the Strip that marketed to locals.

"Hey, I'm grabbing a hot dog," Sam said. "And some nachos. You want anything?"

I waved him off. "I'll eat some of your nachos."

"No, if you're going to eat my nachos, I'll buy you nachos too."

"But I don't want a whole thing of nachos," I said.

Sam grunted. "Then don't eat them all. Dude, you're such a chick sometimes."

"I'm always a chick!" I yelled after him. Sometimes he was something that rhymed with "chick."

Mom laughed. "I wish you could see how cute you guys are together."

Annoying PS—despite Camille's constant presence and the fact that I'd been friends with Sam for so long without any signs of feeling anything, Mom thought Sam and I were Made for Each Other. She was so into the idea of Sam and me hooking up that I exploited the crap out of it, telling her that I was going out with him so I could get a later curfew, always omitting the four to six other guys going with us. "Don't go there, Mom."

Mom shrugged. "He's a nice boy. Might be nice to settle on one guy for a while instead of dating an army of them."

"You're dating someone in the army?" Dad asked.

"You had to be there." And I didn't date an army. I had a policy on boys. I would go out with almost any boy who asked (well, there was a formula involved, but . . . I won't go into it. Suffice it to say potential serial killers factored out of the equation). The more times I said yes—only to dinner, of course—the more boys felt comfortable asking. I wasn't prettier/smarter/funnier/skinnier than any other girl. I was just approachable.

By dating a lot, I avoided having relationship talks with guys, allowing me to say yes to another date at any time. No guy could object because we never had clear boundaries. Most guys didn't go too far, because we weren't together enough for too far to happen. Really, the theory was so golden, I could bottle it up and hawk it at county fairs. *Men! Get your men here!*

The slogan wouldn't stop Mom's relationship chiding. At least she dropped the topic and fell into comfortable conversation while I waved and grinned at anyone within ten feet of our booth.

No one came by. We were boring, our space was boring, we needed a gimmick, something—I don't know—*Spectacular!*

My parents didn't seem too concerned about the lack of customers. Dad was telling Mom about his latest photography project—a series of fruit slowly rotting. He always had artistic projects on the side, though the chapel was his main gig. Mom told him about a local literacy charity she'd started to volunteer for and blah-blah-blah. They were married eighteen years, divorced almost six months. So why did their conversations sound like third-date stuff? *Oh, you took a picture of a moldy peach? How fascinating! Yes, I like the color red as well. It's so reddish. My, it is rather warm in this building.*

Do you ever repeat a question over and over again in your head that you wish you could just ask out loud? I constantly did that with my parents. *Why did you get divorced?* What if I just blurted that out during their conversation on lawn maintenance? Would it surprise them enough that they would give me an honest answer?

Finally, a girl in a red sailor dress lingered near our booth. I set my grin to enthusiastic as she read through our brochure.

"Hi! Are you a bride-to-be?"

"I am." She didn't look up.

"Well, great! Congratulations! We're one of the oldest chapels in Las Vegas, family run, lots of class and charm. We'd love to be part of your special day!" I'd already reached my quota of exclamation marks, and I'd talked to her for only ten seconds.

"Do you do musical weddings?"

I leaned in. "Excuse me?"

"Like, make the ceremony a musical instead of just saying it." She stuck her hand on her hip in a theatrical pose. "Like *Annie* or *Rocky Horror Picture Show* or something."

I flitted a glance at my dad.

"We don't." Dad gave his head a firm shake. "We're a more traditional establishment."

She stepped back from the booth and gazed down the aisle. "Do you know who does?"

"We don't *currently*," I corrected. "But if a musical ceremony is something that interests you, we're happy to put on our jazz hands."

She flipped the brochure back and nodded. "Okay. Great, thanks. I'll add you to my list."

My parents stared at me, gape-mouthed, as the bride wandered to the next vendor.

"Put on your jazz hands?" Mom rubbed her eyes. "Did you start taking singing lessons and not tell us about it?"

"Do you guys have a better idea?" I asked.

"Yeah. Say no to musical ceremonies," Dad said.

Maybe it was sitting through my parents' pleasantries earlier that made me so grouchy, or maybe it was the fact that they had yet to spring into action on behalf of the chapel, except for showing up at Bridal Spectacular and chitchatting the day away. "I don't know if you can hear it, but there is a time bomb ticking, and at the end we all lose our jobs."

Dad frowned at Mom. "When did this one become such a realist?"

"We know it doesn't come from your side of the family," Mom said.

Dad brushed my bangs out of my face. "Honey. I'm glad to see your enthusiasm, but you know Grandpa hated kitschy."

The gold urinals proved otherwise, but I didn't address that. "I hate kitschy too. But that bride doesn't." I opened my arms to the crowd. "A lot of people here don't. And if we want to make more money and save the chapel, we have to try new things. Even things we don't like. Even things Grandpa wouldn't have liked."

"*Give them what they want.*" Dax's words weren't something we had to live by forever, but why couldn't my parents see that we were in survival mode here?

"I guess a show tune or two wouldn't hurt." Mom looked to Dad for agreement. I almost told her that she didn't need Dad to agree with her anymore. They weren't married.

"I can't believe I'm hearing this." Dad furrowed his brow. "Dad gave you the chapel so you would honor it, not bring in show tunes."

"Grandpa gave me the chapel to *save* it."

Dad stretched his legs under the table. "Okay. Fine. We can . . . I'll do some promotional photo shoots or something. Get us a bride and groom, go out on location. Stick it online."

"That's a great idea!" Mom beamed.

"Sure, that's a start. But that's not enough. We have to change our business model. We should be offering broader packages to all our couples. More destination weddings."

"You're seventeen, Holly." Dad's voice hardened. "I'm sorry, but you don't know business models."

I loved this chapel even more than Dad did. He only worked there part-time, snapping staged portraits in the little back room. Grandpa never taught *him* how to polish the pews or deal with disgruntled customers. I'd been business modeled my whole life. "Now I understand why I got the letter and you didn't."

Dad's breath hitched.

Mom shut her eyes and shook her head. Dad stood. "I'm sure that letter didn't instruct you to disrespect your parents."

"Of course not." I rubbed my forehead with a shaking hand. How did our conversations keep turning into fights? We never had conflict before. We never had . . . anything. "Look, Dad, I'm sorry."

A bride walked up then and asked Mom a question, so we all had to turn on our smiles. Dad's didn't quite go full throttle. I hated that I hurt him when he already had the hurt of his dad's death, but I had pain too and I wasn't ignoring the facts.

"Hey, I'm going talk to some vendors. Network and all of that. Are you guys good?"

Mom flashed an exaggerated A-okay sign. Dad didn't answer, didn't look at me.

I could see where James learned to handle conflict. Go, Dad.

✦ ✦ ✦

I found Sam tragically nacholess next to a catering booth, sampling penne pasta in little cups.

"Where are my nachos?" I asked.

"I'll buy you some in a bit. I had to call Camille, and I didn't want your chips to get soggy while you waited."

"How sweet. It would have been sweeter if you got me nachos instead of calling your girlfriend."

"Eat some penne."

The chef glared as we downed two more samples before hitting the convention floor. I literally pushed up the sleeves of my white work blouse before diving in.

I worked that floor harder than a prostitute on Fremont Street. I dropped off business cards and brochures at Angel Gardens, the reception hall we referred our couples to who wanted dinner or dancing. Our unique collaboration set us apart from most chapels on the Strip. Then it was on to the dress tailors, florists, ice sculptors, and videographers. I gave them my number, gave them smiles.

Basically, *I* was the business model.

"Dang, girl, let's not hike up our skirt too much," Sam said in between the Priceless Memories booth and another reception hall.

"These are dress pants," I said.

"I mean, you don't need to be so easy. If you're too eager, it's going to look desperate."

I shoved my hands into my pockets. "We *are* desperate."

"We're going to be okay. I promise, you're doing a good job, and the chapel isn't going to fall to the ground. At least not today." Sam paused in front of a bridal lingerie booth. "By the way, if

Camille's parents call the chapel to check her hours again, she worked today."

"She's not scheduled."

"And I'm off in thirty minutes. So it's perfect."

I made a face. "You guys aren't going to make out in a convention center, are you?"

"We aren't tacky," Sam said. "We'll go in my truck. Oh man, the Crystal Yummy Cakes booth."

Wedding Mecca. Free mini cupcakes. Sam and I always made up a story about our fake wedding if they asked questions, but we could get in a good three or four bites before anyone noticed us. I shoved a toasted coconut bit of heaven into my face. "I would get married just to eat this cake."

"Camille and I are doing lemon on our top layer. Vanilla for the borings, maybe red velvet bottom."

I almost choked on the coconut. "Sam, you haven't seriously talked about wedding cakes, have you?"

"I'm eighteen, Holls. We've been dating for fifteen months. It's not a weird conversation to have."

"Grown adults who have been dating for years don't even talk like that. You haven't picked out baby names, have you?"

"Well, of course we're doing Sam if it's a boy because it's family tradition."

I swallowed. The crumbs stuck in my throat. "Oh, Sam. No."

"You've never had a boyfriend," Sam mumbled. "You wouldn't understand."

"Understand what?"

"True love."

I almost spewed on him. "That's ridiculous."

"You are my *girl* best friend. This isn't the kind of reaction you're supposed to have, especially at a *bridal* convention. Five minutes here and girls will marry a hairbrush."

"So?"

"So you sound too much like Grant and Porter. Don't razz me on this." He flicked some crumbs off his cheek. "Camille is the real thing. She's my forever. As soon as we're both out of school, we are getting married and leaving Vegas. We need to get away from her parents."

I felt sick to my stomach. They'd only been dating fifteen months. You can't know forever in fifteen months. And how could they know each other at all when they spent 81 percent of their time together hooking up? I gave Sam's arm a squeeze. How could a kid with such big muscles be so stupid soft? "I'm just worried that if things don't work out, you're going to crash hard."

Sam shrugged me off. "Then I do. Just because something might not happen later shouldn't stop me from making plans now."

"But why make them before—"

"I think that guy is waving at you."

I followed Sam's gaze. That guy was Dax, and he was a mere fifty feet away at the tuxedo booth. He saluted me again. The combination of delicious food and a delicious Dax almost made me faint. I could never accuse Camille of acting Victorian again.

Sam patted my back. "You okay?"

I wiped off my mouth. "That's Dax," I said.

"Dax who?"

"Cranston."

Sam whirled around. "Why is a Cranston saluting you? Who salutes?"

"Don't embarrass me. He's coming over."

Sam narrowed his eyes. "Tell me you're not serious."

"He's just a guy I've talked to, like, twice. And he's in the wedding business, so we're going to run into him. No big deal. Act professional."

"Professional? You look like you're undressing him with your eyes. Does he look good naked?"

I squeezed my eyes shut. "I swear, Sam. I swear I will rearrange your schedule so you don't ever work with Camille again."

"Fine. Jeez. Protest much?"

Dax weaved around a booth until he was only, what, three feet away from me? It had been eighteen days since I'd seen him. Those eighteen days had treated him well.

I'm not going to pretend that I hadn't thought about Dax. I wasn't pining away, but I did see his chapel every day, and naturally that was going to lead me to think about who was inside. I kept wondering if things would be different if we had met in another way. If he wasn't him and I wasn't me. What if he was just some guy at my school, lending me a pencil or sitting at the table behind me in the cafeteria? Could there be more between us then? Would he want that? Would I?

"Hey, Holly. Glad to see you here." His smile was lazy and self-assured. His accent made my name sound like a ballad.

Yes. Given different circumstances, I would want more. There was a lot to potentially want when it came to Dax Cranston.

"Of course she's here." Sam slipped his arm around me protectively. "We always attend Bridal Spectacular. It's a competitive market. Have to keep being excellent if we're going to stay on top."

"Agreed," Dax said.

I squirmed away from Sam. "Dax, this is Sam."

"How you doing, man?" Dax held out his hand.

Sam wrinkled his nose before giving Dax a limp shake. "Decent. Holls, we better go."

I gave Sam a look. He gave it right back. We actually had a ten-second conversation consisting of grunts and grimaces. Finally, I said, "Sam is my *employee.* We were just tasting cakes, but we're done. Sam, why don't you skip on back to the booth?"

"What about you?" Sam asked.

"I was just headed over to the fashion show if you wanted to go?" Dax asked.

I'd witnessed the bridal fashion show before. Under any other circumstances, I'd rather gouge out my eye with a bridal veil comb than attend. But here was an excuse to talk to Dax for a bit. Just talk. He may have been off-limits when it came to physical things, but he might prove to be an excellent resource when it came to . . . brainstorming effective business models.

"That'll be great. See you, Sam."

Sam pulled me to the side. "What's with the fake Southern accent?"

"It's not fake."

"Where's he from then?"

"I don't know. I told you, I barely know the kid."

"If he goes Cranston on you, I swear I'll drive my truck into their lobby."

"That's your solution for everything," I said.

"Just because it's always my answer doesn't make it the wrong answer."

"You are such a country song."

He looked at me sharply. "Camille told you to say that."

"There happen to be some things Camille and I agree on."

"I just . . . I have a bad feeling about this guy."

I let out an exasperated breath. "And what feeling do you have exactly?"

"Like . . . this doesn't end well. For anyone."

"It's a bridal fashion show, not a Shakespearean tragedy."

Sam huffed away.

Dax let out a low whistle once he was out of earshot. "Boyfriend?"

I made a face. "Gross. No."

"Ex-boyfriend?"

"No, he's practically married, and I am very not interested." I wanted to do something girly then, like flip my black hair, but a pixie cut didn't give me anything to flip. "Sam is my best friend. Sometimes best friend, except when he acts like that."

"Well, is your boyfriend here, then?" Dax asked, peering around the convention center.

My stomach dipped. Checking on my relationship eligibility.

I should have said Sam was my boyfriend so this little flirty flirt would end cold. "No, he hates wedding events."

Dax deflated slowly, like a hidden leak in an air mattress. Which I hated, so I tried to make him smile again. Up you roll, emotional yo-yo.

"Because . . . he went to the shooting range before his cage-wrestling match," I said. "We're going to eat dead animals with our bare hands later tonight."

Dax rewarded me with a smile. There was a dimple under the stubble. I tried to shield myself from all that adorable. It was a thick shield.

"Sounds like a keeper."

"He would be if he were real. A girl can always dream."

Dax started walking toward the stage. "So Sam is an employee?"

"Well, I mean, we work together. With his girlfriend, Camille. They're fun when they aren't sucking face. Do you have any friends at your chapel?"

"Not unless you count Minerva, at the front desk. She makes me peanut brittle sometimes."

"I met her, I think."

"No, that was Millicent. She's Minerva's twin sister. They've worked for us since we opened. Besides those two, we have pretty high turnover. My poppy isn't the easiest person to work for."

"Then is Millicent your friend?"

"No. She hates me. She asked me to bird sit for her once and somehow I traumatized Mr. Tompkins."

The fashion show was already in full swing, which would be 34 percent swing if you were to compare it to any real fashion show. Dax raised his chin so he could see over the crowd. I counted nine girls with "I'm the bride!" nametags.

Models in wedding finery twirled down the catwalk while an MC shouted expressions like "Gorgeous! Dynamic! Breathtaking!" One groom burst into the splits during a nineties hip-hop song. Spectators catcalled and fanned themselves with wedding brochures. It was, to say the least, the worst.

"I love this dress!" The announcer's voice was one pitch away from a dog whistle. "Looks like she's walking on a cloud."

"Clouds are just visible vapor, so if you walked on them you'd fall through and die, and it would be a humid death," I said.

Dax grinned. "Unless you were wearing a cloud sweater, remember?"

"That's a large 'unless.'"

"So I take it you're not in love with the fashion show?" Dax asked.

"We don't sell dresses, and we already refer to a bridal rental store. This isn't applicable to our chapel."

He looked around the convention center. "Then did you want to go look at floral arrangements instead?"

"Not really."

"Limos? Seamstresses? You do know I couldn't care less about any of this, right?"

"Oh."

Why was he looking for excuses to talk to me? More important, why was I looking for excuses to talk to him?

I scanned the convention center. We couldn't be within view of my family. The ideal spot would have been the hair and makeup booth, where you could try out a wedding style for free.

Oddly enough, Dad was already there, talking to one of the stylists. She was younger than him, but not too young, maybe late thirties. Dad was laughing and smiling. Flirting. Even from across the room I could see that. Did my dad flirt with women now? He could, of course. My parents could flirt, or even date, or hook up with other people or get married again.

But it wasn't until I saw Dad touch the arm of that hair girl that I saw the truth. The truth and the future, that my parents, no matter how well they got along, were each other's past now. Our family as it was *was* past now. We were the Used to Bes.

I was shaking, not like it was cold in there. I expected my dad to feel my stare at any minute. To look at me, his daughter, and feel ashamed for how he was acting. Because it was shameful. Mom was back at the booth; they had just laughed together and discussed my classes this semester. How did he move so seamlessly from one role to the next?

"Holly?" Dax asked. "You okay?"

I didn't want to go *Parent Trap* on my parents. I got that they were done. I sort of got it, because I didn't know *why* they were done, but I could deal. It's just, my dad shouldn't be having flirtatious conversations in the same space that I was having flirtatious conversations, certainly not at a wedding show when he was recently divorced.

Plus he was *old* and this was *weird.*

"I should go back," I said. "To the booth." To my mom. Sam.

"I'll walk with you," Dax said.

I tore my gaze away from my dad and that woman, who looked like she might unhinge her jaw and devour him at any moment. "No. If my family sees me talking to you it could be World War Three. Well, Four. I think World War Three went down when our families had that little chat at the funeral."

"I have bruises from that chat," Dax said. "Your sister can kick."

"She went back to school, so you're safe there."

"I get it." Dax jerked his chin toward my booth. "You don't want to be seen with me. I should probably be careful too. We don't do a booth, but Poppy sends us to network. Minerva is walking around somewhere . . ." He breathed out. I don't know why, but I felt more centered when he breathed, like he was taking in oxygen for us both. "Or, if your best friend and/or fake boyfriend wouldn't mind, we could get out of here."

"Here?"

"And go somewhere."

I stared down at my hands and smiled. Why was eye contact so hard? Those moments when it happened with Dax, it felt like he was seeing the things I didn't say.

I glanced back at my dad. He had his phone out now, and I had the sinking feeling he was getting the girl's number. It's not like I could work now with Mom and pretend that I hadn't just seen Dad score a girl's digits. And work-wise, it didn't matter who was manning the booth. It was the same five questions again and again. Camille could cover for me, even if it meant Sam had to miss his truck time. "Yeah, I can sneak away for a bit. You want to go walk around?"

"I love walking."

I sent Sam a text, telling him I wouldn't be back for a while. I'd pay double. I didn't respond to the tirade he wrote back.

It's not like I lost all ability to think logically. I knew what I was doing. I might not know *why* I was doing it, but I knew going somewhere—anywhere—with Dax was a stupid move for more reasons than even I could count. No matter how much I rationalized that Dax and I were just talking, we were doing more. Now we were *walking* . . . somewhere . . . and with each step I took, I was moving in a direction I shouldn't go.

Maybe that's why I went. The scandal of it all. Maybe it was some sort of rebellion after seeing my dad in a new light.

Mostly, I think I just needed to see where "somewhere" would take us.

CHAPTER 8

Dax and I left without a sighting, hiking up the hill to the parking lot, discussing everything from bridezillas to the kind of shoes Dax was wearing today—navy blue boat shoes. He had on the same dress shirt from the funeral, tucked into khakis. Made me wonder what clothes he wore when he didn't have to dress up like an accountant, or if always dressing up was some Southern boy thing.

The conversation jumped around more than I was used to with boys, but I liked Dax's randomness. When we made it to the street, we looked right and left. This was the cultural side of Las Vegas Boulevard, not a place you walked around, like the Strip four miles south.

"I've never really hung out down here," Dax said. "My dad used to take me to baseball games at Cashman, but otherwise . . . wow, there's a library across the street?"

"You're kidding." I pointed to the Lied Discovery Children's Museum, a red-and-gray building with a cylindrical concrete tower. "You never went there on a field trip? Or to the Natural History Museum?"

Dax gave an apologetic shrug. "I'm not much of a native. I was born here, but my parents moved to Birmingham when I was two."

"That's where the accent comes from," I said.

"It sure don't come from living in Nevada," Dax said, pouring on the drawl. "My mom and I just moved back here last summer."

Just Dax and his mom? I tilted my head. We had more in common than I thought. "Yeah, my parents are divorced too."

Dax stared across the street. "No. My dad died. Poppy felt bad for my mom, said he'd take care of us until we got our life back together." He circled his foot on the sidewalk. "It's been almost a year. She's doing a lot better now. Poppy treats her like she's his daughter. He's not so bad."

"Wow. I'm so sorry."

"I appreciate that."

At least I didn't ask how his dad died. That was something I'd learned since Grandpa Frank passed. When you discuss a death with someone who didn't know the deceased, the second question was often, "How did he die?" The more I was asked that, the sadder I got, because that's the one snippet of information you share about the deceased—their demise. No one questions how they lived.

And I didn't know the answer; no one knows the answer.

How did he die? Did he fall asleep when they put him under for the surgery or did he wake up first? Did he feel his breath slipping away or was it one big breath and then a fade out?

Dax probably got that, the replaying, but to a bigger degree, because his dad had to be young, and so his death was probably something instant and sudden, like a car accident. Maybe every time Dax got in a car, he wondered what the sound must have been like and how long it took the pain to register, if it registered.

Or maybe he's not a grotesquely morbid person like I am.

"No, but seriously. I am sorry. About your dad."

He exhaled. "There needs to be a bigger word than 'sorry' for death, you know that? I use the word 'sorry' when I spill water on someone's floor."

"What were you thinking?"

The blue in his eyes deepened, swelled. "It'd be a mash-up of swear words."

"But soft too," I said. "To express regret."

We hadn't established where we were going, if we were going anywhere. We stood there on the street corner next to a sunburned man in a 49ers sweatshirt and oily jeans. Swears, euphemisms, and cheesy Hallmark words like "condolence" popped in and out of my head. Finally, I blurted, "Suckafugsadagus."

"Suckafugsadagus." His face split into a grin. "That's . . . terrible. Really, that's the best we can come up with?"

"I came up with it. I don't hear any ideas from you."

"Okay. Fine. Suckafug . . . what's the rest?"

"Suckafugsadagus. I think."

"Forget weddings, I'm going into the funeral business. Ditching eulogies and just printing banners with SUCKAFUGSADAGUS, and everyone will understand our word."

We had a word. It was a word to balloon sorrow, but it was ours together.

The crosswalk light turned to walk. I shielded my eyes from the sun. "So . . . are we actually going somewhere then? I don't know how much time I have."

"I thought we could be spontaneous. Do you ever do that?"

Sure. Like . . . today. So, that would be . . . once. "Where do you want to go? Most of the stuff is to the right. There's this cool ice cream factory, or we could go to the Old Mormon Fort. I've never been there. I don't know what it is."

Dax glanced behind him. "What's that Neon museum?"

I hit him on the shoulder, harder than I'd meant. "Shut up, you've never been to the Neon Boneyard?" I grabbed his hand and started dragging him down the street. "I can't believe you haven't been here. This is the coolest thing in Vegas."

Dax tripped after me. "I told you, I don't come down here."

"Our wedding chapels are only two miles away."

"Two miles in Vegas is ten hours of distractions. What is it, just some old signs?"

I stopped dead in front of the entrance to the museum, a white shell-shaped concrete building, and pointed aggressively at the facade. "Yeah, just some old signs. And Vegas is just a couple of slot machines. Dax, this building? It's the old La Concha Motel reception area from the sixties, isn't that amazing?"

He shrugged. "I guess. So it's a dead motel? What's it doing on this side of the boulevard?"

"It wasn't always here. They took it apart, moved it with huge trucks, and restored the whole thing. Only in Vegas would they do that. The sign and desk inside the lobby are original too. And!" I pointed to the neon glass slipper on the median across the street. "They restored popular signs, lit them up. History, it's our . . . Las Vegas history."

"I take it you want to go inside?" Dax asked, opening the door. A whoosh of heat welcomed us in. The shell served as a gift shop with just a few hipster-style T-shirts, coffee mugs, and books about Vegas. There was actually a picture of Rose of Sharon in one of those books, but I didn't want to bring up work with Dax. The subject felt taboo, even if that chapel, or at least Grandpa, was what brought us together.

Dax took out his wallet, a flimsy Velcro thing that had molded into the curve of his butt. "Can we get two tickets?" he asked.

I whispered. "I'll pay for myself."

"My mother raised me better than that."

"Come on."

"If you pay, then I can't call this a date."

Date date date date . . . DATE? We couldn't call this a date. Fifteen minutes ago I wasn't even sure if I should walk a hundred feet across a convention hall with this guy.

But I said nothing. I didn't try to pay. Because the idea of this being a date . . . it wasn't the worst idea ever.

The girl pointed to a clipboard on the blond wood desk. "It's one-hour tours. We start every half hour—we have openings in the next one if you want to jump in."

Dax checked his watch. "I'll have to make up an excuse to Minerva for not going back to the convention. Do we have an hour?"

"I have some sway with the boss."

The Boneyard was behind the shell, a two-acre dirt lot with pathways of signs arranged in creative displays. We joined a group of about fifteen others, mostly senior citizens, some tourists, some locals. Our tour guide—gravelly voiced and with thinning hair—took us around the hundreds of rows of signs. Some were just pieces of an old facade, some were letters, some were words, and a few complete signs rose three stories high. Almost every sign had a story attached to it; you just had to point and ask, "What's Sassy Sally's?" and our guide could name the date the hotel went up and, usually, when the hotel went down. There was an area with old motel signs, relics from a time when Vegas was just a gas stop between Salt Lake City and Los Angeles. Somewhere around midpoint, we fell behind the group and Dax whispered, "This place was here this whole time and I didn't know it?"

"And you thought that bridal show was spectacular."

"You're really into it, aren't you?" he asked.

"What, the graveyard? Who wouldn't be? It's magic."

"No, Vegas." He waved his arm like he was creating a big bubble. "Your chapel, the history. I hate living here. It's the sort of place where one day you arrive and just never leave."

"How can you hate living in Las Vegas? It's sunny two

hundred ninety-two days a year here. You can eat at a buffet at four in the morning. Every band comes here for a show. And let's not forget Bridal Spectacular."

"Two hundred ninety-two? Is that an exact number?"

"It's an accurate average."

Dax kicked at a rock. "Okay, what about the heat?"

"It's a—"

"Dry heat. Yeah, yeah. There is nothing dry when it's one hundred fifteen degrees outside. And no one is from here. Like, for generations. There are no roots. In Alabama, I knew everyone on our block, and here . . . I'm pretty sure our next-door neighbor is running a meth lab."

"Like Alabama doesn't have meth labs."

"Alabama sings 'sweet home.' Nothing here does, except maybe Poppy's chapel."

"Cupid's Dream? What's home about that?

"Familiarity? Family? Fun? Pick one. The rest of the town is just half-empty strip malls and cloned stucco houses."

"This is Las Vegas you're describing, right? The City of Blinding Lights?"

"I've never heard it called that. I think that's New York."

"'City of Blinding Lights' is my favorite U2 song. So I say it applies to Vegas—"

"That's what sucks about Vegas, that it rips off other cities—"

"Fine. The entertainment capital of the world."

"Arguable."

"Dax!"

"You know I'm not talking about entertainment. I'm talking about . . . Say you move away, come back in twenty years. What are going to be the places you remember? Some hotel? That will probably be redone then anyway. There's nothing *homegrown*."

I squatted down next to a piece from the old Golden Nugget sign. A hotel, I should note, that might have grown and morphed but was still in business after seventy years. "My dad was at a photo shoot once for this local Vegas magazine, some high-fashion thing with a girl wearing a flowing gown in the desert. The lighting guy was sweating and swearing about how bright the sun was and kept saying that anyone who would choose to live here had to be as godforsaken as the town. Then the sun started to set, and you know how sunsets are here. Pink and infinite, like anything is possible and you're part of something vast. And Dad said the guy sort of twirled around, taking in the sky, and said, 'Okay, God. I stand corrected.'" I shrugged. "I think living here has taught me to keep my expectations low and to appreciate those moments when life proves you wrong. Or right."

"So you're impressed with everywhere else because this place sucks that bad?"

I stood. "You're still new here. You have to get used to it. It's not freaking Hawaii, it takes a little work. But I can show you. Show you all the places that make Las Vegas great."

"Personally?" Dax crossed his arms, amused. "I'll say I hate a lot more things if it means you'll make it your crusade to prove me wrong."

"I didn't mean I would take you there myself . . ." But I did mean that. I was already picturing us hiking Red Rock Canyon and peering over the side of Hoover Dam, like these were activities we could ever actually do together. Like we could ever actually *be* together.

The guide shuffled the group to the next row of signs. Dax and I stayed back, our voices dipped.

"Can I tell you something?" he asked.

"We should catch up to the group."

"I almost called you the other day," Dax said. "At the chapel. But I didn't know if you were working. So I went out to the parking lot and tried to guess if any of those cars were yours."

"I don't have a car."

"Yeah, I didn't know what I thought was going to clue me in. A HOLLY bumper sticker? And then another time I actually saw you in the parking lot, just walking in with a bag like maybe you'd picked up lunch. And I put on my coat and was all ready to come outside and then Poppy asked where I was going, and I couldn't say to talk to you." He rubbed his nose. "And while I'm confessing, that wasn't the first time I've noticed you in the parking lot. I did, before I saw you at the funeral. I have for months now. In my head, you were Parking Lot Girl, and I'd sort of invent a story of what you were doing each day you walked into your chapel." He laughed to himself. "I wasn't stalking you. Just noticing you."

I'd never had someone tell me they love me, but I couldn't imagine it feeling any better than having Dax say he *noticed* me. It took this . . . the talking, the walking . . . the DATE . . .

to a whole other level. The confession made me consider what would happen if I ignored the whole Cranston/Nolan feud and pursued something with this guy.

What if I went out with him, officially, to see what happened? My parents weren't the grounding type, and they had James to worry about. That would buy me time, time with Dax, time to decide.

Staring at Dax in the afternoon light, I decided it was worth the risk. Dax was the kind of guy who was worth a lot of risks.

"Maybe I should give you my number so you don't have to parking-lot stalk me anymore."

He raised an eyebrow. "That was a little cheesy."

"Give me credit for being direct and not naming you Other Chapel Boy while I sat around and did nothing."

He coughed. "Great. But . . . are you okay with this?"

"Maybe?" I tried to force lightness into my voice. "I'm not one of those girls who likes sneaking around with boys. I see Camille and Sam do it, and it looks like a headache. I don't keep things from my parents."

"Neither do I," Dax said. "Well, I never did with my dad. And I don't with my mom."

"But maybe we could hang out a few more times, see if there's anything to even, you know, tell them."

"So you're asking me out."

I was asking him out? I was. I had never asked out a boy. I'd never even let one in this much. "I guess I am."

He pulled out his phone. "We switch numbers. You text me

the time and date. Because if you're asking me out, you plan the date, okay?"

"Now it's a date?"

Dax smiled. "Yes. I like to put labels on things. And you better go big, show me something spectacular in Las Vegas."

We switched phones. He added himself as "Dex," I was "Hallie." He took a step back and nodded his head to the right. "Let me get a picture of you standing in front of that big letter *H*."

I crouched by the lone *H*, which was in a font that looked like an old gambling hall. Half of the bulbs were missing, the metal a rusty red.

"Now let's find *O*," Dax said.

"Ho?"

Dax bent over, laughing. "I was going to spell your name, but I'm glad to hear you have such a high opinion about yourself."

We found an *O*. We found two *L*'s. And it was somewhere in our pursuit of a *Y* that Dax yanked me into the giant pirate skull sculpture, a Treasure Island relic from the family-friendly Strip of the nineties. "Hey, ho," he whispered.

"You know how to talk to the ladies." I breathed out.

"Maybe I should stop talking," he said.

And then he kissed me. *Dax kissed me.* To the point I couldn't remember if my name was Holly or Hallie. I'd spent the last three weeks pretending that I wasn't thinking about his accent or stubble and now that I wasn't pretending anymore, reality felt so good. Family, business, dying wishes . . . who cared at that moment. I just wanted his lips on mine for those four whole minutes until we came up for air.

"Kids!" our tour guide called. We pulled away. The tour had moved forward, but the guide must have forgotten some anecdote and come back. With the group. An old man with a cowboy hat flashed Dax a thumbs-up sign. "You have to stay with the tour. If you can't see us, we can't see you."

Dax took my hand and we shuffled behind. Throbbing, pulsing, whirling, wheeling. Every inch of my skin crackled with electricity. I wanted to plop down in the dirt and rip off his shirt.

"I haven't been listening to the guide for the last half an hour," he said. "Just waiting for a chance to do that. Thought the skull was the most romantic sculpture."

I hit his arm. "Come on, this tour is interesting."

"Of course it is. But my *company* is fascinating."

Our grins were delirious. We made it to the end of the tour, the large neon duck once owned by a dry cleaner. Afterward, the tour guide pulled us aside. I thought he was going to scold us for talking and/or kissing the whole time, but instead he walked us back through the displays. "You guys missed a good photo opportunity with all your chatting."

"Sorry about that," Dax said.

He waved a dismissive hand. "Please. If I'd had a girl like this when I was young, I wouldn't listen either. Did you like the tour, sweetheart?"

I hated being called "sweetheart," but I forgave the man. Kissing a family enemy had put me in a forgiving mood. "I did. Thank you."

Dax's face erupted into a smile. "It was the least boring tour in the least boring museum in the least boring town in the world."

The guide shuffled into a loop of signs and jutted his chin behind him. "Sometimes the lovebirds like to get a picture by this one."

The sign was so perfect it probably sounds like I'm making it up. That amid the crumbling facade of Bugsy Siegel's 1940s Flamingo Hotel, or the statue of the smoking pool player, there could be this. A blue arrow with a red-bulbed tip and words in white: WEDDING INFORMATION.

"I know you kids are too young to be thinking of that stuff, but it's a memory."

Dax and I looked at each other. Just like that photographer with the sunset, the moment was so brilliant and right it made everything seem possible, like Las Vegas was the romance capital of the world and we were the mayors. "Are you in?" he asked.

I kissed him while the guide took our picture.

Yes. God forgive me, but I was in. And I might have already been gone.

CHAPTER 9

Sam was weird to me after Bridal Spectacular, and that's without my telling him about the Neon Museum. I considered calling him on his BS. I considered it but didn't, because I needed Sam's help.

I needed everyone's help.

I made a trade with my friends, offering to help them study for our economics test if they would meet at Sam's house Wednesday night to fold brochures, make signs, and stuff envelopes.

Sam's mom, the Everyone's Mom, set out a sundae bar with whipped cream and hot fudge. We couldn't have fit the ice cream into The Space, forget the friends and sprinkles. Once Sam's mom had finished fretting, she padded upstairs and left us to our own devices. Grant started to sift through the cabinets. We clearly had differing opinions on what those devices should be. The bar was locked up, but sometimes after a party they accidentally left something in the cupboard underneath.

"Bingo!" Grant held up a bottle of Kahlúa. "Who wants a float?"

"Extra sprinkles!" Porter squirted some whipped cream directly into his mouth.

"You guys," I said. "Put that away. It's probably under there because it's expired."

Grant glanced at the bottle. "Does alcohol expire? I thought it got better with age."

"Do you really have to do this tonight?" I asked. "It's important."

Grant set the bottle down on the counter and made a ten-scoop sundae. Victory, I guess.

"It's not a big deal, Holls." Porter ruffled my hair like I was five. "The game is on. As soon as it's over, we'll help."

I folded envelopes alone at the table for fifteen minutes, annoyed that they couldn't multitask for my sake. There was *always* a game on, no matter what time of year it was, and the world had to stop every time.

My dad used to do that to my mom. On Saturdays she'd want to go on family adventures, and Dad would flip up the leg rest of his recliner and say, "Can't, game's on." Do you know how long a football game lasts? Or eighteen holes of golf? What does a non–sports fan have that allows them hours of justified screaming at a screen?

Which is why I learned to watch sports, to understand sports, to join fantasy baseball leagues and memorize stats and spreads. To connect. To communicate. To *belong*. Maybe that was part of my parents' problem. My mom couldn't tell you the difference between a touchdown and a field goal.

As soon as the game was over (college basketball, beginning of season, UCLA won by ten), I turned off the TV. "All right. Start stuffing these envelopes. Mike and Camille, you are the only ones who have nice-enough handwriting for signs."

Grant wiped whipped cream off his face. He was such a pig, but I could name at least ten girls at our school who would love to be that whipped cream. Not that West had the highest population of cute guys to compete with. "I don't get why we're doing this. Why aren't your mom and dad working?"

"They *are* working," I said. "They're doing other stuff. There is a LOT to do when it comes to running a business." My voice had taken on that know-it-all tone that always seemed to come when I talked to my friends. They hated it, I hated it, but maybe if they weren't always such idiots, I wouldn't have to point out their idiocy.

"Just sell it." Mike spread the Sharpies on the table. "No offense, but wedding chapels aren't the biggest moneymakers in the world."

"Says the boy who buses tables at a Mexican restaurant," I said.

"Well, yeah. For now. But not forever. Are you really thinking about working there forever? Like when you're an adult?" Mike wrote, SAY "I DO" AT THE ROSE OF SHARON CHAPEL in nearly calligraphic cursive across a poster board, then added some fancy doodles. "What about college—you'd have no choice but to go to UNLV."

"Yeah, we're not busting our humps at West just to waste away at Un-LOVE." Porter had finished his sundae and went back to the Kahlúa, opening it and giving it a sniff. "What's this supposed to smell like?"

"Alcohol," I said drily.

"Cheers to that." He sniffed some more but didn't drink. "Anyway, you don't want to go to UNLV for real. It's a commuter school; that's not a college experience. Sam's just hanging here for a year and then he's out, right Sam?"

"Yep," Sam called from the couch, where he was tangled under a throw blanket with Camille. "We're out of here as soon as Camille graduates."

"We are?" Camille sat up. "Where do you think we're going? Washington? Ooh, Sam, I have family in Washington. Let's go there!"

"Forget college." Mike finished the sign and started on another. He was good at this, helpful. I just wish he would shut his mouth. "What about when you're twenty-two or thirty-eight? You can't move anywhere else . . . ever. You can't take the chapel with you. You're stuck in Vegas for life."

"Mike, shut up." I could feel anger and tears boiling up, and I pushed them down with all the emotional strength I had. "I'm doing this because I have to. *I have to.* So, seriously, write another sign in your girly cursive or get out."

The boys gave a collective "Ooooh." I swear Mike even smirked, happy he'd provoked me. He had no idea what it was like to be me. He came from a rich suburban family. He worked at that Mexican place because he liked the chips and salsa.

None of these guys had ever *wanted.* If there was a school trip, they went. If they wanted to buy new shoes, they bought them. They thought keeping this chapel was a *choice* for me.

It was conversations like this that made me wonder why I hung out with these guys. They acted like it was such a privilege that I was the solitary girl in their group, that I was above the other girls who temporarily came into our fold, the girls who laughed too hard and flipped their hair too much, until eventually the guy she was dating got tired of her and sent her on her way. Or I was below other girls because I wasn't incredibly hot. They could actually speak to me, while the other girls they only spoke of with chauvinistic reverence. They had a group text chain with a photo of some redhead in a cut-off NFL jersey with subject lines like "Tappable?" Sometimes I was in those chains, sometimes I wasn't. Sometimes I actually wanted to be included, sometimes I didn't.

Because, the thing is, they were funny. And charming. And oddly caring. I mean, even as Mike went off about how I should live my life, he still sat here making signs for me. They never noticed what I wore or dissected our conversations. If I brought them to The Space, they didn't passive-aggressively comment on the square footage: they just opened the fridge. When we got in a fight, it was over within minutes, squashed. Last year, when James got a black eye, they drove over to the junior high just to sit out in the parking lot and intimidate James's assailant. That's love, right? Some twisted form of friendship?

I wondered what it would be like to sit around with a group

of girls right now, girls who watched reality TV dating shows and crammed cookies into their mouths between mumbled "I shouldn't be eating this." Would I like that any better?

"Look, let's just . . . finish. Give me twenty minutes and then you can all go plan your non-Vegas futures together. Mike, I hope you move to Connecticut."

"Don't be that way," Porter said. "Mike is sorry, right, Mike?"

Mike gave a noncommittal shrug. "I mean, sort of. I'm just looking out for you."

"Yeah. Thanks," I said.

Grant leafed through a stack of brochures. "Mike's on the rag, ignore him. Your wedding chapel is fine."

"You guys don't know what you're missing." Sam and Camille untangled themselves from the couch and joined us at the table. "Dude, I would work at the chapel forever too."

"Thanks, Sam." At least I had Sam. I would always have Sam.

"Especially now that Holly is hanging on the guy at the chapel across the street. Proximity."

I considered poking out his eyes with sprinkles.

"Now this makes sense!" Grant slapped his leg. "Let's stuff us some envelopes then. Save her business so she can get up in this guy's biz-nass!"

"Who is this guy?" Mike said defensively. "Were you ever going to tell us about him?"

Camille clapped her hands together. "This is so great! Is he adorbs? We can go on a double date."

I'd rather go on a double date with my parents.

Sam was getting a pay cut for this. The last thing I needed when things were just barely starting with Dax was having my friends made aware. What if they told my family? What was there even to tell so far? We'd kissed twice. We'd exchanged a few texts. I thought about him constantly. I'd named our first three children.

So what?

"A double date would be fun." Sam kissed Camille on the cheek. "I'd love to get to know Dax better."

"Great, say his name, why don't you," I said.

"Ooh, she's getting angry." Porter took a swig of the Kahlúa straight out of the bottle and nearly choked. "Nasty."

Sam laughed. "I think my dad poured all the leftover alcohol in there. He was going to throw it out."

Porter spit into the sink. "Why didn't you tell me that?"

"Because this was more fun," Sam said.

They worked for another half hour, and we were almost done when a hockey game came on and I lost them. Camille hovered next to me by the table until I finally set my marker down. "Can I do something for you?"

"Look," she whispered, shooting a look toward the boys. She didn't need to worry. Except for Sam, they never listened to what she said. "I know why you don't want to talk to the guys about this. They are so antirelationship it's amazing they haven't faked Sam's death so I would stay away."

There had actually been a discussion on this before. Grant had offered his bedroom. They figured Camille would move on in two weeks, then they could release Sam back into the world.

"But all I'm saying is, if you do want to talk to anyone about this Dax guy, or any guy, talk to me. Or Sam, but only when he's alone, because we both know Sam isn't always Sam when the Penis Parade starts."

I stared at Camille. This was not the high-voiced, frail puppet Sam had been dating the last fifteen months. Who was this relatable, foul-mouthed creature? Is this why he loved her? "Uh, yeah. I guess . . ."

"Now? Let's talk now!" Camille pulled me into the guest bedroom, which was a little dramatic, but whatever.

She perched on the edge of the plaid bedspread and primly crossed her legs. "Okay. So tell me about Dax."

This is the weird part. I did. I told her the little stuff, the details I'd been holding to my heart, like this little tick he had where he nodded his head when he was excited and how unbelievable his jaw was and how he made jokes about dead relatives in a sensitive way. And I told her about the Boneyard and the kiss and how I liked him so hard I was physically hurting from it.

"This sounds amazing," she said.

"Or awful." I rubbed my forehead. "What do I do?"

"Okay. So he works at the gross chapel across the street and your families hate each other. Which is, you know, Shakespearean. Whatever." She sighed. "Love doesn't always follow the rules. I mean, look at Sam and me. Do you know what he does for fun? Goes up to Mount Charleston and shoots cans. My parents are gun-control activists, I'm not even kidding. If they didn't already forbid me from dating *any* guy, they would forbid me from dating *him*."

"But you *are* dating him," I said.

"Exactly. Because I love him. Maybe I'll tell my parents about him someday, and we'll have a big blowup, and we might have to run away together to Detroit, or wherever you go when you run away with a boyfriend."

"So you're saying I should tell my parents soon so we don't get so far from the truth that we can't go back."

"No, I didn't say that. If you tell them, they'll try to get in the way and your relationship will be dead before it starts."

"But you just said you're going to have to run away with Sam someday," I said.

"Or break up. Someday. The point is that now I want to be with Sam, and my parents can't know. Just like you and Dax."

"But that doesn't make sense. Why not just get it over with and tell your parents?"

Camille gave me a weird look. "They would totally ground me."

"But you'll have to at some point, right? Like, when you get married."

Camille refolded a blanket on the bed. "Well, that's all a big 'if.' I was only kidding about Detroit. I'm sixteen. I'm not committing to forever yet. Sam talks like that sometimes, but that's only because we work in a wedding chapel, you know?"

I ducked my head. This is how I wanted her to react, because you shouldn't plan a wedding before a graduation party. But Sam had been so assured at Bridal Spectacular, like there was no question that they'd get married someday. I did not want that kid to get his heart broken by a girl who spoke in circles. "We don't talk about that."

"Good." She patted my shoulder. "Besides, you and Dax are forever away from that. You've had a kiss and an accidental date. Let's get you into more solid territory before you start strategizing."

"But that's what I do, Camille. I strategize. It's like an online dating site is constantly running in my head. I have rules and boundaries and I like to have an idea what the ultimate outcome is going to be."

"Not every relationship is an equation," she said.

No. But adding some logic to the mix didn't hurt. If my parents had done the math, maybe they would be together still. Or maybe they wouldn't have been together at all. They always told us this story of a whirlwind romance during a college spring break trip. I couldn't picture them in college, or at spring break, but there the story is. Dad's friends heckled him into some nineties MTV dating contest, which he lost, but when he was walking off the stage, he bumped into my mom, who had just broken up with Lenore's dad and was in Mexico alone to find herself. And then they went out to eat and got food poisoning and stayed sick together and fell in love and Mom moved to Vegas for Dad. They would end the story with "And two kids later, here we are."

And that's where my family was, for quite a while, with parents who didn't fight, still told how-we-met stories, and finished each other's sentences. Which is why the divorce was so completely unexpected for James and me. Not like Porter's parents, who'd been fighting forever, house-shaking arguments that made divorce such an inevitability that Sam actually threw him a party when Porter's dad moved out.

When my mom picked me up from school one day and casually said she had something to talk about, I thought some great-uncle had died or that my room was too dirty. No. The only explanation I got was, "Your dad and I totally respect each other and love you kids, but we feel like staying married isn't the best for either of us, so we're getting a divorce." She'd glanced in the rearview mirror right then, like she was checking if I had on my seat belt. Safe? Good. Emotionally sound? Swell.

I was so shocked in that moment, dumbfounded really, that I'd only asked if she was sure. "We've already signed papers," Mom had said, which was a double blow. This wasn't a night-before decision. This had been in the works for months, while meanwhile we're having family dinners and going to James's piano recitals like everything was ordinary and fine.

James reacted very differently from me, and maybe that's why I never pried more into the matter. They had his outbursts to deal with, and Lenore's . . . Lenoreness. All I did was count—the holidays since the divorce (three), the weekends I'd slept at my dad's (eight), and the days it took for Dad to move out (five). And still I was haunted by one question.

Why?

"Holly?" Camille touched my arm, bringing me back. "I know you're new to girl talk, but you're supposed to respond when I say something."

"What if this ends badly?"

Camille shrugged. "A lot of things end badly. But that doesn't mean you don't start something anyway."

"That was profound," I said.

Camille tapped her head. "It happens, every once in a while."

Someone burped so loudly we heard it from the other room.

"So I'm going to go out with him and not tell my parents," I said.

"Right. And go into the date with an open mind. Be emotional. Be passionate. Think about . . . what did you first like about him?"

"Besides his lips?"

Camille grinned. "Nice lips can get you pretty far."

We went back into the game room. I grabbed Grant's Kahlúa and dumped it down the sink. Porter threw a foam football at my head, which actually kind of hurt, but I didn't say anything. Camille snuggled right back into the crook of Sam's arm. And I wondered if any of them could tell how different I was from a few days ago, or a few weeks ago. I'd experienced heavy loss and extreme like and I didn't know how long both sets of emotions could take up residence in one girl.

CHAPTER 10

The thing about a loved one dying is that everything that person touched becomes a part of who they were, leaving this trail of emotional land mines along the landscape of their life. You expect this immediately after the death, when you're cleaning out their room and find reading glasses perched on the pages of an open book, pages that will never be read, at least not by the deceased. But other times, you see someone on TV wearing a beanie, and you're reminded that The Edge from U2 always wore beanies, and that your recently deceased grandfather loved U2, and you loved him, and so on, day after day, week after week. Scents, songs, street corners . . . a day filled with razor-edged reminders that tear open your heart. Maybe the moments fizzle out after time, maybe the pain dulls. For me, each whisper of my grandpa wasn't a jab; it was a jolt.

That feeling was the reason I waited outside the Golden Steer. I chose this place for my date with Dax because, as the sign stated, it was the oldest restaurant in Las Vegas, full of historical intrigue. It was also close to our chapels and easy to sneak away to. But now I was reconsidering the recommendation. Grandpa Jim took me here when I "graduated" middle school, told me how it had survived decades of hotels going up and crumbling down. "It doesn't look like much on the outside," he'd said, peering up at the cheesy gold-spray-painted statue and mustard-yellow sign. "But this is about as close to preserving history as we get in Vegas."

The waiting room had a bar along one wall. Dax sat at a high-top table, sipping a soda, his eyes glued to a football game on the small TV. He had on a fitted polo, cracked loafers, and . . . reddish-pink pants. For serious.

"You wore your pink party pants," I said.

Dax looked up. "They're salmon."

My friends were already shouting taunts in my head. "Then salmon's your color."

"I know, they're loud." Dax laughed. "You can take the boy out of the South, but not the—"

"Salmon pants out of the boy."

"I'm trying to decide if it's your beauty or kindness that I like more, Holly Nolan."

"Who's playing?" I slid onto the stool next to him. I wasn't arguing the pants. He pulled off the look. Then again, Dax would look sexy in overalls and rain boots.

"Crimson Tide and Georgia Bulldogs. SEC championship. It's un-American that we're missing this game. In Birmingham, the whole town shuts down."

"I hate the Crimson Tide."

"Do you even know who they are?"

I rolled my eyes. "University of Alabama. In Tuscaloosa. They're a dynasty. Won three or four National Titles in the past few years. Always bullying everyone in the SEC."

"I would have been excited if you could tell me the state they are from, but . . . wow. That was otherworldly. Are you a cyborg or something, sent here disguised as the perfect girl?"

"I am a human," I said in a robot voice. "Pay no attention to my perfection. Alabama football is evil."

The hostess called my name and led us to our table. Dax slid his hand along the small of my back like it was the most natural gesture in the world. I usually wasn't so physical with the guys I dated. Nathan Gulliver took me out six times without touching me once.

"You know, I'm sad that you don't roll tide," he whispered. "Alabama is my favorite school. My dad went there. So did my poppy."

"Are you going there?"

"I was . . . but I doubt it." He straightened his shoulders. "I'm West Coast now."

"West Coast football sucks even more than Alabama."

"Not Oregon."

"Do not even get me *started* on Oregon."

"So we don't agree on football teams. Got it." He made a fake check in the air. "Anything else we should veto?"

"Besides our wedding chapels? Rats. I hate rats. And spaghetti."

"And rats *in* spaghetti. But who doesn't?" He stared at me then, like he was trying to find a good quality, and by the way he lingered, I'm sure he found a few. "I like your hair like that."

I touched the little braid that I'd managed to twist my bangs into. Camille had e-mailed me a hair tutorial. I'd used more hairspray on that spot than I had on the rest of my head all week, but at least I'd found a way to make my short hair look different.

"Thanks."

"No compliments back?" he teased. "I bought new deodorant. Old Spice Mr. Swagger Sport Action-Hero Fresh, I think."

"Are you asking me to sniff you now? You're weird, know that?"

Most of the circular booths in the restaurant were named after dead celebrities who had eaten there at some time: Elvis, Marilyn Monroe, John Wayne, notorious members of the Mafia. I breathed a sigh of relief when the waiter sat us at the Sammy Davis Jr. booth, one that was usually reserved. The waiter gave us a quick backstory of the restaurant. This was the original leather booth that Sammy used to sit in. In the fifties and sixties, the other restaurants still wouldn't serve a black man, so the whole rat pack ended up joining him here, and a Vegas institution was born.

Once the waiter left, Dax unfolded his napkin into his lap. "This place is something else."

I wiped my hands on my dressy jeans. Camille also e-mailed me outfit guides, designed on some fashion site. It must have taken her an hour, but I learned how to mix prints and colors, a far cry from my usual monochromatic black/gray/white. I'd even stopped by the Forum Shops at Caesar's Palace yesterday to buy a rose-colored blouse. Or top. Blouse? Shirt. I had on a new shirt. "Thanks. I thought it'd be fun to do something sort of . . . special. Las Vegas special."

"That's right. You're converting me to Las Vegasism." He nodded. "I've driven by here a million times and thought it was a dive."

"So you shouldn't judge everything based on your first impression. Like this city."

"I told you. I'm happy to be proven wrong. It's just going to take a lot of proving." He scanned the darkened room. "This is definitely a step up from Chili's."

"Sorry you don't get your Bloomin' Onion," I said.

"That's Outback."

"Oh." I laughed. "I don't usually eat at chain restaurants."

"I see." Dax shook out his menu. It was the same menu they'd always had. There was so much comfort in knowing a place hadn't changed in a lifetime. "Now your flaws are really coming out. You're a chain snob."

"No. I'm an I-want-to-eat-something-that-wasn't-frozen, dropped-on-the-ground, and flash-fried snob."

"So I won't be using my Olive Garden gift card on you."

"You can. I'll brave the salad." I sipped my water. "And I'm not a snob, you know."

Dax set his menu down. "Everyone is a snob about something. You're a chapel snob, a chain snob—"

"Then what kind of snob are you?" I folded my arms across my chest.

Dax didn't even pause. "A shoe snob. I could spend a fortune on shoes if I had the money. I'd rather buy shoes than eat this steak."

"I'm paying for dinner," I said. "We can go shoe shopping after."

"Then you really are the perfect woman." Dax squinted at the ceiling. "What else? I'm a TV- and movie-editing snob—I hate when in one scene a girl is putting on her jacket, then putting it on again, or an actor drinks coffee that is supposed to be hot but there is clearly nothing in the cup. Baseball . . . I can only watch entire baseball games in person, because if I'm watching at home, I know everyone at the ballpark is getting a better experience, with hot dogs and pretzels. Oh, and butterflies."

"What do butterflies have to do with baseball?" I asked, entranced.

"Nothing. Sorry. Next snob thing—I loathe butterflies. I think they steal all the thunder from moths. Moths go through metamorphosis. They have wings. But no one tattoos a moth on their lower back, there are no poems about *moth* kisses. Just because moths are drably colored, except for the luna moth, of course, and they mostly come out at night instead of the day."

"That's exactly why no one likes moths. Butterflies are beautiful."

"Well, it's absolute species racism. Moths get the shaft."

I couldn't think how to reply. I was finding that to be a problem with Dax, that my pauses were a little longer, because everything he said surprised me. I didn't talk like this with guys I dated, not about things that were actually interesting. Compatibility had never been standard for me. Now a guy I really, *really* wanted to date came around, and I saw all the cracks in my system.

"So sounds like your snobbery is far reaching," I said.

"It comes from my name. You can't have a name like mine and not be a little uppity."

"Dax? Dax sounds like a surfer name."

"Short for Dax*worth*."

"Oh. I'm . . . I'm so sorry."

"I appreciate that."

I nudged his leg. "Where'd you get that name?"

"My mom's name is Consuela. She's like a quarter Puerto Rican, grew up in Mississippi, completely Americano. She felt like her name held her back, that people destined her to be a housecleaner, when she's the principal at a middle school in Henderson. So she gave me the whitest, most Southern boarding school name she could think of to automatically get me into Harvard or something."

"What have you done with the name?"

"I'm thinking community college."

"Long live Daxworth Cranston."

"Just next year. I'm going to transfer, hopefully, maybe to a California school. I don't know, I'm just hanging out right now."

"But it's December. You should be collecting your letters of recommendation. Looking at requirements. You're just . . . hanging out?" I didn't mean for it to sound pathetic, but that's how the words tasted. I'd never in my life just hung out. I always knew that I wanted to go into business, maybe help my grandpa expand and build another chapel. I'd already talked to counselors at UNLV and I was still a year away.

"I was fixing to play baseball for Alabama. My dad and I were already talking to scouts. There was big interest." He did that shrug, where his left shoulder rose higher. "I used to pitch."

That was better than "hanging out." "You must be really good if you were going to pitch at an SEC school."

"I was really good. I know that doesn't sound modest, but I was."

"You know, we have baseball in Las Vegas too."

"I said I *was* good." Dax's eyes flashed. "I messed up my shoulder. Can't do any competitive sport now. I'm a racehorse put out to pasture."

I softened my voice. "What'd you do to your shoulder?"

Dax focused on something behind me and nodded his head. I turned around to see Bart Andrews, an old friend of my grandpa's, clutching his hat, frozen.

Oh boy. Bart Andrews. Retired owner of a small limo business. Also not a fan of Victor Cranston. "Holly Nolan, what are you doing with a Cranston? If your grandpa knew—"

I held up a hand. "Bart. It's fine. We're here, we're here for . . ."

"Business." Dax stood up and held out his hand, which Bart did not take. "Hello, I'm Dax Cranston. Holly and I were just honoring a meeting I'd set up with her grandfather months ago. Trying to reconcile some professional differences."

Bart gave a curt nod. "Your grandpa is no professional, boy."

"Yes, sir," Dax said.

They just stood there, staring. Dax smiled, but Bart would have none of it. That's what I get for taking Dax to a popular hangout in my grandpa's social circle. This wouldn't have happened if we'd gone for the Bloomin' Onion.

"Holly, your family is in our prayers," Bart said. "Be smart and . . . take care."

"Bye, Bart."

Dax stayed standing until Bart walked out of the room. He slid back into his seat. "I've never felt so popular."

"Bart had a run-in near the courthouse with your grandpa a couple of years back."

"It's fine. The family name evokes all sorts of . . . emotions."

"Don't worry about him," I said, although I probably agreed with anything Bart thought about Victor, except that his grandson was evil by association. "Bart's kind of crazy. Grandpa said Bart thinks the government has implanted mind-controlling microchips in every kid born since 1990."

"That's where the voices in my head come from!" Dax reached across the booth and took my hand. "So you're not embarrassed to be seen with me?"

"No."

"Good."

I scooted closer to him. This booth had been here for over sixty years; think of who'd sat here. Surely there'd been more scandalous diners than two business rivals. "Good. So you were just telling me about your shoulder."

"Come on, I'm not some old-timer who goes on about sports injuries."

"I want to hear about it. Did you have to get surgery?"

"Lots of them." Dax sighed. "I seriously don't want to talk about it. Instead, let's talk us."

"Us?"

"I've been thinking about you the last couple of days."

I blinked. Smart subject change. He hadn't even said it flirty; his tone of voice could have just as easily said, "Think I'll order the chicken."

"What were you thinking?" I asked, also without flirtation. It just seemed like a direct statement like his could have some detail.

He jiggled his ice with his straw. "About your smile. You scrunch up your nose when you're thinking, know that? And you're thoughtful. I feel like you practice your words before you say them."

"Um, I don't, but thanks? I think?" I paused. "I think about your stubble a lot."

"My stubble?" Dax rubbed his chin. "Really, my facial hair makes the biggest impression?"

"Yeah, how often do you shave it? Or do you just trim it? And when did you start to grow facial hair, ten? It's like model stubble."

"Model stubble?"

"You're supposed to say thank you when you receive a compliment."

"I'll remember that when you give me one."

We glowed at each other. Beamed. Radiated. I did not know that like could be like this. Like love, just not fully realized. I did not love this boy, because to love someone is to know them. But every moment I was with him made me happy, and every moment I wasn't with him, a small piece of me wondered where he was and what he was doing, like there was a satellite in our hearts.

He rubbed his hands together. "So. This is the second date. The getting-to-know-you date, not to be confused with the first kissing-next-to-rusted-neon-signs date. I'll just tell you everything on earth there is to know about me, then you can edit that."

"You could edit *yourself*."

"Not as fun. Now. Daxworth Cranston entered this world almost nineteen years ago. . . ."

"Birthday?"

"June twenty-seventh."

"One hundred ninety-six days away. You're still closer to eighteen."

"What was that?" he asked. "Did you just add that up in your head like that?"

I stuck my hand across the table. "Hi. I'm Holly. And I can add."

Dax shook his head. "That wasn't adding. That was math whizzing."

"I count things." I shrugged. "I can also tell you how many times you've rubbed your jaw in this conversation."

"Yeah?"

"Five."

The waiter came. Dax ordered a well-done steak; I went with the fish, despite the whole part in the e-mail Camille sent about dinner selection. Dax grinned as we handed back our menus. "So, numbers girl. I should have had you around to take stats at our baseball games."

"But then I would have to go to a baseball game, and I only go to professional games."

"Ha, fair enough."

When I didn't say anything else, he shifted in the booth. "What about you? Give me Holly 101."

"There's not too much to say. I go to school, I go to work, I go out with my friends."

"I might not have known you very long, Holly Nolan, but I'm sure there is much more to say than that."

His adorable. It almost hurt.

"I like . . . history. Actually. All kinds. Romantic, tragic, controversial. You know the Mafia used to hang out in the back room here, right?"

"Of course I didn't. I didn't know this place existed until tonight."

"But it's a mile away from where you work."

"I'm not always great with details. You are though, aren't you? Numbers and facts and making it all sound interesting. And you're in the wedding industry, which is detail heaven. I bet you actually like all the little nitpicks brides care about."

"It's their day." I twisted my napkin. "Don't you?"

"Not at all. *'No, I want white flowers!' 'Where is my something blue?' 'I think I'm in love with the groomsman.'* It's a crazy-person's job. No offense." He shuddered. "I only work there because that's where my mom and dad met."

"Really? When was that?"

"Early nineties. Dad was a groomsman for a college buddy. Mom was there for her sister's wedding. They met in the lobby. Dad told Poppy he should buy the place because it had to be lucky. My parents actually got married in the lobby too. Had a wedding anniversary dinner there." Dax smiled wistfully. "Sometimes, when I'm closing, I just lie in the middle of that room and think of every story that has walked across that floor." He laughed softly. "I guess I like history too. I'll have to find out how many Mafia men we've married there. I'm sure there's a few."

I grabbed his hand. "I take it back, when I said your chapel is tacky."

"You never said that."

"Not to *you*. That's a beautiful story. I think it makes up for the dusty carnations."

"What's a carnation?"

"Shhh. Don't ruin it."

He told me more about his life in Birmingham. His Dad coached from Little League on up, even in high school, where he taught chemistry. Dax talked about being an only child and living alone with his mom, then more about moths, although every fact was completely and ridiculously made up.

"Moths are also the most intelligent winged insect."

"Have you heard the expression, 'like moths to a flame'? They're idiots."

"You're a dream crasher."

The waiter came by and made our salads tableside with homemade Caesar dressing. This is how Vegas used to be, Grandpa would say. Dinner was an event and you took your time, none of this shorts-and-Hawaiian-shirts-with-black-socks-and-sandals.

I told Dax about my business program, about Sam and Camille, Grant and Porter. Icky Mike. I didn't say anything about my family. They felt too tied up with the chapel, and we weren't touching that territory. "And I did cross-country freshman year to get a PE credit, but it was kind of a hassle since I had to go to another high school for practice, so now I just run for myself."

"Do you miss being part of a team?" Dax asked, which was the weirdest question ever. Cross-country never felt like a team, not at my low level. It was just a mass of people moving from one spot to another.

"The only thing I like about organized sports is betting."

"You're joking," he said.

"Grandpa Jim liked to gamble." I thought about how much of the chapel loan must have gone to his gambling habit. I thought about how I must have contributed to it. "I read up on all the spreads, the player's statistics . . . it's pretty easy, if you take the emotion out of your choice."

Dax leaned back in his seat. "And you can do that? Just cut off emotion?"

"Of course. I don't care which team wins. I don't even care about the sport. No heart, more money for my grandpa."

"But sports are all heart."

"Professional sports are about money. It's business."

"And what about life? Can you do that? Just tune things out?"

"Mostly." I'd somehow tied a knot in my cloth napkin by now. "It makes things easier, don't you think?"

"No." His voice was monotone. "When my dad died, I tried that. Trust me. It doesn't work. Your emotions keep existing whether you want them to or not."

"Then what do you do with your emotions?"

"Feel them. Sometimes I numb them. Either way, your truths play on."

Bart Andrews walked by our table again, all judgmental stares and old-man head shakes. I knew what he was thinking, or what he would think if he knew I was falling for the grandson of the man who would love to destroy everything Grandpa Jim had worked for. Grandpa might as well have given the chapel to Donna—at least she wasn't romancing the enemy.

Although, I mean, if I were romancing the enemy (not in a calculating way, purely by coincidence) it didn't hurt to at least ask what, exactly, his grandfather knew about the chapel. And what Dax wanted to do about it.

"I can't believe you're this seasoned sports better and all I've done is snuck into bingo with Minerva," Dax was saying, oblivious to Bart and his Accusing Eyes of Accusations. "Poppy gambles a lot. He's a poker guy."

"Yeah. About him." Bart was gone now, after completing the most drawn-out restaurant exit of all time. "I know we said we wouldn't talk about our chapels. . . ."

"Yep." Dax looked me dead in the eye. "We did say that."

"But, look, I don't know if you know what's going on, but at the funeral, your grandpa said he knew our chapel was in trouble. How would he even know that?"

"I told you. We can see how many customers go in there—"

"But that's not what he was talking about. It's like he knows . . . things, and I don't want him to be another obstacle for us."

"*Another* obstacle?"

"Any obstacle."

"But he's a competitor."

Our main course was served. I tried to think of exactly what to say as the waiter cleared plates and presented food. Dax ran his finger along the rim of his water glass.

"*I* own the chapel, okay?" My voice shook. And not what I

was planning on sharing. See? Emotions don't help anything. "My grandpa gave it to me. I'm in charge. I'm supposed to save it. And I'm doing everything, everything I can to make it succeed, but it doesn't help knowing that Victor Cranston is over there sharpening his devil horns, trying to bring us down somehow."

"That's my poppy."

"Right. And he's also one of my biggest problems."

"I just work there part-time. It's not like I'm privy to the inner workings of the place." Dax gave a heavy shrug. "I'm sorry if he's making it hard, but—"

"You're not going to do anything about it," I said.

"There's nothing for me to do." Dax smacked his hand against the table. Our silverware rattled. "If he's fixing to hurt your chapel, he's going to do it. Just like before your grandpa died. Nothing has changed."

"Except it's *me* he's messing with now. Not my grandpa."

"I don't want to talk about this."

"Fine." I cut into my fish, cut into it until it was just a sea of mush. Dax ate some steak, poked at his potato. It was the longest stretch of silence we'd ever shared.

"What would you do?" I clanked my fork against the plate. "How would you feel if my grandpa were alive and yours was dead and we were trying to put *you* out of business?"

"Awful. Both sides are just awful. I wish this wasn't an issue. I wish . . . I wish you were just a pretty girl I met at a funeral and our biggest problem was choosing a chain restaurant for dessert. But that's not our reality, and the truth is, your grandpa has been trying to put us out of business for years."

"No, he hasn't."

Dax let out an exasperated breath. "Holly. He has. There are the lawsuits, the pranks, all the rumors he's spread within the industry. That Bart guy probably hates my grandpa because he was told to. I'm sure he was a good man, but it's a two-way street."

I pushed my plate away. "If I don't save Rose of Sharon, I'm losing the closest thing I have to home. Do you understand that?"

"Completely. More than you even know." Dax rubbed the back of his neck. "I'm not saying I want you to lose. I'm just saying I don't think there is anything I can do about it."

"You don't *think*." I stood. "Thinking isn't doing. It's not trying."

Dax stood up too. It wasn't easy, being in a booth. There was scooting and fumbling and people watching us. "If I say anything, he's going to know we're dating, or whatever this is we're doing. He'll know, your family will know, and they'll go all Montagues and Capulets on each other. The chapels would be the least of our worries."

I could not listen to his reason. "I . . . I need air. I'll be back."

I hurried outside and plunked myself onto a chipped bench underneath the GOLDEN STEER sign. I stared up at the gold cow statue, vaguely remembering some biblical story of God's chosen people building a golden calf to pray to and Moses getting mad about it. I would pray to it now; I would pray to anything or anyone.

Dax came out after a few minutes. He slid onto the seat next to me and didn't talk for seventy-two seconds.

"I paid for dinner," he said. "They're putting our food into doggie bags."

"I said I would pay."

"And then you ran away."

"I didn't run."

"You walked briskly."

"Don't joke."

Cars whooshed past us on their way to the Strip. All those people had expectations about how they thought their evening would go, just like I did with my careful outfit selection and giddy flirting with Dax. A lot of them would end up just as disappointed as me. They wouldn't meet that person they hoped they would meet, they wouldn't win the money they hoped they would make. Vegas was a dream, but a pipe dream that could never be realized.

Dax touched my arm, tentatively. When I didn't pull away, he cupped my face in his hands and kissed me. This kiss was so much softer than our last one—sweet, apologetic, warm. I was glad I didn't eat any of my fish. If someone in that moment had asked me what I cared about more, Dax or that stupid chapel, I would have handed over the deed to that place and jumped into Dax's arms. They were much softer than our pews.

"I'm sorry," I said.

"Me too."

"So that's it," I said, resigned. "You're Team Cupid's Dream."

He touched his forehead to mine and whispered. "I don't want it to be Team Chapel. I just want it to be Team Us."

I kissed him again. I would date Dax. I would save the chapel. It wasn't either-or for me. I wanted an *and.*

CHAPTER 11

In my parents' quest for the most amicable divorce ever, they were aggressive at keeping holidays "normal." They scheduled us alone time with each parent as well as a combined activity of some sort. The Fourth of July, with two barbecues, two sets of fireworks, and a family movie, all while sandwiched between Lecturing Lenore and Jaded James, was one of the most exhausting days of my life. That was, of course, before Christmas.

The day started off at The Space. Mom chose our postdivorce, three-bedroom apartment because it was by the bus stop. At one time, the apartments might have been considered nice, but this would have also been a time when Rollerblades were considered cool. Every few years a new company came in and renamed it some serene Spanish or Italian name, like Sienna Sunrise or Alicante. No matter how many times they repainted the stucco, maybe added some faux stone or spruced up the landscaping,

The Space was just a holding cell, a spot you lived in until your credit cleared or you found a boyfriend with a nicer address.

Aunt Sharon, in town from Phoenix, slept on the couch with her baby, who screamed all night. Mom almost had to use physical force to get us out of bed and in front of the Christmas tree for presents.

Presents. It really was Christmas. The first Christmas where we hadn't woken up to the smell of breakfast and the sounds of our parents' voices. It was the first Christmas without married parents and the first Christmas without Grandpa Jim here to make his *chile verde* eggs.

No one could ever make eggs like him, because no one would ever be Grandpa Jim. I would have other relationships in my life, love other people, but I wouldn't have *that* relationship. I wouldn't love anyone else in the same way that I did Grandpa Jim. The lack of togetherness and traditions magnified that truth.

Holidays are evil.

And so I started the painful process of trying to ignore emotional triggers as my family went through the motions of opening presents. James was all animated about his new war-themed video game (who doesn't want to arm their emotionally unstable child with a virtual weapon?), Lenore wanted everyone to know her hand-knit scarves were made out of organic yarn, and that baby just cried and cried.

By the time we were done and everyone started debating whether we should hit up a casino buffet or Denny's, the stress of holding things in got to be too much. I locked myself in the bathroom and curled up in the tub. The hexagon tiles were small enough that I could count for a while. I thought I might cry, but I didn't, just breathed, until I decided that I was going to implode if I didn't connect in some way with someone.

If I texted my friends on Christmas morning that I'd locked myself in here to count bathroom tiles, they would either not respond because they didn't know how to respond, or completely miss the hint that I needed help and start talking football. And really, it's not the easiest emotional clue to pick up on, so I shouldn't expect anything.

I slid my phone out of my pocket. Maybe it was needy, desperate, I don't know, but I texted the only person I could think of to text.

ME: Hey. Christmas is hard.

He wrote me back in one minute.

DAX: I'm Jewish.
ME: Oh. Really?
DAX: When it comes to Christmas I am. I'm anything other than any religion that makes today the Worst Day of the Year
ME: Maybe not the worst. I got a juicer. I can drink my vegetables now.
DAX: That must be where the expression "yuletide glee" comes from.
ME: Ha. Yeah.

Then I had nothing. If I couldn't text the people I knew best a feelings-themed text message, I shouldn't do it to Dax. I was starting to write, "Well, thanks for writing, talk soon," when he wrote:

DAX: First holiday is the hardest. Promise.

It was scary, being understood by a person I'd known less than two months. Today had to be torturous for him too, with just his mom and his douche bag of a grandpa. There was this whole other life he would be living if his dad were around.

ME: Thanks for understanding. Hope you get through the day.
DAX: I've been getting through the day for the last nine months. Time to light the menorah.
ME: Wait, so are you joking?
DAX: Mazel tov.

I washed my face and joined my family. Lenore and James got me a basket of fruits and vegetables to go along with the juicer, so we drank lemon, apple, carrot, kale, and mango for our Christmas breakfast. It kind of sucked, to be honest, but it could have been worse.

✦ ✦ ✦

That afternoon was James's Christmas Day piano concert at a church in nearby Henderson. Dad was supposed to meet us at the fountain outside the church at two o'clock. Dad didn't do so well with *supposed to*s.

The baby had a diaper explosion, so Aunt Sharon and Lenore hurried to the church bathroom. I counted the cars that drove into the parking lot. Twelve. None of them Dad's.

"I've got to go in." James stuck his hand into the fountain and scooped out a quarter. "I'm the main musical event, and Mrs. Georgia is going to be mad."

Mom glanced at her watch and sighed. "This isn't like him."

"Flaking out?" James asked. "Yeah it is. Dad flaked out on us. Open your eyes, woman."

"James, what did your therapist say about calling me 'woman'?" Mom asked.

He bit at a nail. "I could call you worse than that."

"James." There was a way that Mom said his voice that made me hurt for them both. Like she loved him, but she was so tired of him, which only made him worse, which just restarted the exhausting cycle.

"Lana," he mimicked.

"We talked about this."

"I'm not doing anything!" he shouted. A few churchgoers walking into the chapel shot us harsh looks. Yep. Loads of Christmas spirit. "I'm here to play the effing piano and you're getting mad for no reason!"

Mom looked up and breathed, like God was going to send a guardian angel or saint specializing in teenagers. "We also don't say 'effing.'"

"We didn't. I did."

"You're provoking me," Mom said.

"Whatever. I'm going in. Tell Dad thanks for not coming." He kicked at the door and didn't look back when Mom called after him.

"Find us after your performance."

"I don't care," he yelled.

Mom and I were silent. It could have been worse. At least he didn't actually call her a name—he'd done that. Or break something or punch a hole in the wall or break his hand punching a hole in the wall. Mrs. Georgia told us that his hands are his outlet for his anger. Without the piano, it would be worse.

"I'm sorry, Mom," I said.

"Next year for Christmas, let's go on a cruise." Mom chewed on her lip. "I should probably go in and save us some seats. Can you wait for your father?"

"I guess," I said. "I didn't want to watch anyway."

"He's coming," Mom said decisively.

I didn't say he wasn't. It might just be *after* the concert that he actually showed up.

The fountain outside was probably considered modern when it was built, but now it just looked like an afterthought sculpture with leaking water. I counted all the coins inside, the number of women wearing hats, and the minutes. I was pretty accurate at knowing how many minutes went by without counting seconds.

Twenty-one minutes later, Dad came huffing up the stairs. "Sorry. Late. Had. A. Meeting."

"It's fine." I checked my watch. Twenty-two minutes. Close. "James will actually have a reason to be mad at you this time. You okay?"

Dad bent over, hands on knees, and caught his breath. "Was your mother upset?"

"Is she ever upset?" I paused. "It's Christmas. What kind of meeting would you have on Christmas?"

"What?" Dad yanked open the lobby door.

"The reason you were late."

"Just some thing for work."

"I know, but what kind of thing?" I asked. Because my dad didn't ever have "meetings." He had "shoots" or "jobs" or even "appointments." But I never heard him say "meeting." And I don't care what job you have, meetings are never scheduled on Christmas morning.

Dad hurried across the hallway. "Wow, third degree. I had to meet someone, okay? How about you, how was your morning?"

"So it wasn't a thing, it was a who. Is this who a she?"

"What's with you?"

He didn't answer my question. Why wouldn't he answer my question? Why couldn't he just tell me the truth for once? Tell me why he divorced my mom and if he was dating someone now. That's not a lot to ask. It's not like I cared all that much what he was doing, I just hated that he was shady about it. If he wanted to protect Mom, fine, then tell me that. Be an adult. "I just wonder at what age you'll start to be honest with me."

"Who says I'm not? You're on one today." He cracked open the door to the theater. "There's your mom. We made it."

"I'm not *on one*, I just want—"

He was already down the aisle, halfway across the pew. He didn't hear me; he never heard me. I don't know why I let in those little pricks of caring. It wasn't worth it. James was proof.

The choir ended, and someone got up and read scriptures about Christ's birth. Our family had always been vaguely Catholic, going to church on holidays and wherever James had a concert. In the last year or so, his reputation had landed him more and more religious gigs, so we were getting closer to churchgoer status.

This particular church I liked because they didn't let the babies in the chapel and the acoustics made James's music soar. James walked across the stage, all slouchy posture and pinched features. He flopped down on the bench, shook out his hands, then tore into his piece, fingers pounding in a frenzy.

Mom put James and me into piano when I was nine and he was five. My brief piano career lasted approximately thirteen months, until my mom learned I was paying the piano teacher, a keyboardist for a struggling Strip headliner, three dollars a session *not* to make me practice. Mom promptly ditched that teacher and hired Mrs. Georgia, who would not accept such a lazy student and used that extra half hour to prodigize my little brother. James went from once-a-week half-hour lessons to hours and hours of tutelage. My parents poured money neither of them had into his magical fingers. James played at churches, colleges, festivals, and competitions. Even with all the angst and turmoil he'd had over the last couple of years, he still played every day, without fail.

Someone coughed a few rows ahead of us, but besides that, the only sound in that church was James's music. Jesus crescendoed to life and died in a stretch of mournful notes. James hit the final part, the part that Mrs. Georgia told him was supposed to be hopeful. The emotion soared from his fingers, but the song was bittersweet. Tears pricked my eyes. The Christmas story was joyful, but I couldn't feel it in James's interpretation. Only longing, so much longing.

James didn't even acknowledge the thick applause, just flicked his gaze to our pew. Dad waved and James dropped his eyes. Those same hands that had filled the church with such harrowing music were now fiercely clenched as he walked off the stage.

I'd never been more stressed about New Year's Eve in my life. This included last year, when Grant got a room at the Excalibur, a Camelot-themed hotel that is more smoke than magic. No matter, we were on the Strip, and the boys would be able to find girls to kiss in the new year. But there was also a curfew, and a cop spotted us the minute we walked outside. Instead, we had to stay in the hotel and play stupid carnival games and couldn't leave until early morning because everything was blocked off, and we all got in trouble and what did we have to show for it? A fake sword Grant won from Skeeball Tickets.

No, this year was even worse. Because after a month and a half, we had increased our wedding numbers by only 25 percent. Great under normal circumstances, but not when we were shooting for 100 percent. That 75 percent was going to take some effort and imagination.

And if not imagination, then Elvis.

I am not exaggerating when I say that almost every single chapel on the Las Vegas strip offered some sort of Elvis package. Although there were only a handful of really good impersonators, there were plenty of guys willing to stick on a suit and snarl their lips. So at any given second in this city, "Love Me Tender" is being serenaded to a giggling bride.

Except, of course, at our chapel. We turned away at least one couple a week because they wanted Elvis and only Elvis. It's not like Minister Dan couldn't do it—he was a private contractor, so he worked at other chapels. At sixty-two, he wasn't the most convincing Elvis, but the Germans and Koreans always seemed to like him. We could use the German and Korean money too, you know. And the British, the Taiwanese, the Brazilian, the Ethiopian . . .

In years past, Grandpa had closed the chapel at seven so we could get out of downtown before the New Year's crazies came out. This year, I scheduled an all-night shift and an all-day shift so we could compete with the round-the-clockers.

I was praying that the crazies came out tonight.

In order to get the word out that Elvis was now in the building, I had everyone, *everyone*, dress like Elvis. Minister Dan got the authentic rental. The rest of us wore cheap knock-offs or homemade costumes. You can guess how this mandate was received.

"This jumpsuit makes me look like I have cellulite on my

butt," Sam said. "I'm too young and too much of a man to worry about cellulite, Holls."

"I think your butt looks cute." Camille gave it a slap for good measure. "And I love the sequins. The world should wear more sequins."

"I appreciate your positive attitude," I said.

She squinted at me. "You need some eye shadow. You can't wear something like that without makeup, it totally washes you out."

"There is a chipped rhinestone falcon on my back. I think I'm making enough of a statement."

"It's New Year's. An overdose of sparkle is like a law. Bride's Room. Go."

And that's how I found myself getting the full Elvis makeover.

Camille talked a torrent as she tweezed, teased, and perfumed. "I don't want you to think I do this all the time. I think it's gross using your makeup on someone else. No offense."

"None taken."

"You need to work what your mama gave you more." She blew a curl out of her face. "A selfish part of me is glad you go for the whole androgynous look so I don't have to worry about you and Sam, but I'm your friend too."

"Camille, I don't think anyone puts as much thought into this kind of stuff as you."

"Yes they do. It's called the fashion and beauty industry. Look, I get that you have this whole wear-black-and-white thing going for you, but . . . you don't really have that going for you. You know?"

"Are you done? You've already insulted me four times."

She turned me around to face the mirror. "And complimented you seven. Now don't let a parking lot get in your way tonight."

I sneezed glitter. "What, like, Dax? He's working. I'm working."

"A hundred feet away from each other. So find some time to work *it*. You look sexy in that suit. I would have told you to go with a push-up bra, but still."

"A push-up bra's not going to matter for you because you're wearing the sandwich board on the Strip."

Camille grimaced. "Next time I give you a makeover, remind me to give you the how-to-hook-a-sister-up talk. You're a failure."

"It could be worse. James and I have to stand in front of the chapel and wave signs around. At least you and Sam get to go to the Strip. If you see anyone coupley, give them a brochure. And please make sure you don't make out all night."

"Would you notice two Elvis's kissing?"

"Yes."

"See? Good advertising. I'll be sure and turn so they see the sandwich board." She blew me a kiss and flounced out with a bag full of flyers.

Alarmingly, I was starting to like that girl.

The adults were in the break room. They stopped talking when I came in. I almost started singing "Viva Las Vegas," but they didn't look up for it.

Mom had on a blue jumpsuit with a wide white belt and white scarf. Dad's was classic black, muted, with only a few rhinestones. Minister Dan looked the best, in a blindingly bedazzled white getup complete with a red-and-gold cape, sunglasses, and sideburns that could almost pass as real.

And then there was Donna. Oh, Donna. A mauve suit today. She might as well have given me the middle finger.

It's not like I wanted to do this whole Elvis promotion either. Yes, the man represented Vegas—he was fake married here for *Viva Las Vegas*, real married here to Priscilla Presley, and headlined for years. But I'd never understood how having some stranger dress up like a dead guy and sing was romantic to people.

"Donna, why haven't you changed your clothes?"

"Because I'm not going to change," Donna said crisply. "I find this whole thing incredibly offensive. You know how your grandfather felt about Elvis."

I wiped my hands on my polyester pants. This suit was already giving me a wedgie. "Okay. I've said it to everyone individually at some point, but let me say it collectively now. We're doing Elvis. We're doing Marilyn."

"Monroe or Manson?" Dad asked.

"Either. Or. And. I understand and agree with everyone that this is new territory for us, territory that Grandpa would rather not have explored. But as I see it, we have about two months to make a miracle happen, and the only way that miracle is going to happen is if we slap on some bell bottoms and give the people what they want. I'm not saying we sell out forever, just a little. Just for now."

"It's your chapel," Mom said. "Are you sure?"

"No, I'm not sure. I have no idea what I'm doing. But I'm trying *something.* So come on, little lady." I knelt on the ground and held up one hand. I tried to do the Elvis lip snarl, but I'm pretty sure I just looked like I had to sneeze. "Who's with me?"

"Uh-uh-huh!" Minister Dan said in a spot-on impersonation.

"I swear this suit is chafing me. Is anyone else chafing?" Dad grabbed a soda and wandered out of the room. Mom started talking schedule. I was still kneeling, waiting for applause. Donna held out a hand. "He might have hated Elvis, but he would have loved that awful speech."

"Maybe he heard. Maybe he's sitting on a cloud watching."

"Maybe." She puckered her lips. "Now why don't you go outside and make sure our next couple makes it into the chapel. Once Cranston gets wind that we've gone Elvis, he's going to start outselling us right in the parking lot."

✦ ✦ ✦

If you wear it, the people will come. They came in jeans, they came in tank tops. Dresses and top hats, wranglers and vests. They came planned, they came spontaneously. They came somber, sober, or drunk. It didn't matter. The people came.

In only six and a half hours, we married more couples than we had on any date in the last two years. I bounced along the street, swaying my hips like I was the King himself. We were in new territory, tacky territory, but also that magical place where the "im" part of "impossible" faded into the casino smoke.

Maybe it was that feeling of infinity that made me text Dax around two a.m. for a little rendezvous. I popped into the chapel to make sure no one would see us, then after a quick breath and face check (still sparkling!), slipped into the rose garden behind the chapel.

Dax leaned against the African sumac tree Grandpa planted after his second divorce. He stepped into the light and grinned at me. "I don't know what to say. I'm all shook up?" He wore a dirtied, bloodied suit and gray makeup.

"I don't know what to say either."

He lurched over to me, moaning and gurgling. "Elvis brains. Good."

"I can't believe you're doing zombie weddings." I flipped my cape behind my back. "Like, plural. The zombie fad is the worst."

He pretended to straighten his tie. "How many ceremonies have you had tonight, Mr. Presley?"

"Well . . . a lot."

"Themes help, right?"

"There are themes, and then there are *themes*," I said.

"So are you lonesome tonight?" Dax asked.

"Here we go."

"Sorry." His smirk spread across his gory face. "Am I being a hound dog?"

"You know, if you wanted to win me over, you'd recite U2 song titles instead—"

"Don't be cruel." He swooped his arm around my waist and pulled me close. "How's this?" His voice dipped deep, his twang brightened. He sang a song I'd never heard, all earnest adulations. Dax should have on the Elvis costume. I would scream and throw underthings at him on stage. He ended, "That's the wonder, the wonder of you."

My breath hitched. "That's an Elvis song?"

"He sang it when he headlined in Vegas. Poppy showed me a video once. Guess I know a little local history that you don't." He leaned in to kiss me, then paused. "I might zombify all that pretty glitter on your face."

He'd morphed Elvis from tired and used to glorious and sweet. I grabbed his face. "I'll take my chances."

Not that this was a new encounter. Since our date at the Golden Steer a few weeks ago, this is how we met—sneaking out to the garden or behind his chapel by the Dumpsters, kissing when we could. Between our work and school schedules, and the fact that we had to hide everything from our families, there hadn't been as much face time as I would like. Face time, neck time. Any time with Dax was amazing. I'd never had a New Year's kiss, and now to be here, with him, was . . .

"What are you doing?" James was frozen in the parking lot. "You're kissing a zombie?"

Dax and I jumped away from each other. Even in the dim light, glitter glinted off his lips.

"Your face is all gray now," James said. "Is that a Cranston? You were sucking face with a Cranston?" James poked me with the large foam hand I'd made him wave up and down the street. "Happy New Year's to me."

Dax stepped forward. "Hey, buddy, how are you doing? I'm Dax."

James didn't even look at him. "Did he just call me buddy?"

"James."

"Just say cheese." James took a picture of Dax and me all disheveled, wearing each other's makeup and guilty faces. He tucked his phone into the pocket of his jumpsuit. "Your dirty secret is safe with me, at least until I need ammo. Like . . . I'm kind of sick of wearing this stupid outfit. I'm going to change. Either of you have a problem with that?"

"You're fun," Dax said.

"James, come on. Seriously, if you tell, ever, it'll . . . think of what Mom and Dad would think. And now, with things how they are at the chapel . . ."

"How are things at the chapel?" Dax asked.

James narrowed his eyes. "I bet you'd like to know. Did your grandpa pimp you out to my sister so you could find out our secrets?"

"No! I'm asking . . . I want to help." Dax cast me a desperate look. "I swear, I . . . Your sister is special to me."

"Your sister is special to me." That's a quote I wouldn't mind knitting into a cloud sweater and wearing every day.

James snorted. "That's the biggest line I've ever heard. Ditch the dude and come inside."

"I'm not coming inside just because you told me to."

"Of course not. Why should you listen to me? Why should anyone ever listen to me? You're just like Mom and Dad."

I didn't see how making out with a boy behind the wedding chapel was anything like our cryptically divorced parents. "Look, this has nothing to do with you. This is my deal, okay?"

"Uh, guys." Dax stepped between us. It was a wasted gesture; it's not like I was going to fistfight my brother. "I'm sorry to break this up, but . . . is that your next ceremony?"

A limo pulled into the parking lot. Let me rephrase that. The fanciest, stretchiest limo I'd ever seen parked smack in the middle of our two chapels.

We gaped at each other in the neon moonlight. Out spilled three muscley bodyguards in black suits. "Hey! Elvis! You open all night?"

James straightened his posture. "Yes, sir. Can we help you?"

"Our clients don't have an appointment, but they want to book the whole place out. They, uh . . . they need privacy. And they'll pay. Whatever. Now, which chapel do we go to?"

A gargle rose from Dax's throat. "Uh, you sure you want Elvis to do it?"

"Don't even," James growled under his breath.

The bodyguard took his sunglasses off. His hands were bigger than my whole upper torso. "Or a zombie. How they acting right now . . . they might get a kick out of a zombie."

Dax cut me a look. Whoever was in that limo had money and perhaps some degree of celebrity, and this was exactly the clientele Victor Cranston adored. One celebrity wedding could bring in months of business. There was a chapel down the street that said, "Michael Jordan was married here." Married in 1992, divorced, and remarried, but people still went there because of Michael.

It would be a jerky move for Dax to tell them to go to his chapel, but it would be understandable. Roles reversed . . . I don't know what I would do.

His eyes flitted between me and the bodyguards. Holly or mystery celebrity.

We were making the choice we said we would never have to make.

"I can't believe I'm doing this." Dax squeezed his hand into a fist and beat it against his thigh. "Fine. It's yours."

"Of course it's ours," James said.

"Dax." I squeezed his arm. He was so good. So good. "I . . . I don't know what to say."

"Just don't tell my poppy." Dax stormed back to the chapel but stopped and turned around. "And erase that picture, kid."

The bodyguard was still standing there, his meaty hands shoved into his pockets. "So, what do I tell them?"

"We're open," I said. "We have a ceremony ending now, but they can be next and book out however long they want."

"Rest of the night?"

James squeaked. I started crunching numbers. "That's a lot. We are supposed to be open until five a.m., and it's our busiest night, and our most expensive package runs up to a thousand dollars, so . . ."

"They'll give you fifteen thousand."

I almost choked. Whoever "they" were, "they" did not mess around. "Then we'd be happy to make this a very special evening for them."

I scrambled inside and started hollering orders. Minister Dan finished up the other ceremony in record speed while we all tidied up the lobby.

Five minutes later, the wedding party appeared. First came the flood of bodyguards, then a string of gorgeous men in suits. I instantly recognized two guys from TV. They weren't name-remember famous, but recognizable enough that even Donna cursed under her breath. Next came the ladies, and three out of four were teen movie stars. They held up the bride, Valerie Hamilton, also a former child-star turned pop sensation. The only thing indicating that Valerie was the lucky girl was the pink BRIDE! sash slipping down her shoulder. Otherwise, she had on a fedora, a holey sweater, and sailor-style jeans.

"She needs a bouquet," star/bridesmaid number one said. "And maybe she could brush her hair?"

The groom, Barry Naylor, was the star of a fake-documentary TV comedy, as well as countless rom-coms. It's what this all was—a big rom-com of a night where I was making out with my sort-of boyfriend behind a tree, had my Elvis-impersonating brother go paparazzi on us, and, the next thing you know, a limo pulled up with a fourth of the money we needed to save the chapel.

"Let me take you to the bride's room," I said. "The ladies can freshen up. Donna, can you get our wedding party some ice water and butter mints? Anything else?"

"Hey, am I seeing double?" Barry rubbed his eyes. "There's a lot of Elvises here, right?"

"You told us to stop because you saw Elvis," the bodyguard said.

"Good." Barry's head rolled to the side. "I thought I was the only one who saw Elvis."

"I'm guessing you didn't stop and get a marriage license?" I asked the friend. He was on a cop show. He played the handsome cop. Or the handsome lawyer. All I could think right then was *handsome.*

"We didn't even know they were getting married until about twenty minutes ago," he said.

Donna visibly cringed behind the counter. Grandpa had been known to turn away last-minute, midnight I-doers if he thought an annulment was in their short future. My quick calculations only gave them a 15 percent chance of surviving the week.

"We'll have the limo take them to the courthouse. Just need to show some ID and sign. You've booked the chapel all night, no rush. Is there anything else I can do for you guys?"

"Wasn't there a zombie outside too?" Barry asked.

"No, just Elvis here," Donna said.

"That was, er, someone from the other chapel."

Dad lowered his camera. "Who from the other chapel?"

"I don't know. Just someone dressed like a zombie. You know how Cupid's Dream is." I prayed that I'd gotten all the zombie makeup off my face.

"Well, I want a zombie. I was in a zombie movie once." Barry hiccuped. "Make it a zombie Elvis."

Donna walked around the counter and pulled me back. "First Elvis, now this? When does it stop? How far will you go before you realize it's all too far?"

"Probably sixty thousand far. Because if I don't go there, we don't go anywhere." I jerked my arm away from her. "Please make a choice to be happy about this."

"You want a zombie?" Donna smiled at Barry. "Holly would love to dress up and make any of your wedding dreams come true. That is, after all, what she does."

✦ ✦ ✦

Forty minutes later, Barry and Valerie said their "I dos." I stumbled slowly behind them as they walked down the aisle, my arms out zombie-style, dirt and ketchup smeared across my face.

We ended up making $21,000 that night. If we could just maintain average numbers and have a decent Valentine's Day, we were going to be fine. More than fine.

Rose of Sharon Wedding Chapel was in business. For now, it didn't matter if it was the kind of business Donna thought we should be in or not.

CHAPTER 13

Since we worked New Year's Eve, Sam decided to host a January fourth party. I asked Dax to go. My mom was driving her sister back to Phoenix, and I didn't work until three the next day, meaning I had no curfew or responsibility.

But it wasn't until Dax accepted that I started thinking about the party, how my friends could be . . . how they were, how he and I weren't really at the meet-the-friends point yet, how being together with someone on a holiday—even a made-up holiday—makes that "being together" more of a thing.

I went to Sam's early to help Camille set up. His mom had chosen a Mexican theme for the evening (for what reason, we knew not), and had a taco bar catered and sombreros hanging from the ceiling and mariachi music playing near the pool. Sam came up behind Camille, shaking some maracas, and kissed her.

Which of course lasted too long, so I pretended the salsa bowls needed to be shuffled around. For five painful minutes.

Camille pulled away and batted Sam on the shoulder. "No more *bessar* for you, señor!"

"New Year's is automatic *bessar*," he said.

She folded her arms across her chest. "Wait, so you think just because you're having another party, you automatically get to hook up with me?"

Sam grinned. "No, I think because it's a day ending in *y* I get to hook up with you."

"Sam Perkins! Stop being a jerk!"

"Hey, babe. Don't get mad. It's New Year's." He started to sing, deep and twangy. *"What are you doing, New Year's Eve?"*

"Tell me that wasn't a country song."

Sam shrugged.

"That's how you apologize? It's not even real New Year's."

"It's *our* New Year's."

"If it's only ours, then why have a big party?"

Sam reached for Camille. "You like big parties."

"No, *you* like big parties. I like . . . I like . . . I don't even know what I like because you never let me decide for myself." She turned around and grabbed my arm. "Come on, Holly. Let's leave him alone with his sombrero."

"There's a U2 New Year song she might have liked better," I informed Sam before Camille pulled me out of the room. I thought it was unspoken that, as Sam's friend, I would naturally side with Sam, but those boundaries were starting to blur.

Sam was out of line, but it was probably hard for him to see that since Camille never took much of a stand.

We went up to the kitchen to, I don't know, check on more salsa. "That boy is getting on my nerves," Camille said. "It's like he thinks he owns me."

"He doesn't think that. Seriously, Camille. He is so far gone in love with you. He was picking out your wedding cake flavors the other day."

Camille looked alarmed. "He what?"

"No, just at Bridal Spectacular. He was saying you like lemon cake but vanilla would be better . . ." I was not helping things. Clearly.

Camille looked down at her hands. "I don't like when he talks like that. I'm sixteen."

"I know! I don't think he means it, not always, he just . . . he loves you."

"He's my first boyfriend. And my parents don't even know he exists. We have a long way to go before we even think about marriage."

"Of course you do. But it is fake New Year's Eve. No sense getting into that now and wasting all your sparkles, right?"

Camille shrugged. "I guess not. I just feel like if we don't talk about things when they happen, then we never talk about them."

"I bet if you go back to the basement, Sam will apologize right away."

"Yeah, he will." Camille wrapped her arms around me like a butterfly in a chrysalis. Or a moth. Dax would prefer I mention the moths. "Thanks for talking. You're better at it than Sam says you are."

"Um. Thank you?"

The doorbell rang. Camille let me go. "Come on, time to play hostess."

Not to rub salt into a wound, but this is what happens when you get into these forbidden, love-of-my-life kind of romances in high school. High stakes, high breaks. Dax and I would be totally different because we weren't in that kind of a relationship, we weren't even *in* a relationship, and James already knew about us. At some point, if we even got to that point, we would tell the family and it wouldn't be a huge deal. Or we wouldn't tell the family, but we wouldn't get so serious that we talked about marriage.

I mean, besides that time we talked about marriage.

Guests poured into the house for the next hour. Dax texted to say he'd be a little late, but 9:30 felt like we were a little past "a little." Camille came back and forth between the upstairs and the downstairs to check on me. She offered me a sympathetic smile the third time. "Did he at least apologize?" she asked.

"Here's what he said, 'Sorry, my ride taking sweet time. Kiss you soon Juliet.'"

"Is that a nickname?" Camille asked.

"I guess so. Because of the chapel thing? It's weird. I don't know."

She squeezed my hand. "Come downstairs with me. You can put a sign on the door. He'll find you."

"I'll give him a few more minutes."

Once she was gone, I tried writing three different texts to Dax.

Did you get lost?

Romeo, Romeo, when are you getting here already, Romeo?

Oh, hey, I'm at the party if you want to come

I backspaced them all and sent nothing. Three blondes, five brunettes, a redhead, and a guy with a shaved head walked in. 9:45. He said he'd be here at 8:00.

I should text him, right?

My phone finally buzzed at 9:53. Text from Dax: Sorry. I'm at the gate. My stomach whirled with butterflies. No, moths. Beautiful moths.

The music pumped downstairs, and kids ran around on the tennis court outside. If I was going to make Dax come to a party at my school, at least it was this party. Not a Harry Potter role-playing event like Sam used to have in middle school. Not that Dax wouldn't be okay with that, I just wanted tonight to seem . . . older. Worthy of his stubble.

The doorbell rang. I watched Dax through the peephole. There was another guy standing next to him, probably someone who rolled up at the same time. Maybe it was the anticipation of wanting to see him all day, but I had never seen a finer peephole-sized specimen. Dax leaned in closer to the door. The moths rammed the lining of my stomach so hard, I thought I might puke.

I didn't mean to fling the door open, but the anticipatory adrenaline gave me superhuman strength. "Dax, hey!"

Dax gave a lopsided grin. "Hey, Hallie, this is Alex. Alex, this is the girl I told you about."

Alex held out his hand to give me dabs. Dabs? I'd been given dabs four times in my life, no times since I was over the age of twelve. "Where's the party?"

I pointed to the stairs. He took them two at a time.

"Friendly guy." I wanted to follow it up with a "and who is he?" But . . . whatever. So Dax brought a friend. He needed a ride and he didn't know anybody but me. Of course he brought a friend.

Dax stepped forward and gave me a kiss on the cheek. "You look . . . whoa." He smelled like beer. Lots of beer. And look, I know it was (fake) New Year's Eve, but this was a date, right? Sort of? What kind of guy shows up two hours late smelling like alcohol with some random kid and all I get is a "whoa"?

Dax threw his arm around me. "I had car problems and Alex had to drive."

"Oh." My voice was small. Teeny-tiny. I hated how mouse-like and disappointed I felt. This night was supposed to sparkle, and so far we hadn't even reached lackluster status. "Glad you made it. Finally."

Dax shoved his hands into his pockets. "This house is huge. Is bringing me here part of your plot to make me like Vegas?"

"It's just a house."

"Where are your friends?"

He was going to meet my friends like this.

Spectacular.

✦ ✦ ✦

Grant loved Dax from the get-go. They had so much in common. Like . . . red Solo cups. That's about it.

Maybe Dax wasn't any different from any other guy. Maybe it was just how I felt about him, and maybe that feeling was unfounded, a by-product of the recent life changes I'd experienced.

Dax caught my eye from across the room and smiled. I could actually see his dimple now that he'd shaved. Nevermind. My feelings were founded.

Porter flopped down next to me on the couch. "So your new boyfriend is a—"

"Don't finish that sentence," I said.

"Is a Crimson Tide fan. Said he used to live in Alabama. What did you think I was going to say?" he asked.

"Nothing."

"You're mad because you wanted him to show up with roses and champagne. Sorry, Holls. I think he already toasted."

"I didn't expect roses." I motioned toward Dax and Grant. They were laughing about something. "I just wanted . . . I don't know what I wanted. Don't make fun of me."

Porter leaned in closer. "Don't let him hurt you. Three out of five Alabama fans are not doctor approved."

"He's not hurting me, it's not like that."

"Good. You deserve better in a boyfriend."

"You're worse than Mike. We've only been out a few times; I don't even know him."

Porter stood. "Then go talk to him. Don't you know that drunk people are the best conversationalists? They spill all their secrets."

I checked my watch. 10:51. I didn't know what I was counting toward. Fake New Year's with a boy who wasn't even paying attention to me?

I sunk back into the couch. At least the party was under control, even if my date wasn't. West parties were different. Kids were smart at our school, smart enough that they didn't party too hard (like Dax) and knew where they wanted to go to college and what they were doing with their lives (unlike Dax).

Why did I invite him here anyway?

Dax weaved around the people and offered me a cup.

"No thanks."

"It's water."

I took the drink and peered inside. Sniffed.

"It's water, Holly," Dax yelled over the music.

I grabbed a water bottle from the cooler instead.

"You want to get outta here?"

"Do you ever stay in one place?" I joked.

"What?"

I pointed to the door. "Follow me."

Sam's family had a big side yard that no one ever used. I don't know why the backyard got all the love when the side yard had such charm. There was a little gazebo with a tea table that Sam and I used as our interrogation room when we filmed home action movies in middle school. I always got stuck playing the Russian spy.

"This is cute." Dax pulled back a metal chair. "Did you bring me out here to have your way with me?"

I took a sip of my water. Another sip. "I don't really feel like joking around with you."

"Oh?" He grinned. "Then what do you feel like doing?"

Would it have been too much to ask for him to be normal tonight?

He scooted closer, got up in my face. "You look pretty."

He didn't smell bad, not really. He still had on cologne, and alcohol can be sort of sweet too. But this guy in front of me wasn't the Dax I knew or wanted to know. Dax was kind, funny. He seemed like someone I could count on, but maybe this was who he really was. Maybe he drank all the time. Maybe he was habitually late.

Maybe he was just like his grandfather.

I nudged Dax off my shoulder. "You're drunk."

He grinned, shiny-eyed. "I'm faintly intoxicated."

"How much have you had?"

He waved a hand. It was a gesture I'd seen him do before, but this time, it was like he was moving in slow motion. "Good question, numbers girl. I should have kept you nearby to count. I always lose track."

"Always? How often do you get faintly inebriated?"

"Intoxicated." He smiled lazily. "Not a lot. Holidays, we've already established, are awful. Hmmm, Tuesdays! Never been one for Tuesdays."

"What did Tuesdays do to you?" I asked.

His smile was a slow fade, like the last gasp of a meteorite crashing into the ozone. "My dad died on a Tuesday. Not a fan."

He was so sad. Drunk sad, raw sad. If he were an angry drunk, I could stay angry too, but he just looked so desperate and needy and my broken-bird instinct kicked in. "It's not really New Year's Eve though. You were sober then."

"Sober but not in my right mind. I can't believe I gave you that limo."

"Is that what this is about, that limo?" I asked.

"How much did you make on them?"

"They pulled in because they saw Elvis," I said. "You didn't give me that limo."

"But I told you to do Elvis."

"Wow. Elvis at a Vegas wedding chapel. Revolutionary idea. Did you want me to make you partner now?"

"I'm just saying, that wasn't the smartest business move I've ever made."

"Neither is making out with your competitor or showing up here drunk." I scooted away from him. "Seriously, are you mad at me now? Is that how it's going to be?"

"I'm not mad at you." Dax peered into his cup. "I'm mad at me. I'm mad at, just . . . I don't know what I'm mad at. I'm being stupid. Sorry."

"Look, Dax. I don't mess with stuff like this. And you shouldn't either, especially given how much your grandpa drinks."

He hiccuped. "You're right."

"I'll get you home and we can talk later."

"But later I won't be able to talk about this stuff."

"What stuff?"

"My mom went on a date tonight." His voice scraped over the words. "First date since Dad died."

My stomach dropped. "Oh, Dax."

"She's . . . she's moving on. There are boxes of his that we brought when we moved from Birmingham. Some of his sports stuff, trophies. Things that mattered so much when he was alive, they're all in *boxes* now. A few weeks ago, she took those boxes out of the closet and put Dad . . . put his boxes in the garage." He threw his cup into the grass. "It's my fault. Did I ever tell you that? It's my fault that he died."

"You can't blame yourself."

"We were in a car accident. Headed home from practice. I was driving. Dad was talking about how much my fastball had improved. He wasn't one of those dominating coaches—just really smart about the game. Kind of like you, looked at sports like a science. Quiet guy. Humble. God, I miss him."

"Dax—"

"There wasn't rain, we weren't fighting, I wasn't texting. I don't even remember what I was thinking about, I just wasn't paying attention, and then I thought I saw something on the road and swerved and hit an oncoming car. Smashed my dad, tore up my shoulder. It was my fault. People didn't try to tell me it wasn't. Everyone just said it was a tragedy. I don't think Mom's even made eye contact with me since the funeral."

Dax buried his face in his hands.

Look, I'd just lost someone too, I knew how much it burned his throat to say these things out loud, but even with all that empathy, I couldn't touch Dax. I felt no responsibility for Grandpa Jim's death.

"Dax, I'm . . . Of course there is nothing I can even say. That's just . . . horrible. That's . . . I'm sorry."

Dax wiped at his face and stared forward. "Me too. I don't understand why it happened. What if practice hadn't gone over five minutes? What if my dad had taken his car? What if there wasn't something on the road? What if that other driver wasn't going somewhere else? Do you know how many things had to line up for such a random thing to happen?"

"If you spend your life agonizing over the what-ifs . . ."

"But you don't. Right? You don't think possibility. You're about probability. Measure it out, move forward. The only moving I've done in the past ten months is from my home to Vegas."

Moving forward? I'd been in the same safe place my whole life. "But you do so much for your poppy, and the chapel—"

"It's fine. Sorry I went off like that. Suckafugawhatever, right?" He laughed hoarsely. "Sometimes I feel like if I could just have that one question answered, why did he die, then everything else in my life would line up."

I looked down at my hands. What was I supposed to do? Hug

him? Hold him? Tell him that everything was okay when it wasn't? I'd never gotten this deep into a relationship. I wanted out of this territory, this zone of caring and worrying and feeling. Dax's vulnerability almost made me like him more, when it shouldn't. It wasn't safe to like him as much as I did.

"I wish I had an answer for you," I said.

"I'm really sorry. You have everything so together, I hate that you're seeing me. Like this. It's not who I am."

"Just don't drink like this around me again, okay? I hate it."

Dax slipped his hand on my knee. "How many dates have we been on now?"

"Actual dates? Two? I guess you could count this as our third."

"What's the etiquette? Am I supposed to tell you this stuff on the third date?"

"We met at a funeral. I don't think there's etiquette after that."

Dax looked around the backyard. "I'm kinda feeling sick right now."

"Physically or emotionally?"

"Both. But more the first."

"Did you want to lie down somewhere?" A couch. Or maybe a bed. I would get Dax situated. Taking care of basic human needs was something I could handle.

Dax raised an eyebrow.

"Shut up," I said. "Seriously, how much have you had?"

Dax tried to stand, stumbled. "Too much. Yep, too much."

I eased him up the stairs to Sam's room, realizing that we

didn't look like the most innocent pair, but better a rumor than Dax throwing up or passing out in front of everyone.

I knocked once on Sam's door and said a silent prayer of thanks when no one answered. I pushed the door open with my foot.

Dax giggled. "Holy Hogwarts."

I would consider myself a fan of Harry Potter. Sam, on the other hand, had a bit of an obsession. Granted, his mom had decorated his themed bedroom in eighth grade, so it was over the top, but he could have changed things since then. The colors were Hufflepuff yellow and black, with a shelf of different wands and Lego creations. The funny thing was he also had some band posters, a girl in a bikini, and a huge 8 × 10 picture of Camille. Did she buy that for him or did he frame it himself?

I eased Dax onto the bed, praying that he wasn't a frisky drunk. He flopped down and stretched. "Hogwarts has comfy beds."

"I'm going to put a trash can by the bed in case you throw up. But please, don't throw up. Sam will hate you forever."

"I really wanted to impress your friends," Dax said, cuddling into a pillow.

"Well, Grant likes you. Although he might not remember you in the morning."

"Tell Alex to come get me."

I tugged off Dax's shoes. "I will. And don't get up. Try to, I don't know, sleep it off."

"I like you," Dax said.

I squeezed my eyes shut. You can't take the things people

say when they are drunk as meaningful. Alcohol is not a truth serum; it's a mask. You never know if it's the person or the drink talking. "Yeah, I like you too. Just not so much when you're like this."

He didn't respond. I checked my watch. 11:22. I was at the door when I heard him mumble, "Really, numbers girl. You couldn't count all the ways you have my heart."

✦ ✦ ✦

Alex, shocker, was MIA. I'd already described him to three different people before I found a girl who said Alex had left with a friend of a friend. Whatever his whereabouts were, it was not Sam's house.

Sam and Camille had repaired things enough to begin a public make out on the bench next to the tennis court. Honestly, they didn't even look comfortable. If this really was love, I was fine if I never left 'like.'

I poked Sam with a tennis racket that was leaning on the fence. "Hey, I need to get a ride for someone."

Sam pulled himself away and grinned. Camille looked like she'd been caught, which wasn't too hard when there were tennis lights *beaming down* on her. "Who?" Sam asked. "Not that very drunk gentlemen friend of yours, right? What's his name again?"

"Shut up. You know it's Dax." I rubbed at my eyes. "I put him in your room."

"If he messes with my Hogwarts—"

"I'm sure Hogwarts is safe." Camille smoothed down her hair. "Dax doesn't seem like the type to draw lightning bolts on his forehead, okay?"

"Just another thing wrong with him," Sam mumbled.

I smacked Sam on the shoulder. "Fine. You two go back to face snarfing and I'll find him a ride."

"Sam, your friend needs your help," Camille said.

"Dax isn't my friend."

"Is your head that thick?" Camille stood. "Fine, I'll take Dax home. I don't know where he lives and my car interior is much nicer than yours, but I will drive him because that's what friends do."

Camille's whole timid Victorian lady thing was a very clever disguise. Girl had bark.

"What are we fighting about?" Grant and Mike sidled up. Great, more input.

"Holly's boyfriend is drunk and passed out in my bed, and she needs to get him a ride," Sam said.

"Boyfriend?" Mike looked hurt. "I thought you'd only been on a few dates."

I let out an exasperated breath. "We have."

"So when did he become your boyfriend?" Mike shook his head. "I have to tell you, I'm not totally comfortable with you defining the relationship this early on, especially with someone who puts you in these kinds of awkward situations."

"Yeah, *Dax* is the one making this awkward right now," Grant said.

“Okay, all.” I held out my hands. “It’s fine. I’ll just call my sister.”

“No you won’t. Your sister won’t come get you,” Mike said.

“Guys, it’s eleven forty-four,” Camille said.

Everyone checked their phones or watches. Grant finally said he would take us home, but not until he wanted to leave. Which, I knew, would be forever. While everyone left to ring in the Fake New Year, I sat crossed-legged on the court and tossed a ball up and down. My phone rang at 11:53, and for one fleeting second I thought it might be Dax, that he wasn’t really drunk, that he was searching the party for me so we could count down together. But it was Lenore, who never called, only texted. I answered. “What’s wrong?”

“I don’t know what to do!” She sounded near hysterical. “Do you know Ren Madfield?”

“Who?”

“He’s apparently James’s friend. James was at his house earlier, I dropped him off there, and now the kid’s mom called and said James walked home, like, two hours ago and just wanted to make sure he got home safe. He’s not answering his phone, so I hurried home, he’s not here and . . . what do I do?”

The noise from the house was picking up as everyone crammed into the basement. I covered my ear with my hand. “Lenore, stay calm. James does stuff like this all the time. What did Dad say?”

“*Your* father isn’t answering the phone,” Lenore said. “This is why I’m never having a family. It’s not fair to thrust this level of responsibility on me when I’m so young.”

"You're twenty-two."

"Exactly!" Lenore cried. "What if he's in a ditch? Do I call hospitals?"

"Just . . . come get me. We'll look for him together."

"Are you still at Sam's?" Lenore asked.

"Yeah. And . . . we need to give a friend of mine a ride too."

"He better live close. This break sucked. I should have gone back up to school early. You know I got invited to a huge party in San Francisco? Instead I ended up at a club with a girl from high school I don't even like that much, with all these middle-aged guys in blue dress shirts leering at us like there is any way I would ever—"

"Lenore. Come get me. Bye."

The countdown started then. I watched midnight hit through the window. Sam hugged Camille and spun her around. Porter grabbed some girl nearby and smacked her a kiss. Confetti swirled around the basement while sombreros were tossed in the air.

I slipped through the back door and up the stairs. Dax was sleeping peacefully. I flopped down on the bed and gave him a soft kiss on the cheek.

"Happy Fake New Year's, you idiot."

CHAPTER 14

Despite Lenore's hysterics, it still took her twenty minutes to show up at Sam's. She gratefully didn't ask too many questions as we stuffed Dax into the backseat. She wasn't the most observant sister; Sam was the only friend of mine she even vaguely remembered or recognized anyway.

"I want to find James before we take him home," Lenore said.

I clicked on my seat belt. "That's fine. He's napping."

"Where does he live?" Lenore asked.

"I don't know."

"I thought you said he was your friend."

I cut her a glance. "He's kind of a new friend."

Lenore whistled. "Sounds like you're having a big night."

I snuck a glance at Dax in the side mirror. "Not as big as I'd hoped."

Lenore twisted around in her seat. "He's pretty, when he's sleeping."

"He's pretty when he's awake too."

"Are you sleeping with him?"

"Lenore! Of course not. Why would you ask that?"

"Look at him. What else would I ask?" She leaned farther. "Wait, is that the Cranston from the funeral?"

"Shut up."

A grin spread across her face. "You know, this is probably the first time you've made me proud."

While we drove back to The Space, I tried James on his phone, but everything went straight to voice mail. Dad didn't respond to any of my texts or calls. I didn't try Mom. She was out of the state, she couldn't do anything, and besides, I didn't want to scare her. Not yet.

When we got home, Lenore stayed in the car with Dax while I ran inside to look for clues. It's probably not too surprising that James wasn't a fan of people visiting his room, but when a thirteen-year-old disappears for almost three hours, all bets are off. I clicked on his computer and checked his browser history. Cleared. I fumbled through his backpack, finding only duct-tape creations and sheet music.

I ran back outside. Dax was awake now, his head against the window.

He winced when he saw me. "I met your sister," he said.

"Yeah, Dex looks like he's had better days," Lenore said.

Dex. He winked, but it was sort of a sloppy blink.

"I didn't find anything," I said. "We need to call Mom if we don't find him soon. I mean, he has a bus pass, but I don't know where he would have gone."

"Should I drive around to bus stops?"

I pinched the top of my nose. He left that party alone. His friend lived maybe a mile away, so if he didn't get on the bus, he could still be somewhere within walking distance.

"Let's go drive around the lake first," I said. "Maybe he's at the minimart."

I took Lenore to my spot, to the minimart, to James's friends' houses. We'd resolved to head back to the house, call Mom and the cops. But as we drove around the north side of the lake, I spotted James on the top of the grassy hill along the community running track.

It was the road that began at the elementary school and ended at the gate to the rich lake houses. He was sitting up there with a block of ice. So he had to have walked over to the grocery store, bought the ice, carried it for almost a mile, and now . . . he was just up there alone. That kid.

Lenore parked the car and hopped out. "James! What are you doing?"

"Nothing!" he yelled down. "Leave me alone."

She shot me an exasperated look. "He's killing me."

"I can get him," Dax said.

"Sure you can." I slid out of the car. "Lenore, babysit my friend Dex here while I save our brother from himself."

"Are you guys dating?" Lenore asked as I started to run up the hill. I didn't hear the answer.

"Hey." I plopped down in the grass next to James. "Ice blocking?"

Wordlessly, James pushed the piece of ice down the hill. It slid across the grass and crashed on the street.

"What are you doing here?" he asked.

"Looking for you," I said. "Ren's mom called Lenore. She's been . . . we've been hysterical. Your phone is off."

"It died."

"Then call us from home."

"I went home. No one was there. No one is ever there. I called Dad too; he didn't answer."

I scooted a little closer to him. He scooted away. "So . . . why'd you leave the party?"

"They're all dumb."

"Why?"

"They started to play spin-the-bottle. What are we, six?"

"You played spin-the-bottle when you were six?" I asked.

"You know what I mean. It was all so fake. The girls were all like, ooh, we want to kiss Jonathan Fickler, who is dating a ninth grader anyway. And there's this girl named Hannah that everyone thinks I like and I don't, okay? That was last year. And Theo wanted to smoke, and I haven't smoked since that scout meeting, that's why I chew seeds, you know?"

I wanted to hug him so bad. There were so many problems in one tirade. I forgot how young James was sometimes, even with his angel cheeks. "That does sound like a sucky night. I can see why you left."

"And winter break is so stupid. It's the last night so we're all supposed to have fun, it's like a law of society. It was almost as bad as Christmas."

I sniffed. "Christmas wasn't the greatest."

"At least I got *Battle at Devil's Creek*." He looked down at his nails. "You got a juicer. What was Mom trying to tell you with that?"

"I don't know. Eat your vegetables?"

"It's like she doesn't even know you. It just sucks when it feels like the people you see every day don't know you."

"But we want to. You get that, right?"

James wiped his nose with the sleeve of his jacket. "Is that the Cranston kid in the car?"

"Don't." I picked at a piece of grass. "We're talking about you. No one knew where you were. That's scary, James."

"*I* knew where I was, okay? Why does it matter if anyone else does? I mean, Mom leaves town and Dad has Lenore watch us because it's an off weekend? Lenore? You're more mature than her."

Two weeks off of break and we'd stayed with Dad once. His apartment was even smaller than ours, but it's nice to be asked. Then again, he might be entertaining female friends like hair girl from Bridal Spectacular.

"So did Dad take you ice blocking here sometime and you wanted to have a good memory?"

"No. Stupid. It's not like that old movie with the Rosebud sled that Dad loves." James pulled five fireworks from his cargo pocket. "I was going to explode that ice cube, but it was too slick. The fireworks kept sliding off the top."

I stared at my brother. "Now that sounds stupid."

He shrugged. "It was. Plus, I got worried I'd blow my hands off. Mrs. Georgia would kill me if I couldn't play piano." He hopped up. "Okay. Let's go home."

"That's it? You're not going to say you're sorry or explain yourself?"

"Sorry for what? If you guys would have stayed out late like you were supposed to, you wouldn't have even known I was doing anything."

"But we didn't. Because we totally care about you."

"Blah-blah-blah. You're too sentimental since Grandpa died. Come on." James shoved the fireworks back into his pocket and ran down the hill.

Too sentimental? Me?

Dax slid over so I could get in the back by him.

"Where do you live?" Lenore asked Dax.

"Henderson."

"You're kidding." Lenore pulled the car into the street. "That's thirty minutes away."

Dax closed his eyes, his complexion stone white. "I see intelligence runs in this family."

"I'm hungry," James said.

Lenore slapped the steering wheel. "You almost gave us a heart attack, and now you think we're getting food?"

"Wendy's is open late," Dax said.

We got Frosties and talked about ice blocking and other outdoor adventures while we drove Dax home. My siblings didn't mention how Dax smelled or how hard he laughed. Dad finally sent us all frantic texts around 1:30, saying his phone was in the car. We didn't ask where he had been. I wrote a curt *Everyone is fine* and asked Dax to pass me some fries.

Somewhere near Dax's freeway exit, I put my head on his shoulder. He slid his arm around me and whispered, "Your grandpa was right. What he said in his letter."

The letter. Dax had never told me what fateful words Grandpa Jim wrote to him. Maybe he did take a truth serum and all would be revealed.

"What did he say?"

"You're a fixer."

"I'm not fixing you, if that's what you think."

"Not me. Your brother."

"What else?"

He kissed the top of my head. "And that you're wonderful. But I already knew that."

"Dax—"

"I know. I bombed tonight. But I'm a fixer too. I'll make it up to you."

"Hey, Lenore," James said from the front seat.

She flicked him an annoyed glance. "What."

"Happy Fake New Year!"

Lenore snorted. James sat back in his seat, grinning out the window like he'd said the funniest thing ever.

I wasn't sure how this next year was going to go . . . with the chapel, with my family, with Dax. But my Frosty was good and the night was clear with the Strip all lit up, and I thought, I don't know, maybe everything would be fine.

Fine wasn't asking for too much, was it?

CHAPTER 15

You don't hear many songs about January weddings, or January anything for that matter. Despite our best efforts, we were lucky to get two ceremonies a day at the chapel over the next three weeks. The upside was I had lots of time at work to get all my upcoming homework projects done so I could be free come February.

Most of our customers were in town for conventions, and there were lots of requests for theme weddings. Minister Dan dressed like Elvis more often than Minister Dan now, and although I was getting sick of the jumpsuit too, I didn't really know what else to do. If it was May, it wouldn't be a problem, but the cold truth was no amount of advertising could produce brides when tourists weren't here to get married.

I was at Grandpa's desk . . . my desk, going through some numbers Donna had set out for me. James slammed my door shut behind him. He paced for a second before jamming himself into a chair, his breathing deep and angry.

"What can I do for you, little brother?"

"When were you going to tell me about Angel Gardens?" he asked.

"Angel Gardens? There's nothing to tell. I sent them three couples last week. They should love us right now."

"Well, they don't. They're dropping us. No more business with Rose of Sharon."

I pushed back my chair. "What, why? How do you know that?"

"Because I've been working there." James thrust his hands into his jeans and came up with a fistful of bills. "I've been playing piano there for two months now. Trying to help out the family." He threw the money on the desk. "When I went into work today, they said they hoped I stayed on now that they were going to be under new owners."

"Someone bought Angel Gardens?"

"Not some*one*. Some jerk. Some Victor Cranston."

"But . . . why?"

"Why don't you go ask your stupid boyfriend?" James wiped his nose with his sleeve. "He should be telling you this stuff. Angel Gardens sends you a buttload of customers. Now that's gone. What are you going to do about it?"

I hurried around the desk. "James. Not so loud."

"Oh, what, you don't want anyone to know your secret?" He drew his fist back like he was going to punch my desk, but stopped himself and instead swiped everything off. The stapler, files, hole puncher, and pencil jar all came crashing down. "Start caring."

I grabbed his arm and squeezed. "Don't tell me I don't care."

James wrenched his arm away. "Fine. You care. But about the wrong things."

It wasn't true. I worked there all day. Every day. All I did was work there in that tiny little chapel. I hadn't really hung out with my friends in months, had only seen Dax in our cracks of time. I was living the life of a twenty-something workaholic.

James picked up the wad of cash. "There's six hundred dollars here. Use it however you want. I'm just saying . . . we can't lose this place. If we lose the chapel, then what else is left, you know?"

I grabbed my brother into a hug. "I'm sorry."

"I'm going to spit on you if you hug me any more." He shook me off. "Sick."

"I think Therapist Whitney would say that throwing six hundred hard-earned dollars at your sister is a sign you want a hug."

"The only hugging stuff we've talked about was to make sure I don't punch people who do it."

"I'm going to visit Victor Cranston." I strode to the door. "I don't know what he's doing."

"But Dax might, right?" James's voice cracked, his cheeks all cherubic innocence.

I paused. "Yeah. He might."

✦ ✦ ✦

Minerva at Cupid's Dream said Victor and Dax were on location at a destination wedding. Luckily, the destination was the Stratosphere, which was across the street.

The Stratosphere was the stark exclamation point on the rambling sentence of the Strip. There was a revolving restaurant, an observation deck, and all sorts of stupid thrill rides. When it got windy, they had to close because the concrete swayed. I took the elevator up over one hundred floors of the space-needle-shaped tower, hoping I didn't miss the Cranstons. Hoping a little bit that I did.

Victor was in a cheap button-down shirt with a purple bow tie. He was intent on the ceremony, intent on uniting two idiots together before they professed their love by sky jumping off a building. The Stratosphere had its own wedding chapel; I didn't know how Victor weaseled clearance to do a ceremony up there.

I held my breath before waving to get Dax's attention. Did he know what was going on? Was he keeping it from me?

Things had been good since Fake New Year's. Dax and I didn't talk about that night again. Anytime I tried to bring up the things he'd said about his dad, he shrugged his lopsided shoulders. I saw now why he was lost; I just didn't know if he ever wanted to be found. He was convinced he killed his dad, and who was I to say otherwise? I wasn't there. I could only be here, now, with the Dax that formed in the wake of that tragedy. It made me wonder, if I'd met Dax a few months earlier, when my life was on its mundane, set course, would we still have clicked?

He loped around a group of tourists. I didn't want to ask him the questions I needed to ask. I didn't want there to be any questions between us, nothing between us, not even air.

"Hey, what are you doing here?"

"Did you know? About Angel Gardens?"

Dax's face was blessedly confused. "No. What's Angel Gardens?"

"It's that reception hall down the block. Your grandpa bought it. You didn't know?"

"What are you talking about? What did my grandpa buy?"

I flung my arms around Dax. My heart felt like it was going to strap on a cord and jump off the Stratosphere with that couple. My guy-I-was-dating had not sold me out to his grandfather. And he wouldn't sell me out. He wasn't like that. He was a Cranston, but he wasn't.

Victor finally noticed us. I don't know what possessed me—spitefulness, courage, honesty, or a mixture of all—but I grabbed Dax's face and kissed him like the world was ending. Dax froze at first, then melted into my kiss. Those sky jumpers had the right idea. High-altitude kissing is amazing,

"You haven't kissed me like that since . . . ever," he said. "Are you trying to send a message to my poppy or is this, like, our two-month anniversary and I don't know it?"

"That depends." I smiled. "Are we together?"

"Of course we're together." He looked surprised. "Why, you aren't kissing other guys like that, are you? I'm worried your lips would fall off."

"Your grandpa is coming over here."

"I'm sure to congratulate us." He glanced back at his fuming grandpa. A flock of tourists blocked his route. "This isn't some rebellion against your parents, is it?"

"It sort of is. Do you have a motorcycle, by the way? Could you rent one just to meet them?"

"We actually have one at the chapel. The bride and groom ride it down the aisle for our fifties ceremony."

"Then never mind."

"So I didn't know about the Palace Angel."

"Angel Gardens."

"Whatever. And you're my girlfriend."

"Girlfriend?" I swallowed. I had never been a girlfriend. "Okay."

"That sounds convincing."

"Yes," I said formally. "I am Daxworth Cranston's girlfriend."

"And I am the boyfriend of Holly Nolan."

"Officially."

"Should I buy us plaques?"

I patted his arm and stepped away. "You might not want to watch this part. Although this is fun talking about your grandpa before he's in earshot."

"Fun for you."

Victor glowered before us. Sweat slid down his face, which was now purple, to match his bow tie. "What are you doing?" Victor screamed. "Why are you kissing this Nolan slut?"

Dax stepped in front of me. "Poppy, careful with your language. This is . . . Holly is my girlfriend."

Victor's eyes almost popped out of his head. Mine probably did too. We'd only officially established that title, oh, seventeen seconds ago, and now he was proclaiming it to the world? To his *family*?

"What, and you had to tell me that *here*?" Victor asked. "In the middle of a ceremony?"

"We need to talk," I said.

"Oh, we're going to talk." Victor snarled at Dax. "Go take care of the couple. They're on the ground waiting and we're supposed to provide chocolates and champagne once they get their safety harnesses off."

"Be nice to her," Dax said.

"Daxworth, I swear—"

"I don't ask you to do much, Poppy. Do this." Dax turned to me. "You good?"

I gave him a feeble thumbs-up. "Good" was a vague word, wasn't it? Shaking and sweating and panic attacking were probably not labeled "GOOD" too often. Why did I think confronting Victor Cranston a thousand feet in the air was a *good* idea?

I counted to twelve before I said anything. "Victor. You know why I'm here."

Victor stormed over to the elevator and poked the button. "To neck with my grandson? You have about two minutes until these doors open and I push you in."

I folded my arms across my chest, trying to create some shield against Victor's ickiness. Neck? Does that mean kiss? "You bought Angel Gardens."

"Yeah. So?"

"So, we have a contract with them."

"Had." Victor grinned. "I don't think I'll be renewing that."

"But why did you buy them?" I asked.

"Because I have plans, Nolan, plans that I'm not going to tell you. But since you seem to be buddying up with my grandson, I will do you a little favor. I'll give you a chance to sell. Fifty K."

"Victor. Our chapel is worth six times that. Rose of Sharon isn't for sale."

"Fifty-one K. Final offer. If your parents sell now, they can get out gracefully." He ran his tongue along the front of his teeth, then spit. "Otherwise, things are going to get ugly."

"Too late for that."

"And stay away from my grandson. He's a good kid."

"No."

"Fine." He shrugged. "Then don't expect me to stay away from your chapel."

The elevator doors scrolled open. I willed myself to look Victor Cranston in the eye. "Please, Victor. Just . . . let us be."

"The ball is rolling. Either you jump on or you get smashed." Victor sneered. "See you in the parking lot, Nolan. At least while there is still a parking lot left."

CHAPTER 16

There was nothing we could do about Angel Gardens. By the end of the week, they'd closed their doors. The doors stayed closed, with no indication that Victor was opening things soon. Which did nothing to help the neighborhood, an empty business in the backyard. I wondered if Victor was going to knock it down and expand his chapel, or if he bought Angel Gardens just to hurt us. It was a crazy motivation, but with Victor involved, it wouldn't be a shock.

I didn't tell my family all the details. The news did nothing for morale, and right now we needed another long-term partnership with a reception hall. And before that glitch could be addressed, we had only three weeks until Valentine's Day.

So we went to our next money-making tactic, an idea inspired by my trip to the Stratosphere.

Destination weddings.

Grandpa did them occasionally to fill a special request, but it wasn't something we'd ever pursued or advertised. I didn't know why—it was an easy-enough process. We partnered with a limo company to escort the bridal party anywhere—Mount Charleston, Zion National Park, the "Welcome to Las Vegas" sign. If they wanted to get hitched at a truck stop in Pahrump, we could do that too. Minister Dan commuted over, the ceremony was performed, and voilà. A $300 destination fee added to our regular package. Deluxe packages and à la carte items also available. See website for details.

We had our first ceremony at Red Rock just a few days after my meeting with Victor. My parents were going to run it alone, but I wanted to take notes on logistics. Come spring, destinations could mean big profit for us. Plus, Dad was going to take some professional pictures for a billboard spot we'd bought just off the Strip.

Plus, I was considering, just considering, telling my parents about Dax.

Mom and I set up a small lattice backdrop for the ceremony on an open stretch of dirt with the stunning Red Rock mountains behind us. The bride wanted a "glamour theme," which to her meant purple and black with loads of feathers. Taste is . . . objective.

"I'm glad you thought to do more destination packages." Mom tied a purple balloon to the backdrop. "The chapel is lovely, but it's fun to see what we can come up with without the limitations of four walls."

This bride would have done better with some limitations. "So you're not mad? That I'm doing more? Dad and Donna seem . . . not too excited about the changes."

Mom glanced back at Dad, who was checking the aperture on his camera. "You're right. He's not. But that's his own issue. There's a reason your grandpa put you in charge."

"Thanks." I squinted up at the sun. Dad wasn't going to be happy about this lighting. "That's, like, the only time I've heard you disagree with Dad."

"Really?" Mom frowned. "I wasn't trying to disagree with him."

"You know, you're divorced. It's okay."

"Mmmm-hmmm." Mom pushed a stray wisp of hair back into her ponytail. "Honey, I've been thinking, you're working yourself to the bone trying to help this place."

I scowled at the subject change. I couldn't think of a time my mom had talked about the divorce since it happened. She might as well have worn her wedding ring for how much the divorce didn't happen. Why did we even have to move into The Space? My parents could have just comfortably coexisted in our old house. "I'm totally fine."

"I just wish you had more time for a social life. You're young."

"A social life. Yeah. About that." Time to spill my recreational activities with Dax, except maybe not the other day when we snuck into the Twilight Wedding Chapel and made out for an hour, because I was still a little creeped out about that myself.

What I could tell her was that even though we'd only known each other a few months, it felt like Dax knew me better than anyone, that he helped me know *myself*, that he wasn't like his grandpa, that he wasn't like anyone. That I had this constant knot in my stomach because I was worried I was in love with Dax, and I worried that I was programmed wrong, worrying about something I should be happy about.

But then the groom's mom came over asking for more feathers for the bride's hair and the moment was over, just like all the other moments and opportunities I had to tell my parents the truth. Saving the chapel was the biggest deal right now, and revelations concerning my love life could wait until we weren't in the middle of a ceremony.

Although it seemed like we were always in the middle of a ceremony.

I sat with James in the back row of chairs. We couldn't have timed it more perfectly with the sunset and mild weather. James didn't look up once, just played a video game the whole time.

They skipped the bridal march and played a Jay-Z song instead. The bride's dress was the fabric equivalent of a belt, and the groom wore a green camouflage suit. He fist pumped when she walked down the aisle. Thirty-eight percent success rate, if they were lucky. I'd rather marry a hairbrush than that groom.

Or forget the hairbrush. Dax.

"Blah-blah-blah," James muttered under his breath. "How do you sit through so many of these?"

"They're not all like this," I said. The bride and groom were slapping each other's mouths with their tongues. Or maybe they thought that was a kiss.

"Are you going to marry Dax?" James opened a whole pack of Smarties and shoved them in his mouth.

"What? No. I don't know. I'm not even thinking about that yet." Or I'm thinking about that two minutes ago.

"Fine. If you want to stay with Dax, you should have Minister Dan marry you. Then you can both die and our families will see that their fighting was wrong and come together and cry. Your only love from your only hate."

"You just summarized *Romeo and Juliet*."

He rolled his candy wrapper into a ball and flicked it onto the ground. "I know. It's a movie. Claire Danes? She used to be kind of hot."

The groom tore off his camo suit jacket and tossed it into the crowd. They'd gone so far off script, Minister Dan just rushed a "husband and wife" and pointed them to the aisle. Instead, they decided to start making out again.

"Is this about you wanting me to tell Mom and Dad about Dax?"

"I just don't know why it's so hard for everyone in our family to be honest."

"Then tell them about your job at Angel Gardens. Or the ice blocking. Or any of the other fifty thousand stupid things you get away with."

"Are you serious? I don't get away with anything. Mom and Dad don't care about me, only my prison record. I'm their annoyance."

"A prison record? You're being dramatic."

James dug at a small hole in his dark dress pants. "Therapist Whitney said it's better to be a punk on the outside than to keep it all in. Mom and Dad know how I feel about things because I show them. You . . . everyone thinks you're fine, but you've got this hidden boy and all the crap with the chapel and . . . I don't know. Tell them or show them how you feel, or one day you're just going to implode."

"I'm not a bomb."

"Tick-tick-tick!" James popped open his hands. "Boom! And there goes Holly."

"Fine. I will." I wanted to go *boom* in James's face. "After the ceremony."

The ceremony was pretty much over. The wedding guests were throwing feathers at one another, and Mom had to run in because they were essentially littering in a national park.

"Everybody! Get in the party bus! I just got freaking married!" the bride hollered.

Finally we were able to pack everything up and send the wedding party away. And just in time. The bride's father and the groom's mom were already making eyes at each other.

"You didn't tell them," James said as he and I walked out to Mom's car.

"Shut up, I know. I'm going to."

"They're going to find out sometime. I mean, Lenore knows, I'm surprised it's not on a billboard." James picked his nose. "And I still have that picture of you sucking face, by the way."

"So now you're threatening me."

"Motivating you. Don't be perfect for once."

I stared at my brother. The sun was down, the weather chilled. There was the faintest suggestion of a mustache on his Pony Boy face. "Just . . . get in the car. And don't try to drive."

I stomped across the sagebrush and rocks. Why should I tell my parents anything when they told me nothing? They were on the other side of the hill, folding the fabric aisle. Their voices carried up, echoing against the canyon wall. The sound clanged, metallic and sharp. My parents were . . . fighting?

"These destination weddings are ridiculous," Dad said. "I can't believe you said yes to this."

"Your daughter did it. Which is more than I can say for you. What have you done to save the place?"

Dad dropped his side of the aisle. Dirt puffed into his face. "What have I done? Who's taking the pictures?"

"That's your excuse for everything, isn't it? I can't be home for dinner. Pictures. I can't pay alimony. Pictures. I'm never going to make anything of myself because *pictures*."

"Oh, right. That's our problem. I have an actual job and pay your child support—"

"I wouldn't call what you pay us supportive." Mom yanked the aisle away and started to fold it herself. Her hair wisped limply out of her ponytail. "It's a joke."

"This! This is why I hate destination weddings. I can't stand being out here with you when you're like this." Dad smeared his hands against his dark jeans. "I hope this place does go under because I can't stand seeing you every day."

"Yeah, well, I can't stand seeing you *any* day!" Mom screamed.

The word "day" bounced across the mountain. Mom didn't scream. That wasn't my mom. These weren't my parents.

"You're making a scene," Dad said.

"You started the scene. And we're in the middle of the desert."

"That's because you wanted to do a destination wedding!" Dad hollered, bringing the conversation full circle.

"Um. Guys?" I called down. Mom and Dad froze midfold. Dad kind of shook out his shoulders before smiling up at me. I realized how rehearsed that smile was now. There wasn't laughter behind his smiles anymore, at least not with us. "How long have you been standing around?"

"Just got here," I lied. "James and I were in the car."

Mom retied her ponytail. The dust swirled around them, clinging to their clothes, testifying that they were there, that the fight had happened. "Great! Your dad and I were just talking about getting ice cream together."

"Uh . . . I'm good." They were crazy. Why were they acting like this? For my benefit? Pretending to be happy for that long when you aren't was enough to make anyone explode. James would tell them that. He would tell them it was okay to say and do whatever they needed to be at peace.

I didn't say anything. I never did.

"No ice cream. I've got a lot to do," I said, like the old lady that I was. "I'll be in the car."

"Great! Be there in a bit!" Dad called.

I left them to fold the chairs. I left them to pick up the discarded feathers.

I left them.

I trudged back over the hill and slammed my door shut behind me.

“So? Did they get pissed?” James asked

I flipped down the visor and checked my eyes in the mirror. My reflection blinked back. My eyes worked. What I’d just witnessed . . . that happened. “No . . . they were . . . fighting . . . when I got there.”

“With each other?” James perked up.

“Like . . . screaming.”

“*Why*?”

Why. How many times had I stared at those two and asked why? Maybe this was our answer. Maybe my parents had this whole other dynamic between them that we never saw. Maybe they *didn’t* like each other. Maybe all the small talk and civility was for show. Maybe . . . maybe they were trying to behave like adults.

“I think . . . because they’re divorced?” I searched James’s face. “Or because . . . people fight?”

“And you didn’t tell them about Dax first? Say something to start it?”

“No. They were already going at it when I got there.” I pushed back my bangs. “They were fighting about nothing. Just fighting to fight.”

James leaned back in his seat, a small smile on his face. “So they do fight, huh?”

“It was horrible.”

"That's great," he said.

Was it great? I flipped the visor back up as my parents cleared the crest of the hill. There was distance between them, but no more than there ever was. There wasn't any visible sign that they'd just lost it. I'd been looking for signs for so long, and I realized they were just experts at disguise.

I twisted back in my seat and smiled sadly at my little brother. "Maybe our family is more normal than we thought."

CHAPTER 17

February 13 was our Third Annual (and likely final once my friends went off to school) Valentine's Bomb, in which we convinced Vegas lovers old and young that they are ready for the commitment of marriage, and that they would like to make that commitment at our chapel. As was customary, I paid the boys and Camille each twenty bucks to pass out a box full of flyers on the Strip. But this year, I also asked everyone to dress up in the costume of their choice.

I preferred to have my face covered during such shameful promotion, so I got Dax and me Hello Kitty costumes on clearance. We waited for my friends at Ceasar's valet. Within five minutes, Dax already had two toddlers hug his leg. One even screamed and begged for a picture.

"Are you sure you didn't get me this costume because you're embarrassed of me?"

I patted his paw. "No. That's totally why I got you the costume. Plus, what if my parents stopped by—"

"I know." Dax did an exaggerated head shake. "You are going to tell them though, right? This is getting old, Holly. You can come to my house now, I want to go to yours. I want to be normal with you."

"We are normal."

"Really?" Dax motioned to his costume. "Even for Vegas, this isn't normal."

It would take a lot of time before I was ready to show Dax The Space. My friends didn't hang out there; I hardly did. And after watching my parents fight, I wasn't sure I trusted them with Dax. They might *say* they liked him, but they were obviously good liars. "I promise, next week. We just need to get past Valentine's Day."

"I don't get why Valentine's Day is so big to you. I know it's a moneymaker, but is one day life or death?"

"Absolutely." A group of preteen boys catcalled. I gave them a submissive wave. "My grandpa had a lot of debt. We're trying to renew our loan, and we need to show a drastic improvement in revenue before we meet with the bank next month. Valentine's Day will put us over the edge."

"That's a lot of responsibility."

"Yeah. Well." I shrugged. "It's over now. That's why I've been doing all this aggressive marketing."

"And here I thought you had a costume fetish." Dax tugged off his head. His frown was even more startling because three seconds ago he'd been sporting an innocent feline face. "There's something I want to tell you. No, I don't *want* to tell you, but I need to. I was going to wait for later, but it's really on my mind."

"Okay?"

"My grandpa and I had a big blowup today. I don't even know if I'm going to work tomorrow."

"Why? Because of us?"

"I just want you to know that tonight I'm here to help with *your* chapel."

"But why did you get in a fight?"

"It doesn't matter anymore. He's just making some stupid business decisions."

"Like with Angel Gardens?"

"Yeah. I don't know if he's serious."

"What is he going to do?"

Dax paused. "I'm not sure yet. I'll tell you more when there are definites. I'm just sorry if I seem off tonight."

"We can go. We don't have to do this." I'd had two awful meetings with Victor; I couldn't imagine what it must have been like for Dax. "Was it bad?"

"You know how my grandpa can be."

"That I do."

"Anyway." Dax shook his shoulders, his hands, like he was shaking the entire idea out of his body. "I just want you to know . . . you're amazing. I can't believe you've done all this."

"Why are we talking about me again?"

"Because you're my favorite topic to discuss." He grinned. "You're up there with moths."

I rubbed my kitty head against his arm like a cat. "Even luna moths?"

"You win." He rubbed at my shoulder. Why hadn't I dressed us like barbarians or something, Dax all shirtless and in a loin-cloth? "You beat anything."

"Thanks. I think you're better than a luna moth too." Good thing we were getting this goof talk over before my friends showed up. If Dax started talking like this once they got here, who knew what they would think. *They* being everyone but Sam. Sam would happily break into a country duet with Dax.

I licked at Dax's paw. "You're sure it's not just the kitty costume?"

"Definitely not." He laughed. "Actually, you should probably know, I love you." And with that, he stuck his head back on.

I went so stiff I swear my tail lifted in the air. Did he just say that? Did he mean to say that or did it just slip out? We were in fake fur tombs, and you don't profess love next to the valet parking. Was I supposed to fill that hollow air between us with the same phrase?

I mean, I might love him. I likely did. But I wasn't a parrot. I wanted to say that when I was ready to say that, and *that* was such a big thing to say, especially after talking about his grandpa fifteen seconds beforehand.

It helped that we had our heads on because I couldn't tell if he was looking at me with expectation. The pause grew staler than the air inside our costumes. I waited . . . waited until something happened so I didn't have to do anything myself.

Something finally did. Sam, Camille, Porter, and Grant rolled in to the valet. A bachelor party behind us applauded when Porter and Grant stepped out as showgirls. I don't know where they found costumes that somewhat fit, or how much it cost to rent the headdresses, but knowing them they'd spent the entire day preparing. Grant actually looked passable, with his long hair teased into a bouffant. Their leg hair poked out through the fishnets and the feathers didn't do much to cover up their goods.

If there was ever a time my grandpa was rolling around in his grave, this was it.

"Your friends are representing tonight," Dax said.

"Yeah." There were four valets. There were ten cars waiting to be helped. Eight luxury cars were displayed along the winding curb of the hotel check-in. One boyfriend professing his love next to me. "Thanks for doing this."

I could go back and ask more about the fight with his grandpa, but he'd leaped so far away from that topic with the L-word drop. Hearing something like that from someone who I could possibly feel the same way about . . . this must be how that three-year-old girl felt when she saw two Hello Kitties standing in front of the valet. Joy and a little bit of terror.

"Do you have any lipstick, Camille?" Porter squished his lips together. "I feel like I need more lipstick."

"My cosmetics are way too high end for you."

Grant opened a tube of cheap bright pink. "Here you go, dude."

"I don't remember dressing in drag being a part of our business marketing plan." Sam readjusted himself in his Elvis suit.

I slipped my paw into Dax's. He loved me.

"Are people looking at us?" Camille asked. "When Sam and I were here for New Year's, everyone was looking at us. It was soooo embarrassing."

Porter stuck out his leg and did a lunge. "Oh yeah, they're looking. And they're liking."

"Where's Mike?" Grant asked.

I tried to glance at my watch but the only thing visible on my wrist was fur. "He said he's coming."

"Can we go get some hot chocolate or something before we start this?" Camille asked. "This cape isn't warm enough."

The doors whooshed open behind us and Mike jumped out, dressed in black and waving plastic samurai swords. We just kind of looked at him and then went back to our conversation.

"Fine. Hot chocolate. Follow me."

We walked over to the pink-striped canopies at Serendipity 3, an extension of the Serendipity in New York. A lot of Vegas restaurants were New York or LA re-creations. I tried not to eat at these too often, knowing it was just another replica of a much better original. I liked my restaurants one of a kind.

The waitress looked pained once she saw us circled around the table. Porter pulled out a small notebook from the confines of his fake bosom. He drew out a rough map of the Strip and started jotting numbers. "Okay, I think last year, going inside to the high enders was a wash."

"High enders?" Dax asked.

"Bellagio, the Wynn, anything at City Center," I said. "Rich people."

"They wouldn't even touch our cheap-looking brochures," Porter said.

"Hey, I designed those. They're not cheap looking," Sam said.

"Guys, come on," Mike said. "You still haven't said anything. I'm a ninja. This is the best costume. . . . Grant, that leotard is riding up your crack."

"You would know it's called a leotard," Grant said. "And why are you looking at my crack?"

"I'm not," Mike said. "You're . . . whatever you want to call it. It's disgusting."

"Dude, your costume doesn't work," Grant said.

"Why?"

I tugged off my costumed head. "How does a ninja make you think about weddings? If you approach someone dressed as a ninja, they'll run away, not take a brochure."

"And Hello Kitty is better? Hello?"

"He has a point," Camille said. "It's like having my Hello Kitty doll talk to me in your voice. Creepy."

"Right?" Mike said. "Now Elvis. Elvis makes sense."

Camille smoothed down her pants. "Thank you, Mike. I added some sequins. You can never have enough sequins."

The boys and I turned back to planning. Camille was the only one who ever took Mike's side.

"So no high enders?" Dax asked.

"Most of the people staying somewhere nice already have their wedding planned, and it's at some swanky hotel, not a little chapel," I said.

"Especially a dive like Cupid's Dream," Mike muttered.

Dax plunked off his head and grinned at Mike. "You'd be surprised how many businessmen love Elvis. We've had almost a dozen celebrities married at our chapel, you know, and it's just a different experience—"

Sam held up his hand. "Hey. Daxter. We're not selling your chapel, we're selling Holly's."

Grant snorted. "The Daxter."

Porter pounded Dax on the back. "The Daxinator."

"Daxerea," Mike said.

I slipped my arm around Dax's and leaned on his shoulder. Dax had to know that he'd just wiggled a millimeter closer to the inner circle. Insults. Nicknames. By the end of the night they would be giving man hugs and planning summer surfing trips.

"Okay, Porter. You clearly know the market. Where do we go and what do we do?" Dax asked.

We sipped our hot chocolate while we finalized our strategy. We broke up into teams of two, with each team given three hundred flyers and the goal to have a conversation with at least thirty different people. Sam and Camille got the airport, where they'd amp up the lovey dovey for couples fresh off their flights. Porter and Grant took the sidewalk in front of M&M's World and The World of Coca-Cola, where the skeevies in costumes would take a picture with you for five bucks.

There were also a lot of illegal immigrants there, passing out advertisements for strippers and escorts that could only be described as porn. By the end of the night, the street was littered with thousands of naked girls. I hoped people didn't drop our flyers with the nudies.

Mike was banished to Fremont Street.

"Fremont?" Mike whined. "For Fremont, I get forty dollars."

"They have those good hot dogs over there," Porter said.

"But all the girls are old and veiny." Mike hit Porter's leg with his plastic sword.

I did not ask him to elaborate on the veiny. "Hey, I know you said Bellagio is high end, but since we're staying outside, Dax and I should work the fountains. Everyone always stops, it's romantic—"

"Romantic for who?" Sam wiggled his eyebrows. He's the only person alive I knew who could actually do that. Before, it was cute. Now, I just wanted to shave them.

"Uh, other couples. Are you a three-year-old?" Romantic for me, Sam. I'd had to endure Camille and him making out all over this town. For once, I wanted some Strip-view romance. Because, as I may have mentioned, Dax said he loved me.

Dax reached for the bill. "Hey, I'll take this. No worries."

We gaped at Dax. No one had ever, ever picked up the bill, not even at Pepe's taco stand. We'd split crepes with the expensive hot chocolate, and at ten bucks a pop, it had to be close to seventy. "You don't need to do that."

"But I want to."

"Wow. Thanks, Daxmania," Porter said.

Dax kissed my cheek. The first time he touched me, I thought my body would explode. And now that those words were between us, around us, I thought my heart would shatter. But I scooped up my heart and shoved it into a box, a box I could open and analyze later, privately, when I could stare up at my ceiling and count every moment that somehow led up to the perfection of this.

✦ ✦ ✦

I had always wanted to bring a guy to the Bellagio fountains. The man-made, Strip-side lake dazzled tourists with the fountain show. Unlike most places you saw on TV or movies, Bellagio lived up to the hype. The final scene in *Ocean's Eleven* was filmed here, meaning George Clooney and Brad Pitt leaned on our same railing. Although in real life they were way too old for me, in that movie, at this place, they were the ultimate Vegas mascots.

Dax and I found a spot and promptly abandoned all hope of passing out flyers. I'd never been one for PDA, but I'd also never dated a boy like Dax. We lodged our costume heads between our feet so we could kiss. Also, to save passing children from horrid Hello Kitty nightmares.

He rubbed my shoulders and grinned down at me. "Bet you bring all your fellas to this spot."

"I don't bring 'fellas' anywhere." I nodded to the next pillar over. "And I usually bring them to that spot. *This* spot is new for me."

He nuzzled my neck. "How many guys have you dated anyway?"

"Like, gone on dates with?"

"Sure."

"Thirty-seven."

He paused midnuzzle. "Knowing you, I'm sure that's an exact count. Seriously, did you start dating when you were eight?"

"No. I waited until I reached double digits. Why, does that bother you?"

"I can't decide."

"Twenty-nine of those dates were onetime things. I don't have a great retention rate."

"Then it doesn't bother me, I think." He resumed the nuzzle. "Do you want to know how many girls I've dated? Or more than dated?"

"Why would I want to know that?"

"Because . . . because . . . every girl I know wants to know those kinds of things. And about earlier . . ."

Either he was hoping for more relationship definition, or he was asking me to say I love you back, which was not happening tonight, even if I fell into the fountains and he rushed in to save my life. These are the things couples discuss in a relationship, not that I'd ever been in a relationship, just watched those relationships at their wedding-day pinnacle. What I wanted for me individually was to kiss this boy while a billion gallons of water shot up forty-five stories into the air for gaping tourists wearing denim shorts in February. That's really not asking for much.

"I know. I can't believe Mike dressed as a ninja."

Dax dodged my kiss and cupped my face. "I'm serious. I want to talk."

"So. Talk."

"I never know where I'm at with you."

"The Bellagio fountains."

"Holly."

"I can only have so many conversations like this."

"This would be our first conversation. First and a half, if you count that time I called you my girlfriend."

"Yeah, and I went with it."

"Went with it? Do you know how unromantic that just sounded?"

I rubbed my hand down my face. "Look, Dax. I love that you are super in touch with your emotions and can share all these things with me. I'm serious. It's great. But I'm not like that. I wish I was. And . . . you didn't tell me what happened with your grandpa. So it's not like I know everything that's up with you."

"Are you kidding? I'm, like, the most open book in the most open library in the open world." He frowned. "And I know I just said open too many times."

"You're always the one asking me questions," I said. "Tell me something you haven't said to someone else."

"Uh, I did. In the valet."

My face flamed. Idiot. He *was* the most open book. And he did mean to say those words. It wasn't an accident. "I mean . . . I don't know what I mean."

"Okay. Fine. Look at this." Dax flipped out his wallet. It was one of the first things I'd liked about him, how worn his wallet was. Loyalty to an accessory speaks volumes about a person.

He dug underneath the credit cards and found an old picture of a couple on their wedding day. "This is my mom and dad."

"Can I look?"

He handed me the picture with care. I held the photo like an ancient map. His mom's dress was all lace and poufy sleeves, her veil dripping jewels. The outfit dated the picture to the early, maybe mid-nineties. "They're so happy."

He nodded. "They always were."

"I thought my parents were happy too."

"But now they aren't?"

"Not together."

He motioned to the tourists surrounding us. "I wonder how many of these people think they're happy, or pretend to be happy." He rubbed at his eye. "I wonder what happy even means."

"Maybe happy isn't forever. Maybe it's just moments, and you save them up and hold on for all the in-betweens." I gave him back the picture. "It's nice that you have this. My grandpa used to send me funny greeting cards."

Dax flinched when I said the word "grandpa."

"Sorry. We can talk about your poppy if you want to. Or not."

"Let's go with not. Let's talk about yours." He slid his picture back into his wallet. "How are you doing? With missing him?"

"Some days it's normal. That he's gone. And some days I forget that he even died at all. Some days I'm mad at him because of the chapel thing, some days I'm really grateful. I feel like I wake up to a bingo game every day, and some ball is going to pop up and decide how I'm going to feel."

"B-5. You're angry."

"G-41. You sit home moping and eat soup. But you know how it is." I paused. "Are you ever going to let me read that letter?"

"Probably not."

"Can you tell me something else in there?"

Dax rubbed his hand along his hair, shaking out the static. "This was weird. Your grandpa knew my dad, I guess. My dad was the one who first came in when Poppy bought the chapel. Your grandpa was really impressed with him, took him out to drinks a few times. Dad never got involved in the Victor/Jim feud. And your grandpa didn't want you and me involved to carry on the fighting either. He wanted . . ." Dax breathed. In and out. "He wanted me to know my dad loved me just like your grandpa loved you."

"What made him even think of that? Did you ever talk to him?"

"Never."

"That wasn't like my Grandpa Jim, to reach out to a stranger like that, especially in some deathbed letter."

"You and I have a lot in common." Dax shrugged. "Maybe your grandpa thought we shouldn't be strangers."

The music to the fountains started then, the white lights blinding. The bursts of water danced and swayed, erupting into the sky and cascading back to the lake. Dax leaned his forehead against mine. It probably sounds dumb, but it was the most amazing, profound, sad, and happy moment I'd ever felt.

We kissed for a while, long enough that I knew people were

watching us, two teenagers in furry costumes. Dax started to say something, but I covered his beautiful lips with my pointer finger. It was a rather dramatic gesture, and I sort of liked the emotion of it all. "I don't know if he meant to, but Grandpa couldn't have given me a better gift than you."

"Besides a cloud sweater."

"Well, of course." I kissed him again, slow and lingering. I thought about saying I love you. I thought how good those words would feel on my tongue. "Thanks for telling me everything. About your dad."

He laughed. "What do I say, you're welcome for showing you how messed up I am?"

The music started again. The fountains went off every fifteen minutes. How had it only been fifteen minutes when it felt like the whole world had changed?

"We're all messed up," I said. "I think life is just about finding the right people to be messed up with."

CHAPTER 18

The fountains went off four more times, and we didn't leave that spot. We kissed, we talked, we found happiness in our little moment. Then this guy with headphones accidentally crashed into me. I cussed him out but ran after him to apologize and gave him a brochure. Which reminded me that we were there *because* of brochures, and we went into a frenzy for the next thirty minutes. One man told me he would give me five dollars if I left everyone alone.

"I'm worried," Dax said, as water erupted around us.

"What for?"

"That you're right. I might almost, sort of like Vegas now. Of course, I'll have to move to the Bellagio to maintain this feeling. But this is on my top-five list."

"What's ahead of it?"

"Well, there is this doughnut place on Eastern that has amazing cinnamon rolls. But Bellagio fountains with my Hello Kitty girlfriend? Right up there."

Around eleven, I texted my friends and asked if we could meet up Monday to figure out who won the brochure handoff. My curfew was midnight and I had to be at the chapel early the next day.

"This is kind of like our Valentine's date, huh?" Dax asked. "Since tomorrow we'll both be working ten hours."

"I'm working eleven hours," I said.

"Are you trying to top me, counting girl?" He took my hand and we walked up to the Bellagio valet.

"I already topped you. I passed out one thousand percent more brochures."

"You passed out ten."

"And you did zero."

He pulled out the stack in his back pocket. "I will distribute these by myself now that I don't have you distracting me."

I swooped in to nibble on Dax's lip. It was the kind of kiss that made me want to forget about work tomorrow and slip up to a room with him instead. But Sam was in the valet loop and the cars behind him kept honking. He was either waving me over or flipping me off, I couldn't tell. I was dizzy when I slid into Sam's car and he sped out of the valet.

I held it together. Don't ask me how, but I held it together. I wanted to sing and sob and ask Sam if this is what love was like and how long everything would last. I watched Dax in the back window as we careened away. I understood every love song, movie, and book ever created or even imagined. With this barrage of emotions, you can see why I didn't initially pick up on the vibe happening in the car between Sam and Camille.

I leaned forward in the center seat. "So did you guys have any luck tonight? Bellagio wasn't biting."

Sam stared at the road. Camille fiddled with the horseshoe necklace she always wore. Neither responded.

"Uh, guys? Everything okay?"

Camille turned so I could see her profile, could see the red in her eyes, the puffiness of her skin. She hadn't been crying, she'd been sobbing, and once I snuck a glance at Sam, it was clear he wasn't doing too well either.

"No," Sam croaked. "Not okay."

I sat back. What should I do? Ask questions? Offer advice? Stay quiet? They'd had a fight, I had no idea what about and it wasn't my business, but we had a twenty-minute car ride ahead of us and Sam was my best friend and I actually really liked Camille now, so I should do something? Nothing?

"We broke up," Camille said just as Sam turned onto the I-95.

"*You* broke up," Sam said.

Camille gave him a hard stare. "You're not going to go around saying that now. You don't have a right to do that."

"I didn't want to break up," Sam said.

Camille twisted around in her seat, her seat belt getting stuck on her high-necked Elvis collar. "Sam wants to get married. Tell him he's crazy."

"Sam loves you, maybe you will get married *someday*—"

"Not someday," Camille said.

"Sam."

Sam glanced at me in the rearview mirror. "Why is that a shock? Why not? I didn't say tomorrow, just as soon as Camille gets done with school."

"Why are you even talking about that now?"

Camille fiddled with her bell sleeve. "Sam . . . Sam kind of proposed. At the airport. By the taxi pickup line."

"I gave you a *promise* ring, that's not a proposal. I'm showing you that I'm committed."

Or he wanted Camille to show that *she* was committed. I knew Sam, and putting a ring on it was his way of protecting his territory.

"But she's a junior," I reasoned. "She's still got a year and a half to go."

"Camille's so ahead that she's finishing her home schooling early." Sam's eyes were back on the road. "She graduates in spring, and told me this week that she might go away to college. Which is totally against our plans."

"Sam." Camille's voice was pleading. "Then we talk about it this summer. Just because I got into all those schools doesn't mean I'm going."

Sam slapped his hand on the steering wheel. "It doesn't mean you *aren't* going, either. We planned this. We would tell your parents after graduation, get an apartment, go to UNLV."

Camille looked down at her hands. "*You* planned that. Then you told me your plans. It wasn't a *we* decision."

"You've never said anything. Anytime I talked, you always agreed."

"I mean . . . I talked about it. But we didn't set things in stone. I was trying out ideas. You *know* I've always wanted to go to school in Washington. My dad's whole family is there. I don't see why I'm the one who has to compromise on everything, why all the plans center around what you want and not me."

"You just never said this before," Sam muttered.

Camille bit her lip. "Well, I'm saying it now."

The only thing worse than their fighting was the silence. Sam flew along the freeway at over eighty-five miles an hour, his beat-up truck rattling along. If I didn't die from his driving, I would die from the awkwardness.

If things were flipped, I would expect Sam to be on my side. But as it was, I thought Camille was completely right. Sam was going way too country song on her, and no girl should have these kinds of ultimatums at her age. Sam had a huge heart, believed in soul mates and first love and forever, and although I was beginning to see that these things were possible, it didn't mean he had to have all the answers *now.*

Sam turned off the freeway and slowed down on the back streets as he reached my community. When we hit the 7-Eleven three minutes from my house, I cleared my throat and stuck my nose back into a conversation that I wished had never started. "Guys, look. This is big stuff. But maybe you don't have to figure it out now? Maybe you wait until summer, see where you both are?"

Camille nodded. "That's what I said. Slow things down."

Sam pulled the car over. I couldn't let Sam know that I disagreed, right? He would think I was choosing Camille—a girl who up until recently had vaguely annoyed me—over him, when I wouldn't choose anyone over Sam.

"Summer isn't going to change things," Sam said quietly. "Turns out Camille and I just wanted different things. I can't change what I want."

"I can't make myself want that." Camille sniffed. "Not right now. It's not fair that you're asking me to think so far ahead."

Sam shrugged. "Probably not. But I'm more far gone than you, aren't I? I'm singing you Randy Travis and you're thinking Blake Shelton."

"What?" Camille yelled. "WE DON'T SPEAK COUNTRY!"

"'Forever and Ever, Amen,' not 'All About Tonight'? Never mind."

They stared at each other again, so ferocious and lonely that I had to get out of there. I mumbled that I'd walk home and slipped out of the car. It was almost curfew, but I stopped by my spot at the lake. I curled into the brittle grass and counted the lights shimmering on the water (twenty-three) until I fell asleep. Then I dragged myself home, texted Dax because I was too tired to call, texted Sam and told him to call me even if he was tired, and fell asleep again in a nest of blankets on my bed.

It was around six in the morning when my phone buzzed with a text.

Sam: It's over. I'm over.

Me: Are you okay?

Sam: No.

Me: But you are alive and plan on staying that way until you get to work and I can talk to you?

Sam: Not coming to work

Me: But it's Valentine's Day

Sam: Salt. Wound. Thanks

Me: Seriously, Sam. I need to know you're going to be okay

Sam: I'm not suicidal if that's what you're asking, Holls

Me: I'll figure it out. I'll check on you tonight. Sorry. Thinking of you, K?

Sam:

CHAPTER 19

Enduring Valentine's Day in the wedding business is like working as a mall Santa at Christmastime. And this was my first Valentine's with a valentine. A valentine who *loved me*. When I saw his car in the parking lot, I blew a kiss.

Camille came in at ten, looking like absolute crap. Mom even stopped her at the door. "Camille, what's wrong? Are you sick?"

Camille just stared vacantly at my mom. "I've been better, but I had to work. Is Sam here?"

"Didn't he tell you he's not coming in?" Mom asked.

Camille gave me a broken look.

"Oh, I was supposed to tell you," I said. "Sick."

"Yeah, something must be going around." Camille fiddled with her necklace. "Hey, can we talk?"

Another couple walked in and Mom was back in planner mode. Camille and I slipped into the Bridal suite. She didn't sit, just stood, wringing her hands.

"I came in because I know you needed me, but I'm quitting after today, okay?"

"Camille, you don't need to quit."

She slumped into the bridal chair, a Queen Ann Victorian with original velvet backing. Grandpa Jim adored that chair. "I was only working here to be with Sam. I mean, I know I sucked at this job."

"No, well . . . sort of."

She rubbed at her temples. "I hope he's okay. He got mad again after you got out of the car. I'd never seen him cry like that, it was awful."

"He loves you."

"I love him." Camille thunked her head against the wall. "Where does that get us? Did I tell you, I told my parents? This week? Not how long I'd dated Sam, just that I had started dating a guy."

"Were they mad?" I asked.

"Not really. Just that I'd lied. They wanted to meet him. I thought . . . I actually thought we would have a chance of, like, making it. And then he had to pull out a stupid promise ring. I didn't even know what a promise ring was until he explained it to me."

"Sam's just old-fashioned about things."

She closed her eyes. "Do you hate me?"

"What? No. Of course not." I slipped into the seat next to her and squeezed her hand. "I don't want to choose sides, but—"

"I know. Sam is your best friend. You were only friends with me because you had to be."

"That's not true." Not entirely. "I mean, yes, of course I'm going to be friends with Sam still but . . . don't tell him this. He was acting crazy."

Camille's eyes flew open. "He's a lunatic! I'm still so mad at him."

"Yeah . . ."

"Anyway, I don't know. I think this is really it, like we're really done. So, I just . . . I'm glad I got to know you, you know? We can't be friends now, I get that—"

"Camille, of course we can—"

"Shut up. We won't. There's some sort of code." She stood up and offered me her hand. "But if you ever need help, like . . . with an outfit or some other girl thing, text me. Sam doesn't need to know."

"You'll get back together," I said without much conviction. Seeing Sam the way he was last night, I wouldn't be surprised if he dubbed Camille She Who Must Not Be Named.

She wiped at her eyes. "I don't know how the human body can produce this many tears." She smiled. "Anyway, it's my last day, so let's go sell some memories."

"Grandpa Jim used to say that."

"I know." She opened the door. "I did pay attention once or twice."

The next few hours flew by. I didn't get a break until three, when I decided to go check on James in the hand-billing trenches.

✦ ✦ ✦

What we did last night on the Strip is similar to the hand billing that happens at the marriage bureau, except on the Strip you sift out the potential customers, and at the marriage bureau, the customers come right to you.

In the past, the couples got their license at the courthouse, and hand billers would sit on the steps and wait for them to walk outside so they could get into their face. People complained, laws were passed, one particularly aggressive chapel was put out of business, and now all hand billing took place in a designated area.

My brother sat on a curb around the corner, spitting out sunflower seeds. There was a seed stuck between his teeth when he smiled. "How many? So far?"

I sat down next to him. "Four couples came in with brochures. You're rocking it. How's the competition looking?"

James flicked a seed into the gutter. "There's a guy who's almost gotten into two fights already. The regulars said he's new. He keeps running after couples and no one stops him. It's making me mad."

"Then he'll get kicked out soon. These guys are usually selling ceremonies so cheap they don't even make a profit."

James wiped his mouth. "Yeah, well, I don't like losing. I care about this chapel too, know that?"

"Of course you do."

"Not like Lenore," he said.

I squinted across the street. Lenore was away at college, this wasn't her problem, but James was mad she hadn't come down to help out for Valentine's weekend. The truth was, Lenore hadn't really helped out *any* weekend. She'd just be in the way if she were here. "She's got other things going on, James."

"Everyone has other things going on," he mumbled.

"You can have other things going on and still care. About a business or friend or family. Hearts have more room than you think."

He looked at me sideways. "So you are feeling feelings all of a sudden."

"I've always felt them. I'm just telling you about it now."

"I'm not going to hug you, if that's what you want."

"Then you've officially ruined my Valentine's Day." I picked up a seed and cracked it between my nails. "Anything else exciting happen?"

"Not really." James chewed on his lip. "Except for your boyfriend looking retar— dumb. In that costume."

I stood up and brushed off my skirt. He wasn't reusing Hello Kitty, was he? "What costume?"

"You don't know? Dude, this day just got so much better." James hopped up and practically sprinted around the corner. I followed him as fast as I could in my pointy flats.

"Look!"

Dax was standing on the corner, hand on one hip, wearing a

cupid costume. If you have ever seen an illustration or cartoon of cupid (you being *anyone*), then you know cupid does not wear a shirt. Just a diaper and wings. Oh, and the bow and arrow. Let us not forget that bow and arrow.

I sauntered up behind Dax and whistled. He glanced back and cursed when he saw me. "Don't start."

"I think this street corner is officially my favorite spot in Las Vegas."

It was the second time I'd seen him without his shirt, the first happening during our spa/heated pool hop at the Golden Nugget last week. Then it was dark, now it was light, and oh, how I saw the light. He had more chest hair than I would have thought, which, considering his perennial stubble, shouldn't have surprised me. Shirtless, I fully believed he had the manly capacity to chop down trees, wrestle a bear, and eat three steaks in one sitting. An angry red scar skirted across his shoulder, begging to be touched. He was muscles and hair and skin and . . . I wanted him. In that cheesy costume involving *a diaper,* I wanted him.

Dax covered himself. "Shut up. It's bad enough that it's freezing out here." He narrowed his eyes at James, who was practically rolling on the sidewalk, laughing. "You said she wasn't coming."

James giggled. "You're wearing a diaper, dude. Like I could stop her."

I covered my mouth, trying my best not to grin. "Dax, I . . ."

"Shut up." He growled. "Every couple walks over to *me* first, even if it is to make a smart remark." He unsheathed an arrow from his quiver, which was actually a rolled-up brochure for Cupid's Dream. It was a corny idea. I wished I'd thought of it. "Poppy called and said we've had twenty-five walk-ins today."

James scowled. "People who would spend the most important day of their lives at a chapel based on a guy in a diaper waving a sign are not the kind of people we are marketing to anyway."

Dax gave James a little bow. "Touché."

James wandered back to the group of seven men standing in the designated hand-billing area. I could spot the new guy right away. Anytime a couple walked out of the bureau, holding hands, the new guy would shout or run over and shove a brochure into their face.

Dax shook his head. "I already called the police. It's going to get ugly when they make him leave."

"Maybe you can shoot him with one of those arrows." I widened my eyes. "Make him act nice."

Dax grinned. "I'll shoot you with one of my arrows."

"That sounds like an innuendo."

"Only if you want it to be."

I wrapped my arms around his bare chest, feeling savagely territorial as cars honked. Dax pulled back and waved at a truck filled with middle-aged women.

"Cupid's Dream!" he called. "For all your wedding needs."

"So this is my Valentine's present."

"I thought I'd manage to avoid you. I should have paid your brother to keep you away."

"Wild horses . . . no, not Greek enough. Wild *chariots* couldn't keep me away."

Dax's phone rang. "Hey, sorry. It's my poppy. I've got to give him some stats."

"So you're at work and you're talking. That's good, right?"

He nodded and stepped away, which is the polite thing to do if you are taking a phone call, but I wanted to hear. When I didn't budge, he walked down the street like he was sharing confidential information with a CIA operative.

I wandered over to the hand-billing area to see how they worked in action. A middle-aged couple approached and started what seemed like an auction. The haggling made me slightly ill.

"Okay, who has packages for under one hundred dollars?" the man called out.

The hand billers started shouting out prices and waving brochures in the air. James ducked under two guys so he was in front. He was a scrappy, hardworking kid when forced to be.

The budget-conscious groom had a red-and-white-streaked beard and one of those T-shirts that is supposed to look like a tuxedo. His bride-to-be wore a pretty navy-blue dress with sequins around the hem. She flashed a shy smile at me while her almost-husband haggled over price.

"I can't believe I'm about to get married. Finally," she said.

"Congrats." I smiled. "I'm Holly, what's your name?" Grandpa always said to do introductions right away and use the couple's name while you speak. It's hard to say no to someone you know by name.

"Julia." She lowered her voice and nodded at her husband-to-be. "Patrick always wants a bargain."

"Of course." I paused. "What do *you* want? I mean, is there a certain chapel you're looking for?"

Julia pursed her lips. "I'm a little more traditional. I was reading online about one that has a drive-through? That doesn't seem right."

I glanced back at Mr. Drive-Through himself, a.k.a. cupid, but he was still on the phone. He was getting animated, waving his hands around. I couldn't tell if he was mad or just into what he was saying. Maybe they were having an amazing sales day.

"Yeah, you can get whatever you like. I can tell you where to go if you want a theme wedding, Julia, but if you're looking for something small and sweet—"

"I am!" she exclaimed. Patrick had talked the pushy hand biller into going down to seventy-nine dollars, and it looked like the deal was almost done. We would lose money if we went that low.

I ducked into the crowed and grabbed a brochure from James.

Julia flipped to the price section first.

"We're a family-run place. My grandpa owned Rose of Sharon for almost thirty years."

"Does he still?" she asked without looking up.

My voice caught in my throat. I'd heard him pitch this place so many times, I could sell to this woman ten different ways. "It'll always be his chapel. But I'm sort of running it now. It's charming, very classy. We have fresh flowers every day; my dad is the photographer."

Her eyes misted up. "It sounds like a dream. But how much?"

The pushy hand biller was already giving Patrick directions to the chapel.

"We're more high end than some of these guys, and our prices can only go so low, or else we can't give that experience. Our base package is one hundred fifty dollars, but we are doing a hundred-twenty-dollar special today."

"Patrick!" Julia called. "I want to get married at this place."

Patrick sidled over. "How much?"

"One hundred twenty."

Patrick balked.

"But it is so perfect, sweetie." Julia flipped open the brochure. "It's family run, one of the oldest chapels." She pouted her lips like a pro. "It's our wedding we're buying, not a used car. Can't we spend more and make it special? Please."

Patrick scratched the back of his neck. It was a difference of forty dollars and *their wedding day.* I would never understand some people. "But I wanted to save some money to see Donnie and Marie tonight."

"Did you get two-for-one tickets?" I asked. Really, I was so good at this. "My mom is at the chapel. She can show you a website where the tickets are cheap."

Patrick brightened at this idea and took Julia's hand. "Then I'm sold, little lady. You should go into car sales, know that?"

"Thanks. I think?" I gave them directions to the chapel, and Julia had already convinced Patrick to go up a package size before they walked around the corner, holding hands. Oh, I just wanted to squeeze them. I totally understood the rush Mom always talked about, selling someone on a place that I loved myself. I turned back to the crowd to celebrate with James, but the pushy hand biller was right in front of me.

A zit bulged in the middle of his sallow forehead. What hair he had glistened with grease. "You think you can just swoop in and steal my customer like that?"

"No one is stealing customers."

He got up in my face and started poking me hard on my shoulder. "This is my territory, got that? If I don't sell weddings, I don't eat. This is the first job I've had in five months, and I'm not going to let some fancy slut come in and tell everyone lies."

The other hand billers kind of shuffled back, a noble gesture that truly spoke to the quality of men who worked out here.

James pushed past them and grabbed the arm of my assailant. "That's my sister. Back off, man."

"James, it's fine."

"Oh, this is your sister?" The man threw his arm around me and squeezed me close. He smelled like pot and BO. "She's pretty. Pretty girls are good at selling love, aren't they?"

James's eyes went dark. I knew that look. This was not the look I wanted in the eyes of my thirteen-year-old brother against a man four times his age who clearly had no problem with trouble.

James didn't say a word before he attacked, just lunged at the guy, who was so surprised he fell down on the concrete. I fell too, but he lost his grip on me and I caught myself on my knee. I ripped a hole in my tights, but that was nothing. James and handbiller guy started punching each other, really punching each other, and the rest of the crowd finally stepped in and tore them apart. Handbiller guy had a black eye and a swollen nose; James was cut up all over his face and holding his hand.

Dax was over me, cursing and holding me and yelling at the other hand billers for not doing anything. A cop car pulled up onto the curb. I started crying and tried to get to James, but a cop was already questioning him. The hand-biller guy was still flailing around and screeching. It took two cops to get him into the backseat of the car.

"Miss? Mind telling me what happened?" the cop asked.

All I saw was James holding his hand. "That guy. He attacked me. My little brother was trying . . . he saved me."

James didn't look up at me, but he was sniffling. I wondered how bad his hand hurt.

The policeman had to fill out a police report, but since all the other hand billers agreed that James was protecting me, he didn't get a ticket or in trouble or whatever happens to thirteen-year-olds with cops. The hand billers seemed pleased—one guy was leaving in a cop car, and three more competitors, one costumed, left in cupid's ride.

"Don't tell Mom and Dad," James said as Dax turned onto Las Vegas Boulevard.

"What, that you win the Brother of the Year award? You're not going to get in trouble. How is your hand?"

James grimaced. "Throbbing. Mostly the two middle fingers and the knuckles."

Dax and I exchanged a look. He drove like we were in an ambulance and everything was touch and go.

We made it to the chapel. I'd never seen my parents more shocked then when we came through the front door, their banged-up children and a half-naked cupid. Dad took James to the hospital straightaway, and then I sort of looked around and realized. Oh. Boyfriend. Shirtless. Mother.

"So, Mom. This, um . . . this is Dax Cranston."

Dax wiped his hand on his diaper and held it out. "This is exactly how I always pictured meeting Holly's mom."

Mom took his hand feebly. "We met. At Jim's funeral."

"Oh." Dax's smile faded. "Right."

Mom clasped her hands together. "Well, I have a bride in the Bridal suite to attend to. Dax, thank you for giving my son and daughter a ride back. I imagine you need to get back to work?"

Dax gave me a lost look.

"Mom . . . Dax is my boyfriend." I sucked in a strong breath. "We've been . . . dating. Since, like, the funeral."

"But not *at* the funeral," Dax added.

Mom swore under her breath. She never swore. Why wasn't I the one who broke my hand?

"Dax has been wanting to meet you," I rushed on. "But things have been so busy. He helped with the chapel too, he has really good manners, he's respectful and usually wears a shirt."

"I see," Mom said. "Well, Dax, I wish the circumstances of our meeting were better. But given the craziness of today, I'm going to cancel this one out and ask you to come over another time. Maybe for some coffee."

Dax beamed. "Thank you, ma'am."

"Holly? Later." Mom's eyes were ice. "We talk."

She marched into the Bridal suite. I took Dax into the office. As soon as I closed the door, I shimmied out of my tights.

"Did you get nicked by one of my arrows? This really isn't the place."

"Ha-ha." I checked my knee. There was a good three-inch cut and a bruise already blossoming. I got a water bottle out of the fridge and a first-aid kit from the cupboard and set to work cleaning myself up.

"So you're okay?"

"As long as James's hand isn't broken, yeah." I poured hydrogen peroxide over the wound and winced. "My brother plays piano. That was such a stupid move. I totally provoked that guy. The whole cupid thing threw me off."

"That guy attacked you because I was dressed like cupid?"

"No, I was . . . I was just too happy that I wasn't thinking straight." I glanced up at Dax and saw all skin and hair again. "Maybe you should put a shirt on."

Dax shuffled toward the door. "If you really are okay, I have to go. Is that all right?"

"Cupid duty?"

Dax's face clouded over. "No. I have to go back to Cupid's Dream. Something came up."

I rifled through the box of Band-Aids. "Does this have

anything to do with that fight yesterday? I thought you weren't going to work. Now you're dressed like cupid."

"I'll let you know about it later."

"Tonight?" We hadn't planned a meet-up, but I'd hoped for something, maybe a quick make out in the rose garden. With the cupid outfit still on.

"I don't know. Maybe. You have to work late, and I don't know how long this will take. I'll call you, okay?"

"I'm sorry." I hobbled up and gave him a squeeze. "About my mom. And James."

"Don't worry. In the grand scheme of life, meeting your mom while wearing a diaper isn't a big deal." Dax gave me a salute and closed the door behind him.

Fifteen minutes later, I got the call from Dad I didn't want to get.

Two fingers. Broken.

There went James's solo at the Smith Center. There went his spring concert schedule. There went his therapy, his outlet.

I squeezed my own hand into a fist and thumped my thigh. This was something I couldn't fix.

Donna and I closed at eleven. We hadn't had a huge rush of late-night weddings, but our day hours had seen back-to-back ceremonies. There was one of those giant thermometers in my head, the kind they put on school billboards during a fund-raiser, and with each couple, I raised the mental barometer that much closer to our goal.

Donna hunched over the books as I paced behind her, mumbling things about James and cupid and Grandpa.

"That one couple got the deluxe package. And he tipped me, I don't know why he tipped me, I just handed her the bouquet, but that's another twenty."

"Holly. Relax." Donna readjusted the ceramic Alpaca figurine on her desk. Apparently, he resembled Herbert the alpaca. Herbert. If I ever saw an alpaca baby-naming book, I would pick it up for Donna.

"Relax? My brother broke his hand and my boyfriend hasn't called and—"

"Boyfriend?"

"Yes, Donna. He was in here earlier. Spoiler alert: it's Dax Cranston. Don't say a word."

Donna puckered her lips. "First you bring in Elvis, now this."

"I know. I know. It's chaos and anarchy at the chapel." I slapped my hands down on her desk. "Now, will you please tell me if the chapel is going to stay? With us?"

"You almost knocked over Herbert."

I slid the alpaca to the center of the desk. "Better?"

"I don't know how much better I can be after hearing that you're dating a Cranston."

"Donna—"

She held up a hand. "But I can't talk. Victor and I had a little whirlwind affair back in 2002."

"Ew, gross."

"The man could kiss. My God, that man could kiss." She readjusted the cuff of her grass-green suit. "I'm sure it contributed to the animosity your grandfather had. Jim could get very jealous."

I thought I might dry heave. "You're killing me."

Donna threw back her head and laughed. "You did it, Holly. With all your cheesy wedding packages and hand billing and kissing the enemy, you somehow did it."

"Did what?"

"Saved it. Saved us. We're three thousand over our goal. Twenty away from the payment. Now all we have to do is go to that meeting with the bank in a couple of weeks, pay them half of the balloon, ask to refinance the rest, and our loan should be extended another three years. Five if we're lucky."

"We did it!" I threw up my arms and collided into a hug with Donna. "We did it!"

I tried to make her jump up and down with me, but she kept her arms at her sides. "Holly. Please. My suit."

"I'll buy you a new suit." I smacked a kiss on Herbert the alpaca. "I will buy everyone in this chapel a new suit."

"Or you could just start paying us."

"That too."

I ran into the parking lot and danced. The lights were on at Dax's chapel, but he didn't come out and join me. I would tell him the news when he called after work. For now, I had to let my family know.

If Grandpa Jim was sitting on a cloud right now, he had to be smiling.

CHAPTER 20

Mom was asleep when I got home, so I wrote a sign and put it on her door as a surprise when she woke up. Lenore texted me some inspirational quotes from her female icons, things like, "Try and you can succeed. Stay pensive and you fail."

I appreciated the gesture, but Bono was so much better.

Dad and James called me on speaker from Dad's house.

"So I broke my hand for nothing?" James asked.

"You broke your hand for everything."

"I got a black cast—you have to sign it with white or gold pen."

"It's the cast of a hero," I said.

"Maybe not hero," Dad said. "Let's not glorify violence."

"Did you see that other dude's face?" James asked. "I effed him up pretty good."

"But what did we learn from this?" Dad asked in the standard parental monotone.

"Kick instead of punch?"

Dad groaned. "James."

"Guess what. Dad said now that my hand is broken and my piano career has gone up in flames—"

"Your career has not ended." My stomach twisted with guilt.

"Stalled. Whatever. I needed a break from piano anyway. Mrs. Georgia always smells like eggs." He sniffed. "So I was thinking, I want to take photography classes. I can still take pictures with my pointer finger. Dad said he'd do it with me."

Lenore would point out that this is the first thing they have done together postdivorce and was thus some pivotal moment in the overall dynamic of our family structure.

I was not Lenore. "That'll be cool. Hey, James?"

"What?"

"Thank you for saving me today."

"Whatever. Oh, hey, I told Dad about Dax."

"You what?"

"He wanted to know who the guy in the diaper was."

"We need to talk about that," Dad said.

"Absolutely." I yawned. "Just not tonight. Let's save some excitement."

"But we will talk."

"Can't wait."

"I saw you making out on the street corner," James said. "I almost punched Dax before I punched that other dude. But it takes some balls to wear a diaper like that, so it's cool."

"Okay, this kid needs to sleep," Dad said. "I'm keeping him here for a few days."

This would also be the first time James had slept over when it wasn't Dad's weekend. And the first time James hadn't yelled at Dad during the conversation. And the first time we all saved a wedding chapel.

"Proud of you, Holly!" Dad said before hanging up.

I tried calling Dax too, but his phone just went to voice mail. He was supposed to call me, right? We were maybe even going to get together. Even if we'd celebrated the holiday unofficially the day before, a little "Way to save your chapel" would have been nice.

I changed into my duck pj's and old cross-country shirt. The Space seemed bigger tonight, the couch more comfortable. Despite the niggling feelings about Dax, I couldn't remember the last time I'd felt this relaxed. Actually, I could. It was before Grandpa died. I'd been bearing that chapel-sized burden for almost three months.

Sam called me after midnight to say he was coming over.

"Tonight?" I was semidozing on the couch, semiwatching a rerun of *The Office*. "No, I'm too tired."

"Too late. I'm at the door."

"What are you doing?" I asked when Sam pushed past me with a pizza under his arm.

"I'm here to offer you congratulations on saving all our jobs."

"Thanks. But a text could have done that."

"No. No. This is an in-person thing. So. You did it."

I played with the string of my pajama bottoms and tried to hide a smile. "I'm sort of awesome."

"But only sort of." He slid the pizza box onto the table. "The real reason I'm here is because I was hungry and I didn't want to be pathetic and eat this alone."

"And I'm the only mouth you could think of?"

Sam sighed. "Porter is out of town. Grant and Mike took two girls from Green Valley out on a double date. And Camille mangled my heart yesterday. So yeah, it's you, Nolan. Eat."

He flipped back the lid and cursed. They'd shaped the crust into a heart with pepperoni slices fanning around the cheese like lace. "Communists!" he shouted.

I reached past him for a slice. "Mmmm, communist pizza."

"Why did they do this? Are they mocking me?"

I slid my knee onto the arm of the couch. "It's Valentine's Day, remember? It's a nationwide conspiracy."

Sam tore the pepperoni off, like that would fix things, and shoved a slice into his mouth. "I was going to give Camille the promise ring today, did I tell you that? Take her to the park where we first kissed, make a picnic of her favorite foods, make it all special." He tore off the crust. "But I'd picked it up yesterday at the jeweler, and when we were by the airport taxis I saw this old couple. He was helping his wife into the cab even though he could hardly walk himself, and I thought, that's how Camille and I will be. Know what she said?"

"Yeah, I know. I was there when you guys hashed this out last night."

"No, about this couple. She said, 'Ugh, I never want to get old.' Here I am looking at this couple and seeing forever, and she just sees an end."

I headed to the fridge for some Cokes. "Sam, you look for metaphors too much."

"You know who else looked for metaphors?"

"J. K. Rowling," I said at the same time as Sam.

"It's true!" Sam cried. "She also was a master at creating complex characters in relationships that promoted growth."

"Sam. I know. I've read the books as many times as you have. And I think J. K. Rowling would also say that when you lose love you need to move on. Or else you'll turn into Snape."

"But Snape never had the love to begin with!" Sam said impassionedly.

"Sam. I am very sorry about you and Camille. I know you love her very much—"

"*Loved* her!"

"Whatever. You don't turn off love in one day."

"Well, now that I see what kind of person she is . . . do you know she told me that she doesn't even *like* Harry Potter? That she just watched the movies because I like them."

"Because that's what you do in a relationship! You compromise. You don't give ultimatums and expect the girl to just bow down to your orders."

"I didn't give an ultimatum." He folded his arms. "I just have standards."

My phone rang with a text. I rushed over to the coffee table, but it was Camille, asking if I was having a better Valentine's than her. Dax and I needed to have a talk about his texting skills or lack thereof.

"Where's your boyfriend tonight?" Sam took a swig of Coke. "Shouldn't you be sharing a heart-shaped pizza with him?"

I rubbed my forehead. "Sam. Look. You just broke up with your girlfriend, and I'm here to talk to you or listen or whatever. But I don't want you harping on Dax tonight, okay? We had a good day at the chapel, but it was long, in part because you never showed up to work. There is stuff going on with my brother and family and I just . . . I can't, okay? I'm going to be a friend to you. But I need you to be a friend back."

Sam slid down next to me on the couch. "You're right. I'm sorry."

I waved my hand. "It's fine."

"No, no, it's not. Here, I want you to have something." He fumbled in his pocket and pulled out the promise ring. It was white gold with a ruby and little diamonds around it. If it was real, it couldn't have been cheap. "Here. The jeweler won't take it back."

"I'm not going to wear your creepy promise ring, Sam."

"Then wear it as a friendship ring." Sam shrugged. "Hold on to it for me. In case I ever find love again."

The ring barely fit my pinky. "Porter would make so much fun of you for this."

Sam gave me a brotherly peck on the cheek. "That's why Porter isn't my best friend. You are." He swiped the remote from the table and started flipping through channels. 'There's a *Battlestar Galactica* marathon on. Want to watch?"

"It's one in the morning."

He shrugged. "We're young."

We finished off the rest of the pizza and watched an episode before falling asleep. My mom came in and put blankets on us. I had some weird dream about Dax dressed as a zombie cupid, and it ended with all my friends dead and my dad eating a pizza.

When the phone rang at five a.m., I was already onto another dream, this one involving alpacas and skateboards. Sam picked up the phone.

"Dax, what's up?" Sam asked.

"What? Dax?" I peeked open an eye. Sam's hair was flat on one side. I couldn't process why Sam and I were on the couch and why he was talking on my phone. To Dax.

I shot up. "Give me the phone."

"It's Sam. Are you okay? No, we must have just fallen asleep." He paused. "Don't worry, it's not like that."

I grabbed the phone from Sam. "Dax? What's going on?"

"I shouldn't be worried about you and Sam right now, should I?"

Sam leaned in close to listen. I pushed him away. "You shouldn't be worried about Sam and me ever."

Dax sucked in a long breath. "I need to ask y'all a favor."

"Right now?"

"Yeah. I'm at Red Rock. I need . . . can you come pick me up?"

"Like, at the casino or the mountains?"

"Casino. You don't have to come in. I'm actually in the parking lot."

"You want me to come pick you up from the Red Rock Casino parking lot at five in the morning? I don't have a car. Where is your car?"

"It's here . . . look. Don't be mad. Or be mad, whatever. I'm just . . . I'm a little drunk. Maybe not even drunk, but I had enough to drink that I shouldn't drive. And I would call a cab but I don't want to leave my car in a casino parking lot thirty minutes from my house."

I rolled my eyes. Sober or not, he had to know how losery this situation was. "We're coming. Stay there."

I hung up and stared at the phone.

"I'm not going," Sam said. "This guy is a dick. It's almost morning."

"It is morning. I guess we're just waking up early today. I need you to drive me so I can get Dax and his car."

Sam hit his head against a throw pillow. "I don't want to."

I held up my pinky finger. "Friendship ring says you do. I can't leave him stranded." I slapped his leg. "Come on."

"You know if I hadn't broken up with Camille I wouldn't be here to help you out."

"I have to pee. Warm up the car."

I changed into a nicer hoodie and yoga pants, brushed my teeth and hair, and pushed Sam to his car. Red Rock Casino is a locals casino, close to Red Rock Canyon, only ten minutes from my house. The mystery was why Dax was there, when there were twenty other casinos closer to *his* house. Or why he was at a casino at five in the morning, period.

We found Dax on the roof deck of the parking lot, lying on the hood of his car, arms open, legs wide. Asleep.

Sam screeched his tires and barged out of his truck. "I drove down. I get the honors." He slapped Dax on the shoulder. "Hey, buddy."

Dax shot up and looked around wildly.

"Sam, stop," I said, annoyed.

"You have a little too much to drink again? Need your girlfriend to bail you out *again*?"

Dax lay back on his hood and closed his eyes. "Sam. Thanks for helping me out this fine evening."

"Do you know how good you have it?" Sam got up in Dax's face, but Dax just lay there all serene, a little smile on his lips. "Holly is like my sister, you punk. It's Valentine's Day and you're hanging out here, instead of with her?"

Dax propped himself up on his elbows. "You're right, man. I messed up. I'm not going to argue with you because there is nothing to argue."

Sam looked confused. "Well, yeah, right. There isn't."

"Don't worry." Dax patted Sam's shoulder. "Tonight sobered me up plenty."

"Well, I mean, whatever." Sam yanked his arm away from Dax. "I'm not trying to give you a public service announcement here. Just get it together."

Thankfully, Dax saw how serious Sam was and did not salute him. I couldn't handle another person getting punched in the face today, especially when the person was my boyfriend. My drunk boyfriend. Every girl's fairy-tale Valentine's dream come true.

Sam helped Dax off the hood of the car and into the backseat. Dax handed me the keys. "So, you drive me home and Sam takes you back?"

"No. You can come over to my house to sober up, then drive yourself home in the morning. Or afternoon."

Dax slumped against the backseat window. I thought he was asleep until he finally said something. "I sabotaged this, didn't I?"

"This?"

"Us."

I didn't look back at him. "I don't know, today was a really insane day in, like, every avenue of my life, and I need to process what is going on."

Dax nodded and looked back out the window. Two minutes later he said, "I meant it, you know. When I said I love you."

I tried to keep my voice calm, but all that came out was a whisper. "You did?"

"Absolutely. I'm in love with you," Dax said, all matter-of-fact. "Deeply, madly, wonderfully, truly, irrevocably . . . I'm sorry, I'm slightly intoxicated, so those are the only adverbs I can come up with right now. But I am. To the point it hurts. Hurtily? That's not a word, is it?"

"You are drunk."

"Honestly. Painfully. Truthfully. Regrettably. That's, like, ten, so I can't be that drunk."

I paused, a beat, an eon. It's just, he knew he was going to say that, he had all the buildup and could plan out the timing and words. Words aren't as smudgeable as feelings. Once something is said, it's forever said, and this wasn't the time. It wasn't *my* time.

"Dax, I don't want it to be like this."

"Me drunk? Or me in love?"

I glanced at him, in the rearview mirror. I wanted him to be more but I could accept that he was less, as long as this following-in-his-alcoholic-grandfather's-footsteps ended now. He looked like a knight who had taken an arrow in battle, pale and hunched over, with a brave face. "Why were you at Red Rock? You said you'd call, you're drunk, I'm driving you to my house . . . what happened?"

Dax's expression went stoic. "No reciprocation to my declaration. You're tough, Nolan." He splayed himself across the backseat. "I promise I had plans to be a decent person this evening. I was going to surprise you, I didn't even know with what yet, but I was thinking about it all week. I'm not saying this to get points, because an I-was-going-to means nothing if there is no outcome. But then I got that phone call and your brother got in the fight. When I went back to our chapel, we had a busy day, a real busy day, and Poppy said he wanted to take me out to celebrate."

"Did you get the message I left on your voice mail?" I couldn't help the smile that spread across my face. "We had a good day too."

"Yeah. I got it." He paused. "That's great. Let's talk about that in a bit."

"Sorry to interrupt."

"No, ma'am. Never be sorry."

We were almost to my house now, and my hands were slick against the steering wheel. Mom wasn't going to be okay with me bringing Dax home at 5:30 in the morning. What would we even do, sit on the couch? I glanced in the rearview mirror. Dax's eyes were half-closed, his arm crossed over his chest.

"Hey, it's almost sunrise. Let me take you somewhere and we can talk. My house probably isn't a good idea with you like this."

Dax gave a sloppy salute. I drove over to the lake and to my spot. I didn't get ceremonial as I led Dax to my little patch of grass. I didn't tell him how special this spot was to me, how I'd never brought someone I liked (loved?) here before.

Dax lay in the dead grass while I got us both water bottles and little doughnuts at the minimart. He smiled when I handed him the drink.

"Thanks. I'm seriously feeling better now. Physically. I was just playing some slots after my grandpa left, and this cocktail waitress kept offering me free drinks and didn't even card me. I'm not stumbling drunk, just I-shouldn't-drive drunk."

"But you drink often enough that you know your levels of drunk," I said.

Dax bit into a doughnut, white powder on his lips. "I haven't had anything to drink since that party. I'm not like that. Not like this. It's just my world came crashing down a little tonight, and when you're cloaked in despair, a free Jack and Coke sounds like a nice idea."

"Why were you cloaked in despair?"

"I'll tell you, but come lie down first. We need a happy moment."

I settled into the crook of his arm. He smelled like casino. Underneath that, he smelled good. Like Dax.

"Look at the sun." He pointed at the horizon. "That's a good one."

The sunrise was much more than a good one. The sky glowed, all oranges and pinks, the clouds wisps and whispers. I hadn't visited my spot enough lately. I slid my hand under Dax's shirt and felt the hair I'd seen yesterday, felt the lines on his abs. He cupped my face and gave me a tender kiss. He tasted like wintergreen gum and whiskey, or what I guessed whiskey tasted like.

"Do you like it here?" I asked.

He rubbed my hair. "I like anywhere with you."

"This is my spot." I tickled his arm. "My number-one favorite place in the city of Las Vegas. If you don't love it here, you are a heartless fool."

"Hey, it's great. Yellow grass. Green water."

"I come here. To think. Count things. Be alone. Be happy." I lowered my voice. "You're the first person I've brought here."

He raised his neck and looked at me sideways. "If this place is so important to you, maybe we should leave."

"Why?" I sat up. "I thought we needed a happy moment."

He picked at a piece of grass. "That's about to end." He sighed. "Holly. First I want you to know I told you I love you, well, because I love you. But also because once you hear this, I don't want you to think I didn't."

The cloak of despair Dax had mentioned drooped over my shoulders. I brushed some dirt off my pants. "Fine. Let's go in the car and you can tell me."

I buckled into the driver's seat, like we were going somewhere, and set my face to stone. This was it. I didn't know what it was, but I knew it would be bad. And I'd totally set myself up for this moment—taking Dax to special places, feeling special because of him. This was the consequence of being in a relationship, of letting myself like. Love. "Okay. Go ahead. What did you do?"

He grimaced. "Whoa. No. That's not what this is. Man, you are fierce. I would be turned on right now if I didn't have the world's worst news." He pulled his seat back into reclining position and looked up at the ceiling. "The reason my grandpa took me to Red Rock was to celebrate. I mean, he picked the sushi restaurant because he knew he'd get our dinner comped, but he was celebrating because he sold his wedding chapel."

"What?" I shot up and smacked my head against the window. "Why? When?"

"How?" He shook his head. "He was always going to sell it. That's what I found out last night before Bellagio."

"Dax, no. That's awful." I tore off my seat belt and grabbed his arm. "Why didn't you tell me?"

"What did it matter? I have no say." He shrugged me off. "It's my job, but it's Poppy's chapel."

"But that's your *place*. Your Vegas home."

"It is. It was." Dax looked out the window. "Poppy is making so much money on the deal that he promised to buy me a new place. Buy my mom a new house. Send me wherever I want to go to college. He's going to be a millionaire."

I snorted. "Sorry, but Cupid's Dream isn't worth that much."

"No, but when you add in that Thai place, Angel Gardens, the tattoo parlor, that skuzzy hotel on the corner . . . Poppy has quietly bought everything but your chapel and the half-finished condos for two blocks. That's what I found out today."

"Who would want that? It's Strip wasteland."

Dax didn't look at me. "Poppy made a big gamble that paid off. He sealed the deal with Stan Waldon today."

"The hotel guy?"

"Yeah. Waldon sold out of his last venture, and now he's looking to revitalize the north side of the Strip. He's the one who owns those sky-rise condos behind us that were never completed. Wants to tear those down and build a new casino called the Phoenix, like he's metaphorically rising from the ashes."

My voice was small. "How big is this place?"

"You know those casinos. There'll be a hotel and pools and upscale shops and parking garages. It'll stretch from Sahara over past the Stratosphere."

"But my chapel . . . my chapel is there too."

Dax finally did look at me, but when he did I wished he hadn't. His expression said everything before his mouth did. "It's not going to matter how much money you raised. If Stan Waldon wants your land, he's going to get it. There is nothing you or me or your friends or anyone in Las Vegas can do about it. Y'all are done."

CHAPTER 21

I drove Dax home in frigid silence. I didn't care if he loved me anymore, I didn't care if *anyone* loved me, because the thing I loved the most was going to be taken away from me, and Dax shared blood with the person doing that.

I would burn down my own chapel before I let Victor or Stan what's-his-name touch it. This wasn't right. This wasn't fair. Grandpa wrote me the letter; I followed all the instructions. Raise the money, the problem would be fixed. Cause and effect. How were things not fixed now? How was it that I gave everything to that place, poured my soul onto that marble floor, only to have it vacuumed back up?

When we got to Dax's house, I slammed his car door shut and tossed him his keys. Without saying anything, I turned around and started walking to the corner. The bus stop was 1.6 miles away. I'd clocked it in Dax's car.

"Where are you going?" he called after me.

"Bus."

"You're not taking the bus. Come in. I'll have my mom take you home."

"No."

"Holly," Dax shouted. "Be fair. I'm dealing with this too. You have to talk to me."

"And say what?" I whirled around. "Say what, Dax? That it's okay? That I'm fine?"

"No, of course not."

"Then tell me what to say." I stomped over until I was inches from his neck, peering up into his stubbly, perfect face. "Tell me what to do. Because it won't matter. Nothing will matter. You try and you work and dream . . . and people . . . still die."

Dax tried to put his arms around me but I pushed him away.

"You really need to stop blaming me," he said.

"Yeah, well it feels a lot better yelling at you than yelling at the sky."

"The sky?"

"At my grandpa, you idiot. Chilling on his cloud. Doing nothing while his empire crumbles. You're right, he is a prick. Leaving me this. Leaving me period." I crouched down on the driveway and swallowed. Swallowed, swallowed, swallowed like tears came out of my throat and I could somehow keep them back. Hoover Dam couldn't keep them back.

Dax knelt down next to me. I buried my face in my hands and cried, sobbed, for the first time since my grandfather died. For the first time since I fell in love. For the first time since my parents got divorced. I'd cried at some point before, but not a flood. Not this river.

"I failed. I failed." I hiccuped. "I should have . . . I should have . . ."

"Shhh." Dax stroked my hair. "You did every 'should have' you could."

"I hate your grandpa."

"Don't hate him. Don't hate Stan Waldon. Hate Vegas. This is just how Vegas is. Nothing stays the same."

"Fine. You win. I hate Vegas too." I wiped at my nose. "We should move to Detroit."

"Detroit? You think things are better in Detroit?"

"No. Camille just said that's where you go if you run away."

He brushed at my cheek. "You can't run away. Not from this. Believe me."

I pushed my sleeve over my fingers and pressed on my eyes. They throbbed underneath the pressure. "So that's why you got drunk. Good reason."

"There's never a good reason to get drunk. I was being stupid. If I was a real man, I would have called you and told you the news right away."

"Daxworth Cranston, you might have some problems, but you don't need to worry about being a real man. You have way too much facial hair." I let out a shaky sigh. A neighbor walked by with his dog and gave us a weird look. I didn't have the energy to flip him off. "'Kay. I'm done. Thanks. You're a good person, even with that stupid name."

"Always so liberal with the compliments." He paused. "I'd

give you a hug but you still look like you might punch the next person to touch you."

"Yeah, I don't do well with emotions when I'm emotional."

"A handshake?"

"How about a wave?"

Dax hopped up. "I'll have my mom make us waffles before she takes you home."

"Waffles can't fix this."

He offered his hand. "Nothing will fix this, fixer. But waffles won't hurt it either."

✦ ✦ ✦

Donna and I met with the bank two weeks later. Without the remaining balance of the balloon payment, they would not refinance our loan. We had to pay the loan back in entirety, or we went into default and the bank would repossess the property in thirty days.

I kept hearing the "fault" part of "default."

When I broke the news to our employees, Mom started looking for a new job and Donna started looking for a loophole.

"I'm going through every paper your grandfather owned." Donna marched down the steps of the bank. "I need to look over the deed again. There is money somewhere. There is something we aren't seeing that is going to change everything."

"I hope so," I said. "Without the Rose of Sharon, what are we?"

"Unemployed," Donna grumbled.

"How much money do we have now, liquid?"

"Forty-three thousand," she said. "Which is about thirty thousand more than your grandpa usually had."

I scrunched my nose. "Do you have a rich brother or anything? Someone we can get a loan from?"

Donna grew thoughtful. "I do have some investor friends who live in Las Vegas Country Club. Rick is ancient and Mandy loves to spend his money. Maybe I could make a cause out of it for them. Save the Rose of Sharon, that stuff."

We stopped in front of Donna's car. "I still don't understand how Victor and Waldon can just do this to us."

"It's not a surprise." Donna pulled her door open. "Victor Cranston is a snake, so he can't help but act like a snake."

I bit at a hangnail. "I guess."

Donna rested her hand on my shoulder. "I just hope that grandson of his isn't a part of this."

I pulled back. "Of course he isn't. He was the one who told me."

"Right. And how did Victor Cranston find out we were in financial distress? Real distress? How does the bank already have third-party interest when we still own the place? If Waldon wasn't trying to buy that place, the bank would have been happy to take our money and give some kind of extension." Donna ducked into her car. "I'm just asking questions. But you probably should be asking them too, sweetie."

CHAPTER 22

The other businesses closed fast. Going-out-of-business sales and boarded-up shops came and left overnight. Our area was already a little dead, but now the block looked like a welcome party for the apocalypse.

Dax and I made a grand show of frequenting each business on their last day—eating mediocre Thai, buying thimbles at the cheap gift shop. I wasn't old enough for a tattoo, and would never get one if I was, but Dax had been talking about it for a while and felt like Tattoo Wonderland was the place to do it.

"Argh, they never say how much it hurts when they show this on TV," Dax said as the artist poked away.

"It's a needle leaving permanent dye in your skin. It's not a massage." I spun around on the barstool across from the tattoo chair. "So this isn't your favorite spot in Vegas?"

"No. Argh! No."

"I still think you should have done a moth. Or maybe a cute cupid on your ankle."

"That stupid costume is already burned in my memory, it doesn't need to live on for eternity on my foot."

The tattoo artist wiped at Dax's left rib cage. "There you go, buddy. Take a look."

Dax held the hand mirror across his body, reflecting the scrolling letters of his dad's initials. I peered closely at the tattoo. "VOC? What was your dad's name?"

"Victor. But he went by Vince."

"Oh."

Dax stared at the tattoo in the reflection. "Poppy's middle initial is G, if that's what you're thinking. So it's fine."

"I didn't say anything." I took the chance to get a full scope of shirtless Dax. "It's your body."

"You don't need to say anything." Dax stuck his shirt back on. "I haven't talked to him for three weeks now. Trust me, I'm not immortalizing that man."

We stood in the doorway of the tattoo shop and took in the dingy store. The funny thing was, we were saying good-bye to places we'd never even patronized. Except for the Carl's Jr. around the corner. I was going to miss their French toast sticks.

Ever since Valentine's Day, things had been different with Dax. There were so many land mines we had to jump around in conversation now that we never really talked. Not like we did before. I worried something might trigger him to drink again, more worried that trigger might be me. And I had this rage boil up at the mere mention of his grandpa. Even if Dax wasn't talking to him, the fact that Victor Cranston even existed made me see red spots.

So we started this Sam/Camille dynamic where we goofed around a little and made out a lot. Sometimes more than I was comfortable with, actually, but I didn't know how to stop. I liked it, I liked *him*, but for me, the physical was just a way to put off discussing, well, anything. The fissures were widening in our relationship, and the only way to mend the tension was to kiss it all away.

"Where to next?" Dax asked as he slid his hand into mine. Mom and Dad had a "talk" with me after they found out about Dax, but for the first time ever, I played the divorce card and asked them if they ever dated. Dad got so flustered, I was never punished. They didn't exactly bestow a parental blessing, but it was enough that Dax and I didn't have to be so stealthy in our affections.

"I think we need to give a formal good-bye to the Twilight wedding room," I said solemnly.

"Can't." Dax looked away. Who says 'can't' to a chapel make-out session? "Poppy has a meeting with some of the demolition guys."

My stomach sank. "Yeah? How are they . . . how are they doing it?"

"They're doing a wrecking ball on the smaller buildings."

"What about those condos? They're brand-new—no one's even lived in them."

"All forty floors. Those are getting imploded. Waldon needs something big so he can do his whole Phoenix theme for the hotel. A party, fireworks, the big countdown. Boom."

"Oh."

I still had two weeks until the bank could seize our chapel. We were still in business, but without the miracle I'd been praying for, nothing would change.

"I wouldn't mind going to the Neon Boneyard again," Dax said. "Actually listening to the tour this time."

"Maybe," I said absently. I was picturing myself walking into Victor's meeting and laying the smackdown. James wasn't the only one in this family who could break a hand.

"There was a shirt I liked in that gift shop too. That old motel."

"The La Concha," I said. The La Concha. The old motel they moved two miles down the Strip when the land got bought out for another hotel.

The La Concha.

I was already making a list. I'd have to ask what it cost to move a structure like that. We're a historical building—maybe if I filed something with the national registrar I could get a grant. The bank could give us a deal since it was the land they wanted anyway. "Dax! The La Concha! You're brilliant!"

"So you do want to go to the museum?"

I pecked him on the cheek. "We'll move it. Do a big drive to raise money, play the historical, save-old-Vegas card. We could, like, donate ceremonies in exchange for help from the city."

"You're talking . . . the wedding chapel? You want to move an entire wedding chapel?"

"Or Donna! Donna knows this ninety-year-old rich guy and we could find another spot. A better spot! There are hardly any nice chapels on the south side of the strip anymore, we would stick out—"

"I don't know," Dax said.

I frowned. I'd broken our unwritten rule, but this could be the miracle I'd been hoping for. Dax knew how much I'd been hurting, and he couldn't even pretend enthusiasm? "What do you mean, *you don't know*?"

"It just sounds like a lot of ifs. That balloon payment wouldn't just go away. You've got two weeks to come up with the same money you made in three months. Moving that building would take even more money. And they're doing the implosion in a month or two."

"They're not imploding my building. I still own it."

"For now."

I dropped Dax's hand. "What's your deal? Why aren't you supporting me with this?"

"Are you kidding? All I do is support you." Dax stuck his hands in his pockets. "I just think you have to accept reality here. It's over."

"Like your chapel is over. What, you don't want to suffer alone, you want me out too?"

"Holly! Listen to yourself." Dax rolled his eyes. I don't think I'd ever seen him roll his eyes. "Why does everything have to be so difficult with you?"

"You think things are difficult?"

"Well, they sure haven't been a walk in the park. You analyze every word I say."

"Whatever." I knew "whatever" wasn't the best way to end an argument, but I had nothing else I could say. Actually, I had a lot I could say. The space between us grew to a gap as we walked down the street toward our chapels. Dax was two paces in front of me. I counted seven cracks, stepping on the last one and pretending the childhood saying was true, except it was Victor's back I broke. I kept my vision on those cracks as I spoke. "Donna asked me something and I really want to know the answer. How did Victor know that we were in trouble with the bank? I mean, that's confidential info, right? The bank can't even share. Yet they're moving forward with this project like they are one hundred percent sure that they're getting our land. Like they know."

Dax slowed his step. "I'm sure you've told people that."

"Just you. Did you tell him?"

"Who?"

"Dax. Seriously."

Dax stopped. "I don't know? I don't think so. Would it really matter if I had?"

"You know it matters."

"Are you looking for a reason to be mad at me? Is that what this is? I haven't talked to one of my closest relatives for almost a month because of you. A *month*. And you're going to get mad because I might have made some comment that you were in financial trouble when anyone in a two-mile radius would have known that?"

"So you told him."

"Yes I told him!" Dax threw up his hands. "We weren't in on some master plan. I told him when I was yelling at him for selling my wedding chapel. Remember that? I got screwed also. I was on your side."

"Was?"

"Oh God. Am. I am."

I swallowed. "But if you hadn't said something, Victor wouldn't have known when our loan was coming up. We would have gone to the bank, and they would have given us an extension."

"Extension for what? You can't keep the chapel. Loan or not, this building is going down. For both of us. There is no one you can talk to, no amount of ceremonies you can sell that is going to change that."

"You're wrong," I said.

"And you're hardheaded."

We'd walked over to the parking lot by now, not far from the purple line my grandpa had painted to divide the spaces. The line snaked up around our ankles, up our stomachs, across our hearts.

There would always be a line. "Is it going to stay like this?"

"Like what?"

"Never mind. I'm sorry I said anything."

"It's like you're waiting for me to say the wrong thing so you can have a reason to get mad." Dax rubbed his foot along the line. "Look. You know I love you."

I said nothing, just like I'd said nothing this whole time. Every

"I love you" bothered me, like he was challenging me to say something back, pushing me further away from a declaration, further from that feeling. It made me lose this argument, when I couldn't say the words back.

"I just hope that the thing that was keeping us together isn't going to break us apart," I said.

"Is that what you want?" Dax scratched at his head. "I don't know why we're having this conversation. Are you in this or not?"

"That's a stupid question," I said.

"It is. So why am I asking it?" Dax shoved his hands into his pockets and turned his back to me. "Honestly, I hope you save your chapel. I really do. I know that's what makes you happy."

No, you make me happy! I do know what I want, I want you. I want the Neon Boneyard and Golden Steer and Bellagio and the wonder of us. I said these things, six times in my head, as Dax walked twenty-four steps back to his chapel.

CHAPTER 23

Donna's investors came by the chapel the next day. Mr. Nottingburg, with a walker and a velvet house robe. His wife, Mandy, forty years younger and full of design ideas.

"Could we wallpaper these walls?"

"The urinals are painted gold. Tacky!"

"Those floors . . . we'll knock them out. Do a nice travertine tile, maybe?"

I gritted my teeth as she flew through suggestions, basically insulting every corner of the chapel. If we were going to make a deal, we needed to do it before the old man died. Each breath sounded like wind through a chimney.

"Well, what do you think?" Donna asked. She had on a brand-new suit today, fuchsia. It worried me that she chose today to expand her color wheel.

"About the chapel in *its present condition*," Dad added. He'd been gargling back insults each time Mandy made a comment. If they didn't leave soon, my dad was going to choke to death.

"So, Stan Waldon is building around here?" Mandy clanked her bracelets together with a flick of her wrist. She did a lot of wrist flicking.

"All around here," Donna said. "But we still own the land and chapel."

"But his big old hotel will be in the way."

Donna raised a manicured nail. "Not if we *move* the chapel. Mandy, we could do a fun show of it! A parade. Get newspapers, all the charities to come while we have a big truck scoop us up and move us to a much more desirable location."

"Like over by Caesar's Palace?" *Clinkity-clank*. "I love those men in togas."

"What did you say?" Mr. Nottingburg asked.

"I said I LOVE MEN IN TOGAS," Mandy yelled. She smiled at Donna. "That's going to cost a lot, right?"

"Yes, but this chapel is almost eighty years old. Did I tell you, this was originally a preacher's home; couples were married in his parlor. We've filmed multiple movies here. There isn't another chapel like it anywhere in the world. You would have a one-of-a-kind investment."

Mandy sized me up, then scratched her nose. "We'll think about it."

"Eighty-five percent!" the old man hollered.

"What's that?" Donna asked.

"We get eighty-five percent. We pay off the rest of your loan. We pay to move this place, and we get eighty-five percent."

"Eighty-five percent, and you pay all expenses?" Dad asked.

"You wait too long and I'll make it ninety, son."

I chewed the inside of my cheek. When I'd heard the word "investors," I thought they would give us money and then be, like, silent partners. Give us our money and go away. Fifteen percent . . . what would that mean? What kind of power would we even have? Mandy was already talking about knocking down the urinals. I loved those urinals—not that I used them, but it was nice to know they were there. "We'll get back to you."

"Or we move the building but lose the weddings. Make it a theme restaurant! Oh, so much possibility." Mandy's bracelets chuckled in approval as she waved good-bye.

Donna closed the door and whirled around. "Well? What do you think? I've been to their house; Mandy has impeccable taste. She's crazy to think we could ever get land by Caesar's, but maybe by the Riviera? They're doing another revitalization over there soon—we could become a landmark."

Dad wilted. "I'm glad my dad is already dead."

"I don't think this is right," I said.

"It's the only hope we have of keeping our jobs."

"What jobs? Mandy would run the show," I said.

"I bet she'll ask me to take pictures of her dogs," Dad said. "Women like that always want dog portraits."

"We'd just be their employees, and we're not getting hard cash out of the deal." I melted into the seat next to Dad. It was so much work. This was all So. Much. Work.

"But you would save the chapel."

"I would save the *building*," I said. "And maybe not even that, once Mandy is through with it."

Donna slid onto the brocade sofa. "I'm trying."

"We know you are," Dad said. "You're like family to us, Donna."

"This chapel is like family too."

"So, now what?" Dad asked.

"I don't think Grandpa would want Mandy Nottingburg touching his urinals." I drummed my fingers on the arm of the chair. I was calmer than I thought I'd be, calmer than I'd been in some time. I did what I could. And it wasn't enough. "I'm calling it. We're going to euthanize this place. Let it die with some dignity."

"And no more Elvis?" Donna asked.

"Elvis who?"

✦ ✦ ✦

So we went out. In grand fashion. We closed our doors on Grandpa Jim's birthday. Besides Victor's, we were the last place open for blocks.

We gave away weddings. If a couple came in with a marriage license, we gave them the same royal treatment that we'd always given our customers. Plus free flowers, free minister, free wedding cakes.

And there was not an Elvis in sight.

I gathered everyone together before our first ceremony. I'd stolen the easel from the photography lounge and stuck up a portrait of Grandpa Jim from the late seventies. His hair was still red then, his mustache wispy. He hated that picture.

"So. Thanks everyone for coming in today, to work or help out." I stood on the tufted ottoman, in front of my employees. Donna, Minister Dan, my family, and my friends. "I know this isn't how we wanted to celebrate Grandpa's birthday. I know this isn't much of a celebration. But we did accomplish our goal. We saved this place." I glanced at Donna. "Even if we lost it right after. Grandpa hated cheesy so I'll let Bono do the talking."

I hit play on a CD player and the song "Beautiful Day" filled the room. We sat and listened for four minutes and six seconds, some of us crying, some stoic.

Around the minute-and-a-half mark, I let my mind wander to Dax. It'd been four days since we had that fight. We texted. I called him, he called me, our conversations fizzling out after ten minutes. We didn't talk about us or what had happened or what was going to happen. The chitchat was excruciatingly close to my parents' communication style. Part of me wanted to run across the street and kiss him, begging for forgiveness. Part of me wondered why he wasn't offering more. Either way, we stayed on our sides of the line and talked sports and schoolwork and how Sam and Camille still weren't talking, even though, ironically, Dax and I weren't talking much either.

When the song ended, everyone left to their post except for Lenore. Lenore, who'd flown in for the big event and had worked exactly five days in the chapel her whole life, had no post.

Lenore pawed through the employee fridge and came up with an apple. "This yours?"

"Yeah."

"Well, this building is going to blow up anyway." She bit into the fruit. "What do you want me to do today?"

There was no sense cleaning. The couples had the attention of Mom. We didn't need to advertise. "Nothing. There is nothing for you here." I let out a shaky breath. "Nothing for me either."

"Ah, chin up, little sister." Lenore flicked my arm. "You can actually do something with your predetermined life, now that the chapel is gone."

"I do something with my life every day," I said.

"Yeah, but you can *choose* what you want to do."

"What I wanted to do was the chapel."

She snorted. "So much for that ambition, huh?"

I rolled my eyes. Camille acted more sisterly than Lenore. Maybe we just took after our separate dads. "You've switched your major five times now, so who are you to talk?"

"Isn't it liberating?" Lenore breathed in an exaggerated breath. "I have all the time in the world to decide. And so do you."

"But I did. Decide." Didn't I?

Lenore tossed the apple in the trash and wiped her hands. "All I'm saying is you can't let someone else's dead dream keep you from finding your own."

I would never say this out loud, at the risk that Lenore might be recording the conversation so she could continuously play back my words, but . . . she was right. Maybe she had learned something of value at that Liberal Arts College You've Never Heard Of.

✦ ✦ ✦

I was seventeen and already married to my job. If we'd saved the chapel, I would have always kept it. I'd been so focused on the chapel, focused on not letting anyone down. Now I didn't know what to be focused on.

"So, then . . . what do I do now?"

Lenore shrugged. "What, you think I'm a psychic? I don't know. Go hang out with your friends or make out with that boy across the street." She sauntered to the doorway. "Oh, and hey, that couch in the lobby. Are we keeping it? I need more furniture for my dorm."

"Ask Donna."

I couldn't believe that my answer didn't come from Grandpa's letter, U2, or even Elvis. Now I wished my sister would fill in the rest of the sentence for me.

When your lifelong goal dies, what do you do with the rest of your life?

✦ ✦ ✦

Around closing, James asked the family to meet on the right side of the chapel for a surprise that "wasn't going to get me in trouble, promise." We gathered in the dirt lot, squinting in the twilight.

"Honey, we have a lot of work to do," Mom said.

"No, you don't. We'll all be unemployed in a few hours," James said happily. "First I want to get a picture of our family in front of the chapel. Dad said this is good lighting."

Dad cuffed James's shoulder. "Caught the old photo bug."

"Yeah, I just need to set up the timer." James ran over to the tripod, his hand fumbling in the cast. My family shuffled into a grouping. Dad took Mom's hand. "Be sad to see this place go. Remember you walking down that aisle—you were the most beautiful woman I'd ever seen."

"Were?"

"You're still up there," Dad said.

Mom laughed. "Guess we're just being symbolic, blowing up our marriage, then the place where we started it."

"But we always go out in style, right, Lana?"

Mom gave him a peck on the cheek. "We always do."

Dump a little more tragedy on the day, why don't you? I hadn't even thought about my parents' getting married here, but they had, just like Dax's parents had at Cupid's Dream. This really would be a new beginning for them, not having to work with each other anymore. Even though I'd seen that fight, seen what they kept hidden, I hated that we were going to split up even more now.

"Okay, squeeze in!" James ran back to us. He didn't put his arm around anyone, but he actually looked at the camera and smiled. "Say Swiss."

"Why would we say Swiss?" Lenore asked.

"Like the cheese, you, idiot."

Lenore flipped her braids just as the flash went off.

Mom sighed. "Can we do another?"

It took four more tries until everyone was satisfied.

"Okay, now close your eyes." James hopped around like we were about to get on his favorite ride at Disneyland. Not that James would ever admit that he liked Disneyland.

"Juvenile," Lenore said.

"Have you ever seen James this excited?" I whispered. "Shut up and go with it."

I caught my parents smirking before closing my own eyes. We waited seven seconds. I peeked once, but there was nothing but the string of cars and the constant shuffle of tourists.

"James?" Mom asked.

The music started then. Live music. We looked at James, looked around. James sprinted around the chapel, and we followed. On top of the gift shop, behind our parking lot, was Grandpa's U2 cover band. Of course, there was some other guy singing now, some young kid. Fake Bono held his arms up to the sky and soared into "Where the Streets Have No Name." Just like the music video, except it was almost thirty years later in LV, not LA.

"Is this really happening?" Lenore screamed. "How did you do this?"

"I'm influential." James jumped around.

Mom and Dad stared at each other, speechless. Everyone from the chapel was already outside. Sam and Minister Dan started line dancing, and a crowd of passersby trickled over. Camille and Donna stayed at the front door with our next couple, bobbing their heads and smiling at the sky.

Dax's car was in the parking lot. He was in that chapel. He could hear the noise. I almost ran over when the door opened, but it was only Victor. He shook his fist and yelled something obscene. For old times' sake.

I didn't let Dax's absence get me down. This was a big day, he knew it was a big day, but . . . no. You can't be down in the presence of Fake Bono.

I grabbed James by his cast and shouted, "Why did you do this?"

"Are you that stupid? It's Grandpa's birthday present."

I don't think I've ever loved someone more than I did my brother in that moment. There couldn't have been a better send-off for Grandpa, for the chapel, for us. I gathered him into a big hug before he pushed me away. "That's so not rock and roll."

"This song goes out to Jim Nolan, the man, the legend." Fake Bono raised his fist to the sky. We did the same. A cop car pulled into the parking lot and an officer got out. "Hey, are you guys redoing that old U2 music video?"

"I think so, officer," Dad said.

The officer mumbled into his walkie-talkie. "Okay. One more song, then I have to shut you down. You don't have a permit for this."

Bono launched into "With or Without You," the song Grandpa Jim used to sing to new couples. Dad took Mom's hand and led her to the fourth parking spot to dance. I wished and wished that Dax would come outside.

He didn't. So I forced my little brother to dance with me. I didn't know what was going to happen to our relationship once we closed our doors, but I still had my family, all the messy pieces of it.

CHAPTER 24

We gave away nine weddings that day. We didn't spend money advertising the freebie, just offered it to whoever came in. The last couple to get married was in their seventies. I loved that we ended by marrying people as old as the chapel.

My friends came over the next day to help me move everything out. Mom had an interview with a florist, and Dad had a gig. Or a date. Who knew, who cared. Visiting the chapel that day was like identifying a body in a morgue. No sense in putting everyone through the trauma.

We packed up the files, Dad's photography equipment, the candelabra. The pews would stay, along with the stained-glass window and gold urinals. Seemed stupid, since it was all going to get blown up, but we didn't have a use for them now. What we kept was going into storage until we figured out what to do next.

"Where are you going to work now?" Porter asked as we stacked Grandpa's gallery of Irish landscapes into a box.

"I'm not. I'm . . . taking a break."

"Do you even know how to do that?"

"No."

Mike squealed as Sam chased him around with a soggy bouquet.

"But I'm sure you guys can teach me how," I said.

Camille walked in, breezing past Mike and her ex. "I got your text. What can I do to help?"

Sam dropped the bouquet. "What text?"

They'd asked me to rearrange their work schedules so they were never together, and I'd complied. But yesterday everyone was there, and yesterday they'd made such a science of avoiding each other that I decided a mini intervention was at hand. I wanted to be friends with both of them, even if they were never going to get back together.

Now I was rethinking the move.

"Holly asked if I could come help out. This place was special for me too, and we're all adults here."

"I'm not an adult." Sam shoved past me. "I'm getting my stuff, then bouncing."

"Sam, don't. Come on."

"Um, Holly." Grant was peeking out through the blinds. "You probably want to see this."

"What now?"

"Uh . . . Dax? Is outside. With, a, uh . . . a chick."

The six of us rushed to the big window of the reception area, crowding around. Dax leaned on his driver's side door, clad in a University of Alabama T-shirt and basketball shorts. The girl he was talking to had the roundest butt I'd ever seen.

"I'd tap that," Mike said.

I elbowed him. I might have cracked a rib.

Dax laughed at something the girl said and gave a modest shrug. I knew that shrug. It wasn't modest. It was his way of saying, *Yes, I know I'm wonderful, but I can't come out and say it, right?*

"Did you guys break up?" Porter asked.

"No. We sort of had a fight though."

Dax gave the girl a hug.

"Maybe it's his cousin," Camille said hopefully.

"I know that dude is from Alabama," Grant said. "But I don't hug my cousin like that."

My stomach felt like the lining had detached and dropped into my intestines. Who was she? When did he meet her? Did he already know her? Why was she there? Could he see us through the blinds? What was I supposed to do?

"Why don't you go out there and do something?" Sam asked.

"Who, me?" Mike asked.

"Yes, Mike. Of course you." Sam smacked the back of his head. "Come on, Holls. Are you just going to let him go like that?"

There was distance between them now. I wish the girl would turn around so I could see something besides her perky butt. "Like you let Camille go?" I asked.

Grant smacked his thigh. “This is so much better than dressing up like showgirls.”

“I didn’t let Camille *go*,” Sam said. “We’re totally different from you and Dax.”

“Dax told me he loved me,” I said. “And then I didn’t do anything about it. You told Camille you wanted to marry her, and then when she didn’t want that, you walked away.”

“It’s true,” Camille said.

“Your boyfriend is out there feeling up another girl and you’re going to give *me* relationship grief?” Sam asked.

“No. I’m just saying we both don’t have it all figured out.” I shrugged. “Dax is across a parking lot. Camille is in front of you.”

“Exactly, I am standing right here, guys,” Camille said.

“Fine.” Sam folded his arms across his chest. “I’ll take that bet. Camille. I still love you. I don’t care if you marry me. I don’t even care if you want to be my girlfriend. I just want to be around you again.”

The room went quiet. Grant whistled until Porter nudged him.

“Oh.” Camille picked a rhinestone on her manicure. “Sam. That would be great. But you should know, I’m seeing someone else too.”

I could almost pinpoint the exact moment when Sam’s heart exploded. Right when Camille hit the second syllable in “someone,” *BAM*.

Grant pulled out his phone. “I don’t know why I’m not recording this conversation.”

"I'm out of here," Sam said.

Camille stepped in front of him. "No, you aren't. I didn't say I was *marrying* someone else, I just said that I haven't been waiting around for you to grow some balls. If you want to talk, then great. *Both* of us can talk. You need to listen, unless you want this to be our last conversation."

"What happened to this girl?" Porter whispered.

"Backbone," I said.

"It's hot," Mike said.

"Fine, can we talk then?" Sam asked. "Or you can talk?"

Camille looked at me. "Is it okay if we take a break?"

"You guys are here for free helping me pack. What am I going to do, fire you?"

"Wait, we're here for free?" Mike asked

I peered through the blinds again. Dax's girl was gone now, probably left in her own cool car to her own cool job that wasn't about to get bulldozed. He was still outside, getting something from his car. He turned his head when Sam and Camille hopped into the truck, a surprised look on his face. Then he looked past them, at my friends and me still standing in the window. From a hundred feet away, I could feel his gaze. I jumped back.

"He saw you," Mike said.

"Okay, I'm filming now," Grant held up his phone. "Run over there and make out with Dax."

"No way."

"But Sam made a bet with you."

"Sam made a bet, I never agreed to it."

"Then what are you going to do?" Mike asked.

I relaxed my hands. I'd somehow balled them up into fists. "What if I go out there and he doesn't want me anymore?"

Porter put his arm around me. I was so glad it was him and not Mike. "But what if he does?"

I shook my head. "It has to be the right moment for me to put everything on the line."

"Just be careful." Mike peeked out the window again. "You wait too long, and that line's going to disappear."

Dax walked back into his chapel. That was pretty much the moment when my heart exploded too.

CHAPTER 25

Sam and Camille texted an hour later and asked if we wanted to meet them at the secret pizza place in the Cosmo. There was no telling if they were back together now or what, but I was happy that Camille was at least temporarily part of the group again. I sent the boys along so I could have a moment alone with the chapel before I locked up.

I sat on the fifth pew in the back, pushing aside my Dax worries to make room for the ghosts of my childhood. I'd knocked out my front tooth right here. There was still a drop of my blood on the cream-colored cushion.

I roamed the hallway, rubbing my hand along the dirty shadows left from Grandpa's collection of Irish landscapes. I flushed the gold urinals nine times, watching the water leak along the edge. I ended in the chapel, on my knees, counting the gray veins in the marble floor.

"It's just a building," I said to the floor. I had to keep saying that, out loud. "It's just a building." Just some stone and drywall, beams and marble, some shutters, some roofing material that I don't even know the name of. Materials. There was no reason to mourn this much for materials.

But it wasn't just the materials. It was my childhood, and my adulthood as I'd always planned it to be. I'd meant to go to business school, take this over, meet a man and marry him here, uttering the same promises I'd heard couples say time and time again. Lenore said I should feel liberated, and in a way I did. The future was a Strip-length stretch before me, a pathway that allowed me to be anyone and anything.

But I also didn't know who I was if I wasn't here.

There was a knock on the front door.

"I'm in the chapel," I called.

I collected my memories and shoved them into my pocket. I told the guys I would take the bus down the street, but they were back to get me, a rare show of gentlemanly conduct.

But it wasn't a friend in the chapel doorway. Or a gentleman.

"Victor?" I scrambled up. "What are you doing here?"

Victor tapped his boot against the floor. "Is this real marble?"

"Yes."

"Waste of money." He leaned on the doorway and appraised the space. How many brides had held their breath at that spot before taking that first step down the aisle? "So, you closed."

"You too."

"Well, we're closing my chapel, but I'm in business. Big

business. Dax might have mentioned that I'm going to be filthy rich now that this deal is going through?"

I drew circles on the tile with my foot. "You're already getting my chapel, do you want a medal too?"

Victor leaned his head against the wall and closed his eyes. "Did you also know Dax hasn't talked to me in a month now? Not a word. I talk to him, he grunts a little. That's all I get."

"But you're rich now, right? So who cares?"

"Listen, darling, the bank already knew this was happening. They wanted you to fail so they could foreclose, then sell the land to us for double."

"What if we had made our payment?"

"The construction would have started around you, we would have blocked entrances and produced a lot of dust and choked you out until you didn't have any more customers. It was never a question of *if* you'd go out of business, just when."

"Is this supposed to make me feel better?"

Victor hiked up his dingy chinos. "I saw you were packing. You missed some stuff."

"Like what."

"I'm going to own this building soon enough, and when I do, I'd like to give you everything inside it. Not the outside, I want the glory of seeing a bulldozer rip it apart, but the business. The pews. The stained-glass windows. You can keep it."

"I don't understand."

"I talked to Donna today. Used to date that broad, but she got crazy on me when I tried to pet one of her alpacas." Victor grimaced. "She wants to open her own chapel. I'm investing some money in it; she's got some rich old fart who wants to do the same. You can take all this crap over there. Start again. That's what Vegas is all about, isn't it?"

"Why would you do that? That makes no sense. We . . . *I* hate you."

"Feeling's mutual." Victor scratched his stomach. "Jim Nolan was the most hardheaded bastard I've ever met in my life. The day he died, I did an Irish jig. I wouldn't care if your whole family got stuck in this chapel when the implosion happened. But my grandson would, and I love my grandson more than anyone." He shook his head. "I just hope Dax gets over his little crush soon. I thought he'd go for a girl with some curves, you know? At least some hair . . . Grow it out."

"So . . . the deal is, you get the land. I keep everything inside and my haircut."

Victor laughed so hard that it rumbled into a hacking cough. "Shake on it?"

It was better than nothing. I'd give Donna all the materials. I'd give her the files. I'd give her anything, let her do her own thing, and just ask that she give us all a job. A part-time job, that I might do forever, that I might do for a few months. I could love the business all I wanted, but I was happy to step away from motherhood and become an adoring aunt.

I spit into my hand and held it out. Victor made a face of disgust.

"One more thing. Can you send Dax over here?" I asked.

"Get him yourself." He smoothed back a strand of oily hair. Maybe I didn't hate him. Just . . . disliked.

"Victor?"

"What? Fine. I'll get him. Want me to call in the Royal Army too?"

"No. Just . . . thank you."

The words tasted better than I would have ever thought.

✦ ✦ ✦

Dax finally appeared in the parking lot eleven minutes later. We hadn't seen each other for four days, unless you count the parking-lot encounter earlier. And I didn't want to count it; I didn't want to talk about it. I didn't want that moment to exist.

"Hey." I slipped my hand into Dax's. My skin sang upon contact. "I want to show you something." We ducked our heads under the archway to the back rose garden. I'd sprinkled a few petals on the cobblestones, just to throw Dax off.

"Holly, I know it's been a while, but I don't have time to hook up right now."

"That's something old married couples who sleep in separate beds say to each other."

"Then do you want to give me a script so I can say the right thing?" Dax pinched a rose petal, crushing it in his hand.

"Nope. I want . . . magic. Just a moment of magic. Can we do that?"

"Do you want to talk first? I know you saw me today. With Daphne."

Dax and Daphne? Matching names were the worst. They had a 0.26 percent chance of relationship success.

"I saw you, and so did my five best friends. Who was she?"

Dax's face reddened. "She's a girl I used to date. She came by because she heard the chapel was closing."

"That's fine. I don't know why you had to hug her in the parking lot though."

"I don't know. You've been distant. I didn't think you would care."

"Are you kidding?"

Dax smacked his forehead. "I was checking to see if you would care. I was baiting you, and you didn't even bite. If I saw you standing in the parking lot with some dude, I'd be out there in a flash. I might even go into a rage. But you didn't even get jealous. And I don't know if I should take it as some sort of sign that you're just not that into me."

"Are you going to see her again?"

"Do you want me to?" Dax asked.

"Yeah, I'd really like you to start spending some time with your ex-girlfriend. And maybe you two could go to a strip club together? Make a party of it. Of course I *care.* I want to shoot that girl in her perky butt, but I have a little more control over my emotions than you do."

"That's the problem. You have too much control. Except for when we mention the chapels, then your eyes go hard and you look at me like I'm the one holding the smoking gun." He frowned. "Then you sprinkle some rose petals on the ground and you think that does it? You keep making all these doomsday comments that we aren't going to last. I'm starting to believe it."

"Just shut up. I'm sorry, okay?"

"Okay."

"I really am."

"I believe you."

"Good. Now I want to show you something." I'd concealed Grandpa's old toolbox under a rosebush. There were likely better, indestructible containers out there, but I hadn't had much time to prepare and had to go with whatever was left in the chapel. The lid creaked to life, rust flaking off the side. "This."

"That's a toolbox," Mr. Obvious said.

"No, it's not." I slowly spread out my treasure. A T-shirt from the Neon Boneyard. A U2 CD, a matchbook from the Golden Steer, a chipped piece of marble, a brochure, the chapel picture of my family James took, and an Elvis figurine I'd found at one of the soon-to-be-destroyed gift shops. "This is a time capsule. In loving memory of the Rose of Sharon."

Dax's face melted to butter. "But Neon Boneyard . . . is us."

"You're part of the memory for me now."

"This is . . . you are . . . amazing. I'm sorry."

"It's fine. We've both done stupid things."

"But I was stupider."

"We aren't going to argue our stupidity now." I scooped up a few rose petals and sprinkled them into the box. I couldn't look at Dax, had to focus on the words so they came out right. "That grass spot I took you to isn't my favorite spot in Vegas anymore. It's all in here. We're going to dig a hole so deep so that the demolition crew and Stan Waldon can't touch it, and then this spot will be all the good of Vegas and us."

"Do you want to know my favorite spot in Vegas now?" Dax cupped my face.

"The tattoo parlor?"

"No. You are. Wherever you are, that's my spot."

I wiped at my eyes, as surprised with the tears as anyone in Vegas ever is about rain. "You can add something in here too, if you want."

"I want." He opened his wallet and took out the picture of his parents. Wordlessly, he slid the photo into the box.

"And this is for you." I slid a folded piece of notebook paper across the cobblestones.

Dax unfolded the sheet. "It's just a bunch of numbers."

I inhaled. Life is just a bunch of numbers, but it's what those numbers add up to that matters the most. "Thirteen = number of official dates we've been on. One hundred fifty-six = number of couples we've married here since the funeral. Two hundred thirty-seven = number of times James threatened me with that photo of us."

"What about the nineteen?" Dax asked.

The blood evaporated from my body. I crumbled into myself, crumbled into Dax's arms. "That's the number of times I've tried to say I love you. I couldn't begin to count the number of times I've felt it."

He grinned. "You should add one hundred twenty-two to the mix."

"What's that?"

"Number of days since I first met you." He brushed his lips against my ear. "And one. Number of girls I've loved. Yeah, numbers girl. I can count too."

Dax added a few more things to the Rose of Sharon and Cupid's Dream time capsule. A dusty carnation. The bandanna to his cowboy outfit. One of the pictures of Victor and a forgotten soap opera star. And this letter, that he let me read before we sealed our beginnings and endings into a creaking metal box, forever.

Dax (short for Daxworth, I hear. What the hell was your mother thinking?)

If things go as I'd planned, you've met my granddaughter, Holly Nolan. Maybe she's standing in front of you right now, tapping her foot, demanding you tell her what's in this letter. Don't. The things I want to tell you are things she needs to learn for herself first.

I asked her to deliver this letter to you for a few reasons. I wanted you to meet her. I wanted her to meet you. I want the stupid rift between Victor and me to end. Everyone likes Holly, you can't help but like her, so maybe you can not hate her and she could not hate you and our chapels can finally be at peace.

I don't know you, Daxworth Cranston. I'm hoping your character is much like your father's and very much unlike Victor's. I met your dad the day Victor bought the chapel. He came in with a basket of smoked sausage and crackers, of all things, saying he was excited to be in the neighborhood and that he'd married his wife in Cupid's Dream. If you're going to have a competition chapel next door, might as well have this guy there. That was before I met your grandpa, of course, and everything went to pot.

Your dad and I went out for drinks a few times when he'd come work at the chapel in the summers. I saw you as a baby. Your dad talked about you 87 percent of the time. He loved you, probably in the same way that I love my granddaughter. He was a proud father and a good man. I know his death was tragic, but his life wasn't, and that's what matters.

Not many men get the luxury to write these things to strangers. They don't get a dying request, but you're getting mine. Be kind to my granddaughter. Be her friend. Help her through this time that I know you understand all too well. That wedding chapel is her everything, and she's probably going to lose it. I didn't tell her that, of course, but I'm a realist. She's a fixer, and by putting her energies into fixing this, I know it will help her with the loss. Staying in business isn't what matters. I just want her to be happy.

She's a good girl. She deserves goodness. If you have any of that in you, please help her. Help me. You'll be helping yourself.

Jim Nolan

ACKNOWLEDGMENTS

I want to thank my childhood, and most everyone in my childhood, for the bike rides, suburban freedom, field trips to the Strip (wherein our teachers mapped out the fastest route through smoke-filled casinos), and friends "macking" in the Forum shops, wherein little "macking" actually ever occurred. Las Vegas, you're an odd home, but you are mine, and so much of who I am is a result of the weirdness that is you.

I especially want to thank Lynn at Wee Kirk o' the Heather Wedding Chapel, a chapel quite similar in my mind to the fictional Rose of Sharon, for answering questions for hours and hours. Also Chapel of the Flowers, Little Church of the West, and Elvis impersonator Shane Paterson for help with all things Vegas.

For tidbits on everything from class schedules to balloon

payments: Katie Erickson, Kim and Ken Scriber, Eric Taylor (okay, fine, I'll call you Dad), Rachel Hawkins, Lisa Schroeder, Tera Lynn Childs, Cailee Kelly, Emily Wing Smith, and the Neon Scribblers.

Paige Bledsoe, Jessica Wilcox, Kassidy and Paige Gammel for childcare. My family and friends for always being there, even when you probably didn't want to be—especially when you didn't want to be.

Sarah Davies, a solid agent who helps me keep my head on straight.

Caroline Abbey, an editor and friend, in equal order.

And to the fabulous team at Bloomsbury: Patricia McHugh, Amanda Bartlett, Beth Eller, Linette Kim, Courtney Griffin, Elizabeth Mason, Emily Ritter, Erica Barmash, Catherine Onder, Jenna Pocius, Holly Ruck, Jennifer Edwards, Claire Taylor, Vannessa Cronin, Mark Von Bargen, and Jennifer Gonzalez.

Viva Las Vegas!